A House Divided

A NOVEL

DIANE STRINGAM TOLLEY

BONNEVILLE BOOKS
An imprint of Cedar Fort, Inc.
Springville, Utah

ISBN 13: 978-1-4621-2086-4

Published by Bonneville Books, an imprint of Cedar Fort, Inc.
2373 W. 700 S., Springville, UT 84663
Distributed by Cedar Fort, Inc., www.cedarfort.com

LIBRARY OF CONGRESS CATALOGING-IN-PUBLICATION DATA

Names: Tolley, Diane Stringam (Diane Louise Stringam), 1955- author.
Title: A house divided / Diane Stringam Tolley.
Description: Springville, Utah : Bonneville Books, an imprint of Cedar Fort,
   Inc., [2017]
Identifiers: LCCN 2017029512 (print) | LCCN 2017031607 (ebook) | ISBN
   9781462128280 (epub and mobi) | ISBN 9781462120864 (perfect binding
   softcover : acid-free paper)
Subjects: LCSH: Women--Religious life--Fiction. | Nephites--Fiction. |
   Domestic fiction. | GSAFD: Christian fiction.
Classification: LCC PR9199.4.T63 (ebook) | LCC PR9199.4.T63 H68 2017 (print)
   | DDC 813/.6--dc23
LC record available at https://lccn.loc.gov/2017029512

Cover design by Katie Payne
Cover design © 2017 by Cedar Fort, Inc.
Edited and typeset by Jessica Romrell and Nicole Terry

Printed in the United States of America

10 9 8 7 6 5 4 3 2 1

Printed on acid-free paper

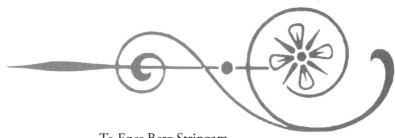

To Enes Berg Stringam
Writer. Mentor. Mother
"You can give without loving. But you cannot love without giving!"

OTHER BOOKS BY DIANE STRINGAM TOLLEY

Daughter of Ishmael

Carving Angels

Kris Kringle's Magic

PROLOGUE

*S*omeone was squabbling, arguing over something. Shrill voices jarred her awake from a soft, dreamless rest.

Hannah opened one eye to a blur of green. She frowned. This was not her house. She tried to open her other eye, but it refused to obey her; tried to reach out to touch it but cried aloud at the pain of lifting her arm.

Then memory washed over her. Cold and bitter, it flowed through her like a knife, cutting her to her tender soul.

Her family—her husband—had stoned her. Her own son had participated, dropping that final, devastating stone, and then left her for dead.

Was she dead?

She tried again to lift her arm and cried out at the pain. No. She was still on earth. Surely there was no pain and suffering in the Spirit world.

Tears began to flow. There was nothing for her in this world. Why had the Lord seen fit to leave her here. Had she not done enough?

Had she not suffered enough?

The harsh voices, still arguing heatedly, invaded once more.

Hannah listened for a moment, but could not make out the words. Slowly, carefully, she turned her head.

The world was rosy with new morning light. The sun had not yet risen, but the air was full of the promise of another day. Hannah's eye widened as she realized it was not a group of people, as she had expected. Rather, a couple of vultures were wrangling over something. Perhaps whether or not she was dead—enough.

At her movement, they hopped backwards a few paces, their eyes on her, their cries silenced.

Hannah rested for a moment, then moved her head again. This time it was easier. She tried her arm and it, too, seemed to be hurting less. Cautiously, she looked all around the clearing. Nothing else stirred. Her family had obviously left her for dead and gone back to their settlement.

And knowing their penchant for late-night celebrations and aversion to the early morning hours, she assumed they would not be stirring for quite some time.

She tried to push herself upright, but she simply did not have the strength.

Carefully, she ran her hand along her body, seeking out injuries. There were several sore spots along her chest, arms, and legs. Her back had been rubbed raw where she had been dragged. And her face and head ached badly from the blows they had received, in particular that last, dropped stone that had been so devastating, both physically, emotionally, and spiritually.

Hannah took a deep breath, listening to the air flow through her body. She felt her heart beating steadily inside her. Strangely, when tears would have been customary, she instead felt peace settle over her.

The Lord had preserved her life.

But why?

Where could she possibly go?

What would she do?

Her family had chosen the path of sin and would receive the wages of such. If she returned to them—and if they let her live—she would be forced to partake of it with them. She, the daughter of Ishmael and follower of the Prophet Lehi. She, who had wanted only goodness in her life. Goodness and righteousness and the light of her Lord and Savior. She, who had instead received the great weight of iniquity. A weight as heavy as the stones her family had used to try to end her life.

The weight of her family's sins already seemed to press down on her.

How would it feel to have the weight of generation upon generation upon generation?

Suddenly, Hannah went still. Stopped breathing. Her hand crept to her belly. Had she really felt—? There it was again. A flutter. Just the tiniest movement.

Was it possible? With all she had endured?

She waited. Surely she was mistaken. Surely—no.

It happened a third time.

Could it be true? Was this the child that Lehi had foreseen? That Mother Sariah had confirmed?

She held her breath for another period of waiting. Then sighed as it came again. Another confirmation.

The child was real.

Real.

In an instant, the course of Hannah's whole life changed. Her work was *not* done. The Lord was calling her again. Giving her another child to raise, even in her age. This time in righteousness.

Forgetting her pain, Hannah found the strength to push herself upright. To work her way to her knees. With many stops to rest, she slowly got to her feet, afraid that any movement of hers might stop that light fluttering. Might prove she was only dreaming.

At last, she stood on her feet. Once more, she waited, one hand on her belly.

There it was again.

Hannah covered her bruised and split lips and stifled a sob. Suddenly her mother's words, spoken in a dream became clear. "— *bring your son to salvation. Your* son. *Remember what I say this day. It is important—when you have a great choice to make.*"

There was a choice to make. For her unborn *son*, she must choose to abandon the family who had abandoned the Lord. And her. She must choose to follow Nephi, her prophet.

With the Lord's guidance, she would find him.

She paused once and looked back at the quiet settlement. Smoke from the ashes of the once-great fire curled lazily into the rosy dawn. Nothing else stirred.

Hannah turned away and, taking a deep, strengthening breath, stepped onto the path leading into the light, her footsteps slow and unsteady, but her mind sure.

CHAPTER ONE

*A*s she stepped from the cool shadow of the trees, Hannah lifted a hand to shade her one good eye, grunting with the effort. Already, her small burst of strength was waning.

Tears of weakness trickled down her face, mixing with the blood and dirt and making dark droplets on her soiled and torn tunic.

How was she going to reach the people of Nephi? She could not even reach the settlement they had abandoned.

She stopped, swaying slightly, and looked around. All was as it had been—was it only yesterday? She had changed so much that it was a bit of a surprise to see that little else was different.

Some fires had been started— supposedly by *King* Laman's followers last night—but little damage had been done. A couple of wood piles were smoking languidly in the morning light.

Hannah started forward again, stopping a few steps further along the quiet street. The partially finished temple stood opposite her, the walls bearing mute evidence of some frantic chopping and scraping, but, again, showing no real destruction.

Next to the temple stood Nephi and Anava's home. Here, there were more signs of a heedless and angry invading force. The door had been wrenched off and it and some of the home's furnishings tossed out into the street.

Hannah slowly made her way to a sturdy chair and, righting it, sat down. She could picture in her mind the frenzied attack. The frustration when so little damage resulted.

She smiled slightly, wincing as her aching lips protested. Then tears came to her eyes. That anger. That frustration. Both had been turned on her.

Taking a deep breath, Hannah straightened. Nothing was being accomplished by sitting here and lamenting what was. How long would it be before someone noticed that her body was no longer where it had been? How long before they came after her to finish what had been started?

Pushing herself to her feet, Hannah tried to think. She needed to get away from here. But how long would it take for her to reach Nephi and his people? First, she needed supplies.

With slow, but determined steps, she entered Nephi's house and looked around for something—anything—that may be of use to her.

There was very little. Furnishings had been tumbled about, but smaller household goods were absent. Either the invaders had taken all that was there; or there had not been anything to take. She suspected the latter.

Hannah opened a large chest pushed back against the wall. Empty.

She straightened and looked around. Maybe in the other room?

Slowly, she made her way into the cooking area. Here, her luck was a bit better. High on a shelf was a lone, clay bottle enmeshed in a woven reed cover.

Her only problem was going to be reaching it.

With many stops for breath, Hannah pushed a chair over to the shelf. Then slowly and carefully climbed up.

Pausing there, she waiting for her head to stop spinning. Then finally reached for the bottle. By its weight, she knew it was partially filled with something. She shook it. A liquid.

Pulling the stopper, Hannah sniffed. Sour wine. Perfect for treating her many injuries.

Afraid to try to get down while holding the bottle, she set it on the chair and slowly lowered herself back to the floor.

Then she froze.

She could hear voices. Someone was coming!

Hannah crept to the window facing the main road, trying desperately not to make any noise. Peering out, she could see two people coming up the street. Her breath caught. Her brother Zedekiah's eldest son, Thaddeus, and one of Berachah's sons, Abishai. Both carried bows and well-filled quivers—Abishai's beautifully embossed and dyed a deep blue.

"Imagine their surprise when we return heavy with game!" Abishai was saying.

Thaddeus laughed. "Do not try to carry home an animal we have not yet caught."

"But we will. And I one of the youngest hunters!" The boy looked around. "I am so happy that we do not have to share the hunting grounds with any from *Nephi's* camp."

Thaddeus snorted. "We do not even have to share Nephi's *camp*."

The boys stopped at the end of the street. "How do you think they did it?" Abishai asked. "Disappeared, I mean. There is not any sign which way they went."

Thaddeus shook his head. "Maybe they flew!"

Abishai gasped and looked at his elder cousin.

Thaddeus laughed at his mystified expression. "They must have some way of brushing out their tracks so no one could follow."

"Lemuel will find them. He is the greatest tracker ever!"

At the mention of her husband's name, Hannah caught her breath.

Thaddeus nodded. "He can track anything. At some point, they will make a mistake, and then we will have them!"

Abishai sighed happily. "It is a glorious new day!" He started to run. "Come. Before the others begin to stir!"

The two young men disappeared into the trees across the road.

Hannah's heart was racing as she walked to the door and peered carefully out into the street. What if others followed? What if the boys returned? She must get out of here!

Carefully, she crept out of the house, clutching her precious bottle. Moving to the shaded side of the street, she paused to catch her breath.

Nothing stirred.

She moved to the next shadow. Then the next.

Finally, she reached the end of the settlement. Again, she turned for a last look behind.

All was quiet. Taking a deep breath, she stepped into the road leading away from the village.

Looking down, she saw countless footsteps. She stopped and frowned. Here was plain evidence of the migration of a large number of people and animals. And only a short time before.

How had Laman's warriors missed this? The tracks were so obvious that a child could have followed them.

'*And a little child shall lead them.*' Her mother's words, spoken so long ago, were unexpectedly clear in her mind and, just as suddenly, Hannah knew these tracks were for her to follow. Only her.

She started walking.

———— ◆ ————

A few hours later, the tracks veered off into the trees. Numbly, Hannah followed them, relieved to leave the increasing heat of the sun for the cool shade of the forest.

A short distance further on, she came across a bundle lying in the tall grass. A blanket, folded, rolled and tied to be worn as a bedroll. Lifting it, she looked it over carefully.

Surmising it had fallen from a wagonload of household possessions; she carefully drew the leather strap over her shoulder, patted the tidy bundle, and continued on through the forest. Now she *had* to find Nephi and his people. She had to return their blanket to them.

Hannah had made many trips through the forest when she was well and healthy. Now she was discovering that this was not to be a simple stroll through nature. Her weakened condition increased her tendency to trip over roots and hummocks. So, while she found the trees a definite relief from the heat of the sun, it was only a partial compensation.

She licked dry lips. And a sip of cool water at this point would not go amiss.

The third time Hannah fell to her knees, she considered simply staying where she was.

Surely death would be an improvement over this!

As she lay there in a deep carpet of old and new vegetation, she realized she could hear the trickle of water.

Pushing herself erect, Hannah slowly regained her feet. Then stood there, trying to decide where the sound was coming from.

Glancing to the left, she saw a thick row of bushes, forming a veritable wall in the forest. Moving slowly closer, she tried to peer over them. It could not be done. Her lack of height and their tightly-meshed growth made it impossible.

Hannah frowned. She was sure the sound of water was coming from somewhere behind these bushes. She decided to turn and skirt them.

Working her way around the little copse, Hannah noted that the patch was roughly circular in shape and quite a bit larger than it had first appeared.

Soon she was again at her starting point. And still the gentle sound of trickling water teased her. It had to be somewhere inside these bushes.

She squatted down and tried to peer under them. They seemed a bit thinner down near the ground. Hannah dropped to her knees and pressed her way inside.

After a few feet, the bushes opened surprisingly into a space. Only a few paces across, it was, at once, cool, dark, and private.

A pool of clear water bubbled in one corner. Hannah knelt beside it in the soft grass and dipped her hand into the water.

It proved to be clear and achingly cold. Hannah cupped her hand and scooped the life-giving water up to her tender lips.

Having drunk her fill, Hannah pulled off her headcloth and her outer and under tunics, and proceeded to rinse away as much of the blood and gore from face, hands, and body as she could. Then she explored the damage to her face with gentle fingers. Her right eye was swollen closed and her right cheek had a long cut that was oozing fresh blood still. There were several sore spots, indicating bruising, but no other significant damage.

On the top of her head, just within her hairline, was the wound that caused her the most pain. Here was where her precious son Samuel had dropped that final stone. The one he had thought to end her life with.

Hannah sighed and traced the wound with her fingertips as slow tears welled. Samuel may not have killed her body with his dropped stone, but something had certainly died.

The tiny fluttering began in her belly again. She grew still and slid her hand over it. Something had died, yes. But something bigger had lived.

Taking a deep breath, Hannah leaned over her little pool and scooped up more of the cool water—splashing it over her face and head.

Then she dipped her headcloth into the pool and, wringing it out, sponged the rest of her body again. The temperature of the water was, at once, refreshing and soothing to her many injuries.

Feeling somewhat cleaner, she sat back and tried to work the tangles from her hair with her fingers. Grass and twigs showered into her lap. Finally, she braided it into one long plait and wound a couple of hairs around the end to hold it.

Tearing some strips from her head cloth, she poured a little of her precious sour wine over them and bound up her injuries as best she could.

Then she donned her under tunic, folded her scratched and bruised fingers together and offered up a prayer of thanksgiving for the sparing of her life and for the Lord's guidance in directing her, and a plea that she would continue to be led until she and her child were reunited once more with the prophet of the Lord.

———— • ◆ • ————

For the next four days, Hannah remained inside the little copse of trees. The first two days because she needed it, and the last two because she had no choice.

Frustrated by her lack of strength, Hannah chafed at the delay. Nephi and his people were steadily moving further away and she feared that the tracks she had been following would dissolve and disappear if it began to rain—which it often did— and her only chance of finding where her people had fled would disappear with them.

But she knew that her only chance of survival—and that of her unborn child—depended on her regaining her health and strength.

She had weighed her options and decided that she could give herself two days to heal and rest.

Her blanket had proved a valuable find indeed, providing warmth against the coolness of the evening hours.

A few times a day, Hannah would venture out in search of food, and was amply rewarded with the discovery of a bed of field-roots and a patch of mushrooms.

By the end of the first day, the bruising around her right eye had healed sufficiently that she was able to see from it once more. After that, she tripped less over roots and outcroppings and her course through the forest became easier.

Early in the morning on her second day, she found a stream—obviously the parent to her little pool—nearby. Frowning, she stood on its banks, wondering why she had not heard its noise earlier when hunting for water. Now, of the two bodies of water, this was the only one she could hear.

The Lord must have wanted her to find the small pool for a reason known only to Himself.

The discovery of a large patch of waternuts drove the thought from her mind, and she spent several happy moments hunting and gathering.

Soon she was back in her little oasis with fresh water and plenty of food.

By the end of the second day, Hannah was feeling much stronger. She had managed to scrub and dry both of her tunics, dry and prepare her store of tubers and vegetables, and, with continued applications of the last of her sour wine, heal her several wounds to the point of discomfort only. She was ready to go.

Dressed in her outer tunic, she had fashioned a pack from her other garment—a pack that was now stuffed with food, a water-filled bottle, and a blanket. Siding her arms into the 'straps' of her pack, she hoisted it to her shoulders and settled it across her back. Then she knelt down, ready to crawl through the bushes.

It was at that moment that she heard a noise.

She went still.

The noise grew louder, and finally was recognizable as a large group of people coming through the jungle toward her. Hannah stopped breathing.

Had they found her?

CHAPTER TWO

*H*annah sank back to the ground and tried to become one with the shadows that surrounded her. The group of people moved closer, finally gathering directly outside her little copse of bushes.

"We will camp here for the night," someone said.

Hannah frowned. Whose voice was that? She thought it might be one of Zedekiah's younger sons.

"Hold!"

Hannah knew *that* voice. *King* Laman was standing a pair of paces from where she crouched.

"We will continue to travel!"

"Highness, your younger warriors are weary. We got a late start and they were up most of the night . . ."

"They are warriors. That is what they are supposed to do!"

"Yes, Highness. But they are new to it. Perhaps if you were to school them in your expectations of a soldier?"

Laman took a deep breath. "Fine. We will camp here for the night!" he shouted.

Immediately, Hannah heard the sounds of people spreading out all around her, moving through the trees, setting up a camp.

Soon, the smell of burning wood permeated her little pocket. Like a frightened rabbit, Hannah crouched in the center of her copse. This place that had seemed so safe and secure short moments before had now become her prison. And ironically, the people she had called family mere days ago were now her jailers.

Now, the reason for the discovery of her little hideaway became apparent.

Please, Father, she prayed, over and over. *Hide me! Make me invisible!*

———— ◆ ————

Ironically, the camp of warriors, after arguing over staying the night, remained for two more days. Listening to their conversations, Hannah learned that Laman was ill. Unwilling to make the demands on himself that he asked of his followers, he remained in his bed the entire time.

For those two days, Hannah hardly dared to breathe. Movements were made only when the group encamped mere paces away were making noise of their own. And even then, she was cautious to the point of absurdity.

Eating and drinking were accomplished with a maximum of effort and minimum results.

Sleeping was out of the question. What if she spoke or made some sort of noise in her sleep? The nighttime hours became a series of cat-naps, from which she jerked awake with a gasp and a renewal of her pleas to the Lord to keep her hidden.

She passed some of the time silently listening to the warriors as they idled near her hiding place, trying to identify them by their voices. Hoping and dreading to hear the one voice still precious to her. But, surprisingly, though she had been around them for all of their lives, she could not recognize any. It was as though they had become strangers to her.

Finally, at dawn on her fourth day, Laman's voice was again heard. "Get them up and ready to march after breakfast! We have an enemy to catch."

"Yes, Highness."

The smell of roasted meats drifted on the morning breeze, accompanied by the usual sounds of meals being prepared and consumed. Then the clatter that accompanied the breaking of camp.

A burst of laugher just outside her walls startled her and she gasped, then clapped a hand over her too, too treacherous mouth.

"Hold him! Hold him!" someone said. "Do not let him go!"

Hannah could hear the terrified snarling and whining of some sort of animal.

"Here. I've got him. Just tie his rope to that tree."

Another burst of laughter. "I guess he did not like that!"

"Well, what does it matter what he likes? He is our prisoner."

"Well, when you put it like that . . ."

"What are you doing?" Someone new had joined the conversation. "He is my animal."

"Jonah is testing his new knife. Watch."

"Stop! He is mine! I found him!" At least one voice carried a note of sanity.

"You have become too attached in these past few days."

"But he is gentle. He can serve us and be a great help."

"Oh, stop whining! You are beginning to sound like an old woman."

"I have just sharpened my knife. This is a perfect opportunity!"

The sounds of several people agreeing loudly over the protests of a single voice.

The poor animal's whines turned to howls of pain.

Hannah crouched down in the very center of her prison, hands pressed tightly against both ears and silent tears streaming down her cheeks.

Finally, the animal's howls were reduced to long whines.

"Well," someone said. "That is one sharp knife! I would say you can take over knife-sharpening duty in the camp."

Laughter.

"So what are you going to do with it?"

"The pup? Leave it. What good would it be? It will be dead before nightfall."

"But—"

"Pack up!"

Within minutes, the sounds of the soldiers had faded away to silence.

Rocking herself back and forth, Hannah remained crouched in the center of her hideaway, dreading the moment when she would have to leave this place and risk being seen—or finding out what terrible thing had been done to another living creature.

Finally, she could wait no longer. As quietly as possible, she donned her pack.

With many stops along the way to listen, she finally made it through her little path. Once outside, she remained on her knees for a few moments, ears attuned to any sound.

The only things she could hear, apart from trickling water and birdsong, were the long whines of the injured creature.

Taking a deep breath, Hannah got to her feet and followed that sound.

A short distance from her refuge, Hannah found a large creature lying in the grass. The poor animal was thin, ribs sticking out and spine clearly visible through its furry coat.

Except that it was much bigger and yellow-eyed and the coat was a mottled light brown and black, it looked like the dogs Hannah's family had left back in Jerusalem.

The animal was watching her approach.

It lifted its head weakly and made a show of curling an upper lip back from long, gleaming white teeth. Hannah stopped a short distance away and it lowered its head back to the ground. She looked at it. Blood was staining the animal's fur down each side of its head.

The heart-wrenching whines kept on.

Hannah moved closer.

Again the lifted head. Again the curled lip, white teeth, and low whine.

Hannah took another couple of steps. She was close enough now, that she could see more blood in the grass around the animal. A lot of blood.

She stopped and thought for a moment. The animal looked as though it was starving. And grievously wounded as well. She bit her lip. She would not be able to help it if she could not get close to it.

Glancing around cautiously, she slid her pack off and dug out one of her precious tubers.

Holding it out before her, she approached the wretched animal.

Its eyes moved between her and the food she held out so temptingly, as though it could not quite make up its mind as to which was most important.

Finally, Hannah was close enough to toss the food over to the poor animal.

The animal sniffed at her offering, then snapped it up.

Hannah regarded it for a moment. Then she dug out another tuber and repeated the entire operation. Again, her present was snatched almost before it hit the ground.

Hannah held out her bottle of water, shaking it so the animal could hear the liquid inside.

Its head came up.

This was the tricky part. Hannah had nothing to pour the water in. She would have to step close enough that she could pour the water out for the animal. And hope that it had strength to take it out of the air.

Stepping closer, she again shook the bottle.

The animal watched her, but no longer curled its lip or showed its teeth.

Carefully, Hannah uncorked the bottle and held it out. Then she tipped it carefully and a small stream of water struck the animal in the face. For a moment, it merely blinked, then it turned its head and began to catch the water on its tongue. Again and again, it lapped at the stream.

Finally, it turned its head away, looking up toward Hannah hopefully. She stopped pouring and corked her bottle. Then she dug out another tuber and dropped it in front of the animal.

Again the morsel of food disappeared.

Even in this short time, the animal seemed stronger.

Hannah took a deep breath. Now she was going to have to examine the creature to see just what damage had been done. Cautiously, she approached the animal.

It watched her, but made no threatening gestures. Finally, she was standing beside it. It lifted its head and looked at her. Then lay down again and gave another long whine.

Kneeling slowly beside it, Hannah reached out with one hand. The animal was watching, but made no move.

Hannah caught her breath as she examined its head. Both ears had been sliced off and the remaining stubs were oozing blood in droplets. For a moment, her eyes filled with tears as she stared at the wounds, wondering at the pointless cruelty of such an action. She turned, biting her lip as she struggled for control. Finally, taking a deep breath, she blinked away the tears and turned to examine the rest of the poor creature. She gasped when she discovered what else had been done.

The animal's tail had been neatly severed close to the body.

Blood was still oozing from the stump.

Hannah sat back and put a hand on her head.

What could she possibly do to help? The poor ears, she really didn't think she could do anything for, but the tail?

Mentally, she went over the items in her pack. Food. Water bottle. Blanket. Leather tie. Headscarf bandages.

Nodding her head, she got to her feet and returned to her pack. Retrieving two of her bandages, she ripped one into thin strips. This time, when she approached the animal, it lifted its bloodied head and when she sat down beside it, licked her arm with a smooth tongue. Hannah jumped and drew her arm back. Then, realizing the creature obviously meant no harm, she sank to the ground once more and shuffled carefully toward the wounds.

The bandage, she bound neatly around the animal's head, covering its wounded ears as best she could. Then, carrying the strips, she moved toward the severed tail.

The animal seemed to understand that she was there to help and, surprisingly, other than more whining, made no protest when she wrapped the strip of cloth around its poor stump of a tail. Cursing the fact that she had used the last of her sour wine on her own bruises and hurts, Hannah made her makeshift bandage tight and sat back.

The animal again licked her arm. This time, Hannah stroked the rough head. "That's all I can do, Little Brother. I hope it is enough." She looked heavenward. "Lord," she said. "I thank you for preserving me these past days. And now I ask the same blessing for this poor creature who has been injured, through no fault of its own. Will you heal it?"

Another lick from a warm tongue. "I guess you approve," Hannah told it.

There was a cord around the creature's neck and Hannah could see that it was tied to a nearby tree. She looked at it. Then at the creature. Deciding the animal was no more of a threat to her untied, she removed the noose from its neck and released the end from the tree.

Getting to her feet, she made a slow search of the area nearby. The soldiers who had camped here, boys Hannah had seen raised and some of whom she had had a hand in raising, were not a tidy group. Bones from animals were strewn about. Many with meat still clinging to them. Already, vultures and other carrion birds were starting to gather.

Picking up several of the meatier leavings, Hannah carried them back to her friend. The animal fell on them eagerly, tearing at the flesh.

Hannah found a small clay pot discarded with the rest of the refuse. Picking it up, she took it back to her friend, filled properly with clear water. Setting it down nearby, she again turned and walked through the camp.

Several arrows had sprouted from the prominent bole of a large old tree. The soldiers had obviously used it as a target. And then had lacked the energy—or initiative—to climb up and retrieve their arrows afterward.

Hannah did so now. She was surprised as she plucked at the arrows, to find a crude knife in their midst. Pulling it out, she turned it over in her hands. Little care had been taken in its making—it was not as smoothly ground as other knives in the settlement and the handle had been formed simply by winding a length of leather cord about the upper part of the tang. But it was very sharp and would serve her small needs admirably. She tucked the seven arrows and the precious knife into her pack.

Hunting further through the camp, she also found another blanket, a small axe, and two earthenware cups and a plate.

Riches for someone in her situation.

Placing everything neatly into her pack, she pulled it on, adjusting the straps over her shoulders. Then knelt down one last time by her new friend.

"I'm sorry to have to leave you, Little Brother," she said, patting the rough fur. "But I cannot wait for you to be strong enough to come with me. I've lost far too much time as it is." She looked at the rope and frowned. "But I can probably use this." She coiled it, looping it over her shoulder. "There." She patted the creature's head again.

The animal licked her hand.

"Good-bye, Little Brother."

She got to her feet, adjusted the pack on her back and, without a backward glance, started off through the trees.

From the tracks they had left, it was fairly obvious the army had taken a course to the right.

Hannah decided to continue straight ahead in the direction she had been following before she had found her refuge/prison.

At the river, she stopped to refill her bottle. A noise made her spin around, heart pounding.

The creature had followed her. Weakly, it approached, trying its best to wag what was left of its sorry tail.

"Oh, Little Brother." Hannah's eyes filled with tears as she patted the bristly fur and saw again the wounds suffered by the innocent creature. "Of course you can come with me." She looked upward. "The Lord will provide."

CHAPTER THREE

*H*annah and her new companion crossed the clear water and continued through the forest.

A short distance from the stream, she reached a point where the sun was shining down through a break in the trees. There she again picked up the tracks of dozens of human feet, as well as those of numerous sheep and cattle, horses and donkeys.

She smiled. "Thank you, Lord," she said.

Little Brother licked her hand.

The unlikely companions continued to walk, stopping often to rest and eat. They found several more patches of mushrooms and tubers. Water was plentiful. And Little Brother proved he was much more than a mere companion when he chased and caught a large, fat rabbit.

Hannah was surprised that, though she ate it raw, the meat was sweet and tasty. She was forcibly reminded of earlier days wandering in the wilderness. She smiled sadly. How bittersweet those memories had become.

———————•◆•———————

For two days, they travelled slowly. Hannah told herself it was for Little Brother's benefit. But in reality, she still had not recovered, and the pain- and fatigue-enforced slow pace was exactly what she needed as well.

At the end of the second day, they stopped beside a great stream of slowly-moving water. The tracks Hannah had been following continued on the other side, so she knew she must find a way across.

Little Brother waded in, lapping at the water. When he was chest deep, he turned and looked at Hannah.

Biting her lip uncertainly, she paused at the very edge. "Do you think it is safe?" she asked her companion.

Little Brother merely looked at her, bright yellow eyes sparkling, red tongue dangling from his mouth.

"Well, if you think so—" Hannah waded in.

The water was remarkably clear and she could see right to the bottom. Flashing slivers of silver darted back and forth in front of her.

"Fish, Little Brother!" Hannah stopped and watched them. "I wish we could catch them!"

She continued forward. The water was cool. Comfortably so. She pushed ahead. The current was slight here and she was grateful because the water was growing steadily deeper.

Lifting her pack above her head, Hannah continued toward the opposite shore. The water climbed to her waist. Her chest. Then, just as she was considering turning back, she realized that it was growing shallower once more. Soon she was climbing out on the other shore, her tunic dripping, but her head and shoulders—and her pack—dry.

Heaving a sigh of relief, she turned to watch Little Brother swim toward her. He waded out onto dry shore and happily shook himself.

Hannah moved closer. Somewhere in the stream, he had lost the bedraggled bandages she had tied around his head and his stub. He turned and licked at the larger wound, then bounded toward her.

Two days of food and attention had made a remarkable difference in the animal. His bones were already a little less prominent and his eyes were brighter and his whole demeanour more alert.

With Little Brother following closely behind her, Hannah turned and walked over to study the tracks which continued in a straight line through the forest. She shook her head. No tracks could have been easier to follow. She lifted her head and looked in the direction

Laman and his warriors had taken two days before. How could they not see?

It was all as the Lord intended. That was the only explanation.

Her heart brimming with gratitude, Hannah turned away and began hunting for a suitable spot to hide away and rest for the night. A place close to the river.

The trees in this part of the forest grew thickly and there was little vegetation in the form of bushes and shrubs on the ground. No comfortable hiding places at all. Hannah was becoming quite discouraged when she noticed several dark spots in the ground ahead. As she drew closer, she realized it was a series of rocky gullies. Most were mere openings in the ground with no way in or out. But one of the larger was partially collapsed and the rubble formed natural 'steps' leading down.

"Little Brother!" she called.

The animal bounded up, eyes snapping and long red tongue lolling.

"Should we camp here?" Hannah stepped down onto the first ledge.

The animal turned and sniffed the air, then started down ahead of her, jumping enthusiastically from step to step.

Soon, he had disappeared from view.

Cautiously, Hannah followed.

The natural steps led down and around a curve and finally ended at a rocky pocket with a sandy floor. Solid rock walls rose all about her and the steps she had followed proved to be the only way in or out. She felt hidden here. But trapped as well. If anyone—or anything— came down those steps, she would have no escape.

She looked at Little Brother. "What do you think?" She made a quick, closer examination of the walls. "Do you think we can safely stay here?"

Little Brother had done his own examination. Now, he curled up against the sun-warmed side of the enclosure and closed his eyes.

Hannah raised her eyebrows and smiled. "I guess that is my answer."

She pulled off her pack and laid out her blanket, knife, and some tubers. Her water bottle was nearly empty. She stood and looked at her companion. "Why not rest there while I go to refill our bottle?" Hannah laughed. "Or you could do it for me."

The animal opened one eye, then closed it again and lapsed back into slumber.

Still smiling, Hannah clambered up the stony stairway. Poking her head above the top rim, she looked cautiously about. Seeing nothing, she climbed out of the hole and onto solid ground.

Everything remained quiet.

Hannah took a different route back to the river, careful of calling attention to herself by repeating any movements.

She reached the shore of the river and knelt beside the calmly flowing water.

Something was floating toward the center of the river and she stared at it as she corked her bottle.

Strange, Hannah thought. *It looks like an arrow.*

An arrow!

Hannah froze, her eyes riveted on the bobbing stick of wood. If there was an arrow here, could that mean there were warriors or hunters here as well?

Several more arrows joined the first, forming a small network of sticks that bobbed quietly as they moved slowly downstream.

Hannah got to her feet and slid into the deeper shadow beneath the nearest tree, silently lamenting the lack of undergrowth in this part of the forest. From this place of relative anonymity, she again looked around.

Nothing stirred.

She glanced over at the water again.

The arrows had moved further downstream and now, Hannah could see something else. Something nearer the shoreline. A quiver!

It too was moving downstream, rolling a bit as the heavier part of it dragged along the river bottom.

A quiver. That she could definitely use!

Darting out from the shadows, Hannah stepped into the shallows at the river's edge and snatched the leather bag from the water.

Then she moved back into the shadows and looked around.

Still nothing moved.

Hannah turned the long, water-soaked bag over in her hands. It looked familiar— beautifully embossed and dyed a deep blue—and she frowned as the memory of where she had seen it before eluded her. She shook her head. Somewhere—

She gasped. This bag had been slung across the youthful shoulder of young Abishai, Berachah's son only a handful of days before. She would swear to it.

But where was the young hunter who had embarked with his elder cousin with such hope in his step?

Hannah looked upstream. Surely the arrows and quiver had come from there.

She detected movement and her heart sped up as her eyes quickly and anxiously sought the source.

There was something in the river. Something moving slowly toward the shore.

Hannah darted behind the nearest tree and hefted her tunic to her knees, prepared to run. She peeped out one last time from her hiding place. The 'creature' in the river had resolved itself into a person.

An obviously weakened one who was struggling against the slow current with only one arm and minimal support from his legs.

The current rolled him over and Hannah's heart stopped as he disappeared from her view.

A moment later, he had again emerged—gasping and coughing weakly—a little closer to her and to the shore.

Hannah stared at him, willing with all her mind for him to make it to dry ground.

She scanned frantically up and down the river, looking for a companion or another of Laman's followers, both dismayed and relieved to see no one.

Finally, just as the figure was about to be carried past her, he managed to heave himself far enough up onto the shore that the river lost its claim on him. Panting he lay there—facedown—still partly submerged, and completely spent.

Again, Hannah looked up and down the river, her eyes darting this way and that, trying to detect movement.

Something behind her growled viciously and she jumped and spun around.

Little Brother had finished his nap and come looking for her. The coarse hair on the back of the animal's neck had been raised and his head lowered as he now regarded the helpless figure through narrowed yellow eyes. Another growl issued forth and Hannah could see the lips curl, showing sharp, white teeth.

She turned back to the person, but he made no reaction to the sound of the animal a mere two paces from where he lay. He appeared to have moved past consciousness into somewhere that pain and panic did not enter.

Cautiously, Hannah crept forward, her eyes darting constantly around her.

Finally she was close enough to touch him. Reaching out, she prodded him with two fingers.

He did not stir.

She prodded him again and pulled back, waiting.

Still no movement.

Carefully, she reached out to grasp the leather vest he wore over his tunic and pull him further from the water's grasp.

Little Brother kept up a constant growl, backing slowly away as she pulled the figure further onto the shore and away from the water. Looking back, Hannah could see a long streak of blood trailing behind him.

With a last burst of energy, she finally heaved him onto a patch of grass away from the sandy bank of the river. He moaned slightly, then relapsed into slumber. Carefully, she turned him onto his back and noted two things. First, that he was younger than she had first expected and second, though he had to be someone she knew, Hannah did not recognize him. His face was badly scratched and bloody, very swollen, and heavily streaked with sand and dirt.

She could see that the left sleeve of his tunic was rapidly becoming stained with blood. She lifted the sleeve hem to see the limb beneath, and then gasped as she realized that there was no limb beneath.

It had been torn away just above the elbow.

CHAPTER FOUR

*H*annah gaped at the torn tissues and ligaments where the young man's arm should be, her mind a flurry of thoughts without shape or purpose.

Then she noted the widening pool of blood beneath the injury.

She blinked, thinking of Little Brother's wound.

Frantically, she tore a strip from her tunic and, pulling the torn skin over the horrible wound, wrapped the strip around the stub of the arm, knotting it tightly. Then she sat back, not knowing what else to do.

Finally, she was spurred into activity again with the thought of further injuries. It was then she realized the man's clothes had been cut and shredded. Long, bloody marks showed in both legs as well as in his remaining arm, and puncture marks about his throat oozed blood steadily.

Tearing another piece of her tunic and moistening it in the stream, she dabbed at the weeping wounds in his throat and tried to sponge off the sand and grit he had sustained when she had dragged him onto the shore.

A hand clasped her wrist.

Gasping, she looked over.

Dark eyes were open and looking at her. "Mother Hannah?"

She frowned at him and nodded. "Yes, it is me."

He tried to smile. "Of course it would be you, Mother Hannah." He coughed weakly. "Only you would stop. Care—" His hand wavered and fell from her wrist and his eyes closed.

Hannah shook his shoulder slightly until the eyes opened once more. She looked into the scratched, puffy, and dirt-stained face. "Who are you?"

He tried to smile. "A-bishai ben Berachah." Again the eyes closed.

Hannah's heart stopped and she felt tears gather. Abishai. Her brother's son. She glanced at the quiver a short distance away. She had been fairly certain, but it was still a shock.

"Abishai! What happened to you?" She scrubbed impatiently at the tears on her cheeks, then patted his face gently. "Abishai!"

The eyes opened slowly.

"Who did this to you?"

"I was to be a—hunter," he said. "It was—time." His voice seemed to be growing weaker. She had to lean far over to hear what he said.

"A hunter?"

He nodded slightly. "Tad—took me. First—big—cat."

Hannah caught her breath. Of course. She could just picture it. He and Thaddeus, the youngest and eldest of the 'young hunters' in Laman's camp, out after the one kill that would make them 'men' in *King* Laman's eyes—the great spotted cats of the jungles and forests.

"Abishai. You were with Thaddeus."

Again the slight nod.

"Son, where is he? Thaddeus?"

He shook his head slightly. "De—"

Hannah's heart froze. "He is dead?"

A nod.

For a moment, Hannah stared at him, unable to comprehend what he had just told her. Then, the cold truth slid down into her chest. Thaddeus. Her father's eldest grandson in whom he had so much hope and been so pleased. In her mind, she saw the little boy who had toddled about on the family's estates near Jerusalem. The young man crossing the waters with them. Grown to manhood in Laman's camp. Now dead. Dead. She collapsed against Abishai's chest and sobbed out loud. In Nephi's camp, these young men would be learning the ways of farming. And walking in the ways of the Lord. Not heading out into the jungle in a vain attempt to prove themselves and impress those who could not be impressed. What a waste of an immeasurably great human life. What a colossal waste. Pictures of little Thaddeus, toddling about her father's estates in Jerusalem

"Mother—H-Hannah."

Hannah straightened and blotted at her streaming eyes with the sleeve of her tunic.

"I'm going to—go now."

"Go?" Hannah blinked and stared at him stupidly. "Go where?"

"Home." The boy smiled faintly. "Home."

Hannah frowned. "You are not strong enough, Abishai. I will care for you here and you can—"

Again he gripped her wrist. "N-not that h-home." He looked up into the trees over their heads and his smile widened. "That home." He turned back to her. "You—you were r-right, Mother Hannah."

"Abishai! Listen to me. Stay with me! I will help you. The Lord will help you!"

"He is. He is h-help—" The hand gripping her wrist slackened and dropped to the ground.

She stared at him for a moment, trying to understand what had happened. "Abishai!" Her cry echoed through the trees. Frantically, she searched for signs of life. She laid her head down on his chest. No breath. No heartbeat. "Abishai!" she cried again.

Hannah lost track of time as she sobbed over the body of her brother's son. Over the waste of a good, young life. Of two young lives.

Little Brother moved closer and tried to lick her cheek. When she pushed him away, he curled up next to her, his eyes on her face.

Hannah's grief turned to anger as she thought about Laman. Of her brother-by-marriage's demands on the young men who worshipped him. For a fleeting moment, she thought of her own husband, whose inability to resist his elder brother had destroyed her family. She thought of Samuel. Her own Samuel. On the cusp of manhood. What terrible feats would he feel compelled to attempt in order to retain Laman's approval?

She felt suddenly sick. Getting to her feet, she just managed to make her way to the river before she lost what little she had in her stomach.

She scooped up some of the clear water to rinse her mouth, then, emotionally drained, sank to the packed sand of the river bank and stared dully at the slowly-flowing water.

What hope could there possibly be in such a world? Where young men were sacrificed upon the whim of those they followed and looked up to?

She slid her hand over her belly as her baby began moving. Her thoughts turned to that spirit who would, in a few short months, be sent to her. Could she find her hope in that time?

Again, her baby kicked.

And suddenly, she was hearing words spoken by her father, long ago when she was still a young girl in Jerusalem. *"Blessed is the man that trusteth in the Lord, and whose hope the Lord is."* And another: *"But I will hope continually, and will yet praise thee more and more."*

Hannah started to breathe again. Her life this far had been based on hope. Hope, not only of a brighter future for she and hers, but hope in her Lord and Savior who would come and take away her pain.

She could not give up now.

Sitting up, she almost smiled when a warm tongue touched her cheek. Turning to the loyal creature that had been her shadow these past couple of days, she saw that the yellow eyes were regarding her steadily.

"We will do what we can for our Abishai, Little Brother. Then we will continue on. In hope."

She got to her feet.

Just as a large, spotted creature dropped from the tree overhead, landing on the sand between her and Abishai.

One of the great jungle cats.

Hannah froze as Little Brother shot past her, growling and snarling.

The creature crouched, ready to spring. Both ears were flat to its head and its eyes glowed green in the late afternoon light.

As Little Brother drew near, the great cat struck out with one paw, razor claws out.

But it moved slowly and Little Brother easily eluded the strike, turning to bite at the larger animal as he whipped past.

The cat turned to follow, but fell sideways on the sand.

For a moment, it kicked its legs weakly, trying to right itself.

Spinning about, Little Brother again approached the great cat, growling viciously. This time, with the great cat helpless on its side, he was able lock his white teeth into its throat . He hung on as the cat's struggles turned from violent thrashing to much smaller movements. And, finally, to stillness.

After several moments, Little Brother finally released his hold and backed away a pace, then circled the creature, looking alertly for any signs of life.

Hannah approached slowly. The animal's eyes, half-lidded, were staring sightlessly.

The great cat was dead.

Hesitantly, she moved forward again, finally touching the cat's spotted hide with the toe of one sandal. She had great confidence in Little Brother's hunting ability, but why had he been able to defeat the vicious creature so easily? She knelt down to examine it further. There were not any other wounds that she could see. She sat back, thinking. Then, getting up, she walked around to its feet. Grasping all four of them and grunting heavily, she managed to roll the heavy animal onto its other side.

Here was the damage she had suspected. Four arrows, broken now, were embedded in the spotted fur. Two in the animal's stomach, one in the neck, and a fourth in its ribs.

She touched the stub of an arrow. Surely one of these had significantly wounded the animal. She looked upriver. Somewhere up there, Thaddeus and Abishai had tracked this creature. Then shot at it, wounding it, but failing to kill it outright. Enraged, it had attacked the boys, killing Thaddeus and fatally wounding Abishai.

The wounded cat had no wish to follow the boy into the stream, so whether he had fallen, or deliberately taken to the water, the act had saved his life.

She looked at the still body of her brother's son.

For a time.

Little Brother had finished circling his victim and now came to her, stub of a tail waving slowly, tongue out and eyes sparkling. He could not know of the heartache she was feeling at this moment. But he did know that he had defeated a large and dangerous enemy.

She rubbed his bristly head. "You are my true hero, Little Brother." Who knew what damage the cat would have done if it had caught her alone, even weakened as it had been? And her with just a knife to defend herself. She shook her head, snorting softly. A knife that was currently with her pack. In her shelter.

Hannah swallowed the urge to laugh helplessly. She could not give way now.

Little Brother suddenly started growling and charged off down the river bank.

Startled, Hannah lifted her hand and shaded her eyes from the last of the sun slanting through the trees.

He had flung himself into a group of creatures.

As Hannah watched, they scattered, most lifting into the air on dark wings.

Vultures.

Hannah looked at Abishai's poor, mutilated body. She frowned. Something must be done to keep him from the creatures that would desecrate his remains, but other than her own shelter, she had no convenient cave in which to put him; and trying to dig a hole in the earth with only her little knife was an impossible task.

A hole in the earth.

Hannah turned toward her cave. There had been several openings there that she had rejected in her search for shelter. Perhaps one of them—

While Little Brother remained on guard, Hannah scanned the area until she found a smaller fissure she thought would be suitable— with a narrow opening just wide enough for her brother's son's young body. Surely it would act as a deterrent to the vultures who would seek to devour his remains.

Slowly and with many stops for breath, Hannah dragged the young man's body to the opening, then arranged him carefully, his one remaining hand across his boyish chest. She regretted deeply her lack of funeral herbs, spices, and bandages. But she would do what she could.

For a moment, she looked at the tunic the boy wore. Two tunics. And a long, leather vest. Surely she could be justified in taking just one. She was in such need.

Her eyes went to the vest. She would take that. But she would leave the rest of Abishai's clothing in the absence of burial swaddling.

Hannah pulled the boy's wounded arm through the sleeve opening. Then she drew the vest to the other side and off his good arm. She looked down at the soaked leather. She could now remember Litha working on this garment.

Tears flooded her eyes once more and, clutching the vest to her, she sank to her knees and wept again for all that should have been.

Little Brother was growling and howling again. Hannah turned. He was happily chasing yet another band of encroaching vultures.

Now they were after the great cat.

Hannah dried her eyes and laid the vest tenderly on the ground. Then she turned back to Abishai and clasped her hands together. "Son of my brother," she said aloud. "I pray the Lord will receive your spirit in righteousness and happiness. That any sins you may have committed will not be placed at your door, but at the feet of those who failed to teach you. Abishai, I give you into the Lord's tender, loving hands. May you find your forever peace."

For several minutes, she sat there, thinking of the boy she had known. Of the budding young man. Thinking, too, of his cousin who had accompanied him and whose body could not even be found.

She shook her head. Time enough later to think on the tragedy. Getting to her feet, she rolled the young man's body closer to the opening. Then, with one final push, sent it down into the opening.

Sinking back onto her heels, her thoughts again turned to those people she had lost since their fateful journey had begun in Jerusalem so many years ago.

Her baby kicked suddenly and she slid a hand over her belly. People lost, but people found as well. Getting to her feet, she whispered one last good-bye, then hurried to her cave to retrieve her knife. Little Brother could only keep the vultures at bay for so long. And she could use the skin and flesh from the dead cat.

Surely some good could come of this tragedy.

———————•◆•———————

Trained in a camp of hunters, Hannah had little trouble stripping the hide off the large cat. She carried it to the river and rinsed it thoroughly, taking the time to lay it on a large rock at the river's edge and scrape off any remaining fat and tissue. Then she cut the flesh from the body of the cat and wrapped it in the hide. She studied the stripped bones for a few minutes, considering removing the great claws from each foot as possible weapons. Then she looked at Little Brother whose sharp, white teeth were happily chewing on a bone and decided she had all the weapons she needed. She stood up and rinsed her hands, arms, and knife in the clear river water, watching the blood blossom out into the stream and disappear.

Little Brother had ceased his chasing and was busily chewing on anything she tossed him.

Hannah called to him and he came, proudly carting a long bone with him.

Darkness was settling over the land when the two of them returned to their little hiding place where they ate their fill of the tender meat. Hannah wrapped the remainder in the hide and stowed it in her pack with her tubers.

Sleep was hard to come by. Hannah's thoughts kept returning to her brother's son slumbering nearby. Finally, she started reciting scriptures. Her mind calmed, and she slept.

The sounds of screeching and squawking awoke her the next morning. Little Brother growled and would have charged up the 'stairway,' but Hannah stopped him.

She still needed to be cautious. Thaddeus and Abishai had been hunting nearby and she had not heard a thing. Obviously, her tracking skills were not what they could be.

She filled her pack and slipped into it, packed her bottle inside Abishai's quiver and hung it too across her back, and then checked her campsite one last time before she started up the stairs.

Carefully, Hannah poked her head above the lip of her fissure.

A group of vultures had surrounded the body of the cat and were loudly competing over what was left. They did not seem concerned about any other predators, so Hannah took that as a sign that she was the only person in the area.

Slowly, she emerged from the fissure, hands clasped nervously about the straps of her pack.

Little Brother shot past her, howling wildly as he charged the vultures.

The birds scattered, protesting shrilly.

Little Brother came back to her, looking quite pleased with himself.

"It looks as though someone needs to teach you the ways of polite society," Hannah said. "And of being quiet."

She walked over to Abishai's grave and stood there for a moment, thinking of the young man and saying a silent prayer and a good-bye.

Then, resolutely, she settled her pack more comfortably on her back. "Come, Little Brother. Maybe today is the day we find our family!" With a prayer for her own safety in her heart, she started forward.

CHAPTER FIVE

*M*uch of the day was spent following the still-obvious trail of Nephi and his people, and Hannah was feeling very blessed that there had been no rain to obliterate the tracks.

The light was growing dimmer. Knowing that the day was waning, Hannah started looking around for a place to spend the night.

The terrain had changed again, with the trees a little further apart and copses of brush and smaller trees here and there.

The last stream had been some time before, but both Hannah and Little Brother had drunk their fill and Hannah had managed to fill her bottle, so she was not concerned about staying near a body of water.

Choosing a likely patch of brush, Hannah first examined it, then, hoping it would be similar to her hiding place of a few days ago, got down on her hands and knees and crawled into it.

Just as she cleared the bushes, something shrieked wildly and struck her on the head.

Hannah stopped and, as the something kept flailing at her, began to back up, bumping into Little Brother.

Growling, he crawled around her, headed toward whatever had confronted his companion.

"Little Brother!" she shrieked. But her words were lost in the vicious noises he was making.

As soon as he passed her, she again heard the high-pitched shrieking.

Forgetting that she had just been attacked, Hannah followed Little Brother, finally emerging in a small space inside the trees similar to the one that had sheltered her.

Little Brother was standing, head lowered and legs stiff, facing a figure that had curled itself into a ball a pair of paces away.

Her attacker was human. Hannah caught her breath. Was this person a friend? Or foe? She moved slowly past Little Brother. "Who—who are you?"

The figure lowered an arm and peeped out at her briefly. Then let out another shriek and buried its head in its tunic again.

Hannah moved closer. "Who are you?" she repeated slowly.

"You are a spirit, come to punish me!"

Hannah blinked. "A spirit?"

"For the evil done to you. You are going to punish the wrongdoers!"

Hannah sat and pondered that for a moment, while Little Brother kept up a steady growl and protective stance.

"I'm Hannah," she said finally.

"I know who you are, Evil Spirit! You have come to punish me!"

"I assure you I am not. And I have not."

"That is what you would say if you were an evil spirit bent on revenge."

Hannah smiled. "I suppose you are right." She was quiet for a moment. "What can I do to convince you that I am not what you think I am?"

"You can leave!"

Hannah shrugged. "Come, Little Brother. We are not wanted here." She turned and made her way back through the bushes to the outside.

Little Brother, still growling deep in his throat followed her a moment later.

Hannah paused, looking around carefully. Seeing no one, she raised her voice a notch. "So are you here all alone?"

"No. My family is with me. And my father is a great hunter and tracker, so you probably would not want to stay!"

Hannah felt a feathering of alarm at the words. She quickly looked around again, then glanced at Little Brother, whose only interest seemed to lie with the person they had left inside the bushes.

"I do not believe that your family is with you. I think you are out here on your own."

Silence from the bushes.

"Were you with Nephi and his people and somehow got separated?"

"No."

"Laman's people?"

"*King* Laman! And why are you asking all these questions, Evil Spirit? Is it not enough that you have trapped me here? Now you must mock me as well?"

Hannah pursed her lips thoughtfully. "I am not trying to mock you. I am trying to discover how you managed to be way out here, several days journey from your home."

Silence.

"Did something happen to you?"

"No—maybe."

"Did you leave? Or did they drive you away?"

"I—why are you asking all these questions?"

"I am worried about you."

"Why would an evil spirit be worried about me?"

Hannah smiled. "Exactly. Why *would* an evil spirit be worried about you?"

"To trick me."

Hannah sighed deeply. This was not helpful. Looking around again and seeing no one, she decided to throw caution away. "Listen. My name is Hannah. First wife of Lemuel. My son is Samuel. I am a daughter of Ishmael; a follower of Nephi and of Lehi before him. My family betrayed me and t-tried to m-murder me." Hannah frowned at the break in her voice. She cleared her throat. "They did not succeed. I survived the stoning and am now trying to find my way to Nephi and his people."

The person inside the copse was silent for a moment. "You are not an evil spirit? One who would torture and kill me?"

38

Hannah laughed softly. "No. I am Hannah. The one who survived."

Another long silence. Finally, "I am coming out."

Sounds of someone crawling through the bushes. A head popped out, followed slowly by the rest of the figure.

Little Brother immediately began to growl again.

Hannah stood up and put a hand on his back. "Steady, Little Brother." She looked back at the figure. "Thank you for trusting me."

A girl, dressed in a torn and dirty tunic, got to her feet. "You can just as easily kill me there as here."

Hannah smiled. "I have no intention of killing you."

"That is what you would say—"

"—if I were an evil spirit," Hannah finished.

The figure pulled back a head cloth and reached out to touch Hannah. "You are not a spirit!"

Hannah laughed. "No."

The girl wrapped her arms around Hannah. "Mother Hannah, it is me, Tabitha."

Little Brother suddenly quit growling.

Tabitha. Daughter of Hannah's own husband, Lemuel, and his second wife, Iscah. Hannah put her arms around the slender figure and hugged back. Then she grasped the girl by the shoulders and held her away so she could peer into her face. The girl she had known had been young and dark-haired and clear-eyed. This girls's eyes, her very countenance, were shadowed and troubled. A streak of white had appeared in the dark hair. Hannah blinked. "Tabitha?"

The girl nodded, then put her hands to her hair and tried to tuck the errant strand out of sight under her headcloth.

Hannah sat down and stared at her. "What happened to you? What did you do to your hair?"

Slowly, the girl took a seat beside Hannah. "Mother Rachel said it is the curse."

"Mother Rachel?" Hannah felt as though she was merely repeating everything the girl said.

Tabitha nodded.

"Could you please start at the beginning?" Hannah patted Little Brother's head absently as the animal sat down beside her.

"Mother Rachel said Laman and his people would be cursed if we did not keep the commandments." She sighed. "When this happened, I knew it was the curse."

"Tabitha, did everyone's hair change?"

The girl looked down and shook her head no.

Hannah sighed. "It is not a curse, my daughter, but a sign of great trial and stress in your own life. What could possibly have been so horrible?" She closed her eyes. She could well imagine—in Laman's camp.

Tabitha touched her hair. "Trial?"

Hannah nodded.

Tabitha sighed. "I knew I should have left with Mother Rachel and Mother Litha."

Hannah's heart seemed to stop in her chest. "Left?"

Tabitha looked off into the trees. "They took their youngest children and left."

Hannah's eyes filled with tears. "They—believed?"

The girl's eyes filled as well. "I believed too. But Mother would not allow me to talk about it or visit the other camp with you." She sighed. "She told me the things I felt were foolish imaginings and if I did not control them and 'root them out' I would become as crazy and tiresome as—" She gasped and put one hand over her mouth.

"As me." Hannah smiled and touched the girl's hand. "I would have loved to have you along."

Tabitha smiled. "There were so many times when I wished I could have gone."

"So when did you leave?"

"The next day after you were—after you left, Mother called me in to tell me that arrangements had been made for my marriage."

Hannah caught her breath. "Marriage? To whom?"

"To Uncle Zedekiah's son, Jonah."

"You did not want to marry Jonah?"

Tabitha made a face. "All he cared about was hunting, hunting, hunting."

"You would have been well-fed."

"But spiritually starved."

Hannah stared at her. "I have never heard you speak like this."

"I have never dared." She looked away for a moment. "Mother had been suggesting it for many months. Since I reached my fifteenth year. But I knew the first time I saw Jonah with his face and body painted in blood that I could never marry him."

"So you decided to leave?"

"Not all at once. I walked over to Nephi's camp and looked around, not really believing they were gone."

"As did I."

"There, at the edge of the town, I saw their trail. I was surprised because King Laman had declared that they had covered their pathway out of town so well no one could follow them. But there were the tracks. As plain as—as my nose."

Hannah laughed and touched the girl's nose. "That is quite plain."

Tabitha looked at Hannah. "I knew then, Mother Hannah, that the Lord wanted me to follow Uncle Nephi."

Hannah smiled. "I received the same sign. It was right after—" She gasped.

"What is it?"

"Thaddeus and Abishai! I saw them then. And they are—"

"What?"

Hannah bit her lip and closed her eyes for a moment.

"What, Mother Hannah?"

She took a deep breath. "Dead. Thaddeus and Abishai. They are dead."

Tabitha's eyes filled with tears. "Dead?"

"I found Abishai yesterday in a river. He was—he was dying."

"And Tad?"

"Abishai told me that Thaddeus was—gone."

Tears formed streaks down Tabitha's cheeks. "How? How did they die?" She peered at Hannah. "Did King Laman kill them?"

"No, Precious One. No. It was one of the great jungle cats."

"The cats they are always hunting. To prove that they are men."

Hannah nodded. "I heard them as they were leaving on their hunt that morning. I was trying to find things to take with me and had been looking in Nephi's house when they walked by. So full of health and life. And all excited to have a successful hunt!"

"It is always the same. The only men King Laman will recognize are those with blood on their hands."

"And all over their bodies," Hannah added.

Tabitha slumped down. "Two more—gone."

"Perhaps it is better for them."

The girl looked at her. "How can you say that? How could it be better for them?"

"Maybe it is better to go home to our Father than it is to stay here bathing oneself in wickedness." She frowned. "Abishai said something just before he—died."

"What?"

"He told me he was going home. And that the Lord was helping him."

Tabitha was silent.

"You see? Maybe he *is* better off."

Tabitha nodded. "Perhaps you are right." She sat in silence for several moments. Finally, she straightened, brushed at her cheeks, took a deep breath, and then looked at Hannah. "You—before you talked of them, you said something about seeing the same things as me?"

Hannah blinked at the quick change of topic. But, she reasoned, Tabitha had been raised in the camp of Laman. Death was, though not frequent, common enough that the people had become accustomed to dealing with it. Even the children.

"Yes," she said. "Just after I saw Thaddeus and Abishai, I saw the tracks. I was surprised *they* had not seen them. I took it as a sign that I should follow." She looked at Tabitha. "And I had nowhere else to go. So I went."

"And now we are here."

"With Little Brother."

Tabitha looked at the animal. "What is it?"

"He is like our dogs back in Jerusalem."

"His eyes are yellow. Were your dogs' eyes yellow?"

"No. That is one difference." Hannah put a hand on Little Brother's head. "And he is bigger with longer legs."

"Maybe that is how dogs are here."

Hannah shrugged. "He does not bark as our dogs did. And only when he is starving will he eat something other than meat. But he has been a good companion and has provided us with our food on many occasions."

"What happened to his tail?"

"It was cruelly taken from him by the knife of one of Laman's warriors."

"They cut it off?"

Hannah nodded.

"Why would they cut off his tail?"

"Why, indeed." Hannah looked up. "It is getting quite dark. Would you mind if we share your shelter? We are happy to share our food."

Tabitha looked at her. "Of course, Mother Hannah. I would be honoured to have you with me."

Hannah followed the younger girl back through the bushes with Little Brother shadowing her closely.

The three of them shared what food Hannah had in her pack, finishing off both the meat and the tubers. Tabitha ate voraciously.

"What have you been eating, Precious One?" Hannah asked. "Since you left Laman's camp?"

"I had found some of those same tubers," Tabitha said, wiping her mouth on her headcloth. "And a couple of times I found some water nuts."

"I have been eating the same. With one or two animals provided by Little Brother."

"What will we eat tomorrow?" Tabitha asked as Hannah started to fold up her cat hide.

"The Lord will provide."

"I like your faith, Mother Hannah. It is—warm—and comforting."

Hannah smiled.

"That also looks very warm and comforting." Tabitha was looking at the fur.

Hannah frowned. "I suppose it is."

"Would you mind if I used it for a blanket?"

"It is not very fresh. I have had meat wrapped in it all day."

"It will be better than what I have." The girl looked around. "Which is nothing."

Hannah blinked and glanced about the small enclosure. Other than what Hannah had brought in with her, there was only the dirt and the surrounding bushes. "How have you survived?"

Tabitha smiled. "The Lord has provided."

"Well, the Lord has helped Mother Hannah provide tonight." Hannah pulled her two blankets out of her pack and tossed one to Tabitha. "Definitely better than a smelly animal skin."

CHAPTER SIX

*H*annah found it both easier and harder to travel with a companion. She finally had someone to talk to besides her four-footed friend and it was immensely comforting to have another human being close by. But now she had to provide for two people instead of one.

If not for the hunting abilities of Little Brother, the two of them may have been in a very sad state.

The next morning, after a prayer, they started out. They found a small stream not far from where they had camped and were able to clean themselves up, quench their thirst and fill their bottle, but though they hunted, they could not find any patches of tubers or water nuts.

Hannah could see that Tabitha was suffering for lack of food, but there was nothing she could do except pray. Which she did for the rest of the morning.

"What do you suppose that is?" Hannah followed Tabitha's pointing finger. Ahead of them was a carpet of dark green leaves, growing where a rare patch of sunlight reached the forest floor. They moved closer, stepping carefully. Peeping out between the leaves, they could see odd, red globes.

Tabitha reached for one of the globes, separated it from its stem and sniffed it.

"Careful, Tabitha. It may be poisonous."

The girl looked at her and smiled. "It is the answer to my prayers, Mother Hannah. I am sure of it." She nibbled one end. "It is delicious!"

She finished the treat and bent over to hunt for more.

"Wait!" Hannah put a hand on Tabitha's arm. "We must give thanks."

The girl nodded and clutched Hannah's hand. "Could you do it, please?"

"Of course." Hannah poured out her heart in gratitude for the bounty before them. Then the two of them hunted through the large patch, at first picking everything they could see.

"Ugh. Pick the red ones, Tabitha," Hannah cautioned, making a face. "The green are a bit . . . tart."

Tabitha laughed as she hunted. The crop was extensive and, before long, the women were holding up their skirts to capture their bounty in the folds.

Tabitha's mouth was ringed with red as the girl happily stuffed herself on the red fruit.

Hannah glanced at her husband's daughter, trying not to remember the last time she had seen someone's face painted in red. She shivered.

"Are you chilled, Mother Hannah?"

She looked over at Tabitha. "No, Dearest One. Just . . . remembering."

Tabitha looked at her for a moment, then nodded. She lifted one of the small red fruits and studied it. "What do you suppose it is?"

Hannah shrugged as she continued searching for more of the red fruit. "I do not know."

"Have you never seen it before?"

Hannah shook her head. "Not that I can recall."

"I think I shall call it—Sweetness."

Hannah straightened and looked at her. "Sweetness?"

"Yes. It is sweet and it is good. Sweetness suits it."

Hannah bent to her picking again. "The naming of the things of the earth was a task given to Father Adam." She glanced at Tabitha. "Not to a couple of women wandering in the wildnerness."

Tabitha laughed and tossed another globe of fruit into her mouth. "Well, Mother Hannah, until Father Adam comes to correct me, I shall call this fruit 'Sweetness.'"

"Trifle not with sacred things, my daughter." Hannah lifted her head and studied Tabitha soberly. "Remember to keep sacred things sacred."

"Are these sacred?" Tabitha looked down at the fruit in her hand.

Hannah smiled. "I think not. But our memories and manner of speaking about Father Adam need to be."

Tabitha nodded and bowed her head. "I meant no offence, Mother Hannah."

Hannah touched the girl's head. "I know you did not. But we must guard our tongues in the small things and then we will be strong enough to guard them in the great things."

Turning, she tossed one of the fruits to Little Brother.

The animal snapped it up and looked hopefully for more.

"We've finally found something Little Brother likes besides meat!"

Hannah straightened and smiled. "Well, that is good. Sometimes I think he will take a bite out of us while we sleep."

"Oh, not Little Brother," Tabitha said, throwing her free arm around the animal's shoulders. "He loves us!"

Little Brother growled. A threatening, angry, dangerous sound in the very bottom of his throat.

The hairs on the back of Hannah's neck reacted.

Tabitha froze. "Little Brother?"

Hannah turned toward the animal, ready to rush to Tabitha's aid.

But Little Brother was not looking at the girl. Instead, he was looking up into the tree which hung out over the patch of red fruit they had been picking.

"What is it, Little Brother?" Hannah asked.

The animal twitched away from Tabitha and moved toward the patch of fruit, keeping his eyes on the upper branches of the tree. Tabitha followed, her steps uncertain. Ahead of her, something dropped out of the tree.

Hannah's eyes widened. A small, furry, black body had appeared in the green tendrils of the fruit patch. The creature pricked little, round ears and bawled loudly, then began to sniff around with a long, dark snout, finding and eating several of the red fruits.

"What do you suppose—?" Hannah smiled. "That looks like the bear!" She turned excitedly to Tabitha. "Years ago, a caravan was driving along the road to Jerusalem and stopped near Father's lands. They had a great brown bear on a chain and the owner allowed me to pet it." She moved toward the busy little creature. "But theirs was much larger—"

A ferocious growl from further back in the trees interrupted her.

She stopped and looked up.

A larger version of the small creature in front of them emerged from the trees. One that easily outweighed either of the women as well as Little Brother. Growling viciously and showing great, white teeth, it rushed forward, reaching Tabitha before she could react.

It lifted a large paw and struck at the girl, spinning her around and flinging her back toward Hannah.

Immediately, Little Brother was between the women and the creature, snarling savagely and showing his own white teeth.

The animal reared up on its hind legs, opened its great mouth and roared.

Hannah gasped. When it stood thus, it easily topped her own height.

Tabitha shrieked and covered her ears.

Hannah grabbed the terrified girl by the sleeve and she and Tabitha scrambled to put distance between them and the two glaring, growling animals.

The larger animal roared again and, dropping to all four feet, made a short feint in Little Brother's direction.

Little Brother charged forward, leaping and snapping at the larger animal's throat.

The animal reared back, seeming surprised by the attack and struck at Little Brother with both front paws.

But Little Brother was faster and the great claws raked the air above him as he dropped to the ground.

Again the animal came at him and again, Little Brother jumped for its throat.

This time, the animal was more prepared and swatted at Little Brother before he came close. The blow caught him on the shoulder and he sailed toward the ground.

Hannah gasped, expecting to see her companion as a bloodied heap.

But Little Brother was tough and far too agile. He was able to use the momentum of the blow. Shifting so his feet hit the ground, he sprang off it and right back at the larger creature.

Again, it reared back, surprised by the unexpected action and remained there, watching Little Brother carefully.

This time, Little Brother dropped to the earth just out of reach of the larger animal. Then, legs braced stiffly, head lowered and yellow eyes glowing in the afternoon light, he confronted his opponent, a deep growl rumbling through his chest.

The larger animal again rose to its hind legs, paused and looked at Little Brother, then lowered itself back to the ground.

For several moments, the two faced each other. Then Little Brother, with smooth, sure movements, slowly began to back away.

The great animal watched him closely until he had put most of the clearing between them.

The smaller creature behind it squalled and the large one turned and moved toward it. Then it, too, started rooting through the green leaves in search of the red fruit. A couple of times, it lifted its head and looked in their direction. But, though it growled, it made no further threatening moves.

Hannah, Tabitha and Little Brother, still keeping their eyes on the creature, continued to move away until, finally, the two strange animals were out of sight.

"What are those?" Tabitha whispered. The girl had locked one hand in the skirt of Hannah's tunic.

Hannah gently disengaged the fingers and squeezed them. Then released them and frowned down at her own hand. "Tabitha? Are you bleeding?"

The girl looked down at her arm. "Well. I guess I . . ." She slid to the ground.

Tabitha did not lose consciousness for long.

Hannah had just managed to lift the tattered sleeve of the girl's tunic when her eyes opened.

"Is it . . . bad?"

Hannah dampened the edge of her headcloth and swabbed gently at the bloodied skin. "I do not think so, Dearest One. I think the animal's claws only scratched."

"I feel no pain," Tabitha said. She moved her arm.

"Wait, Dearest. Let me have a good look." Hannah had seen wounds before. In a camp of hunters, someone was usually getting clawed or bitten or gored. She finished cleaning the wound.

"There are three long scratches." She leaned forward and peered down at them. "They are not deep. Truly, the large animal almost missed you."

"What did you say that was? That animal?"

"I do not know for certain, but I think it may have been a bear." She repeated to the girl her story of the caravan and the bear she had seen. "Their bear was kept on a chain and it was sweet and friendly. I remember the soft, brown fur when I was allowed to pet it." She glanced back the way they had come. "It too was able to stand on its hind legs and the sound of its roaring was similar."

"But it was brown?"

"Perhaps, like horses, they come in different colors."

"Is the small one a bear as well?"

"I think so." Hannah shrugged. "Perhaps it was a baby."

"They were eating the red fruit. But the large one had such great, sharp teeth."

"I am not certain, but I think bears eat more than just meat. I know the people with the great bear back in Jerusalem fed the animal everything they were eating. Bread. Cheese. Fruit."

Tabitha laughed nervously. "I am glad for that!"

Hannah nodded. "As am I." She tore a piece off her headcloth and tied it snugly around Tabitha's arm. "There. That should keep it from bleeding. I do not think it will cause you any permanent discomfort."

Tabitha laughed. "Whenever one of the hunters was wounded, I was never invited into the room where he was being cared for. The sight of blood and I—we are not friends."

50

Hannah smiled. "A great handicap when one lives with hunters."

"It made me—unpopular among the other young women."

Hannah shook her head. Had she been so immersed in her own troubles that she failed to notice those of the other people in her camp? Their struggles? Her two sisters-by-marriage had believed. This young Tabitha had believed. And Hannah simply had not noticed. They could have supported each other. She sighed for the things that might have been.

Tabitha nodded. "A great handicap indeed." She looked down. Her uninjured hand was still clutching the hem of her tunic. Even frightened and hurt, she had somehow managed to retain her small harvest of red fruit. She grinned. "I kept my red fruit."

Hannah looked down and smiled. "You did. Now that is heroic!"

"You are always heroic. Just now, you were able to move. To act. I was filled entirely with fear." She looked at Hannah. "I wish I could conquer my fear as you have."

Hannah shivered. "No, I was very frightened. I guess as one gets older, one grows accustomed to hanging on, even when things look very dark."

Little Brother came over and she knelt down and hugged him. "Thank you," she whispered into one ear. "Thank you!"

The animal turned glowing yellow eyes on her, then swiped at her cheek with a red tongue.

"Ugh!" Hannah scrubbed at the wet spot with the sleeve of her tunic.

Tabitha tipped her head to one side and looked at her. Then she laughed.

"What is it?" Hannah rubbed at her face again. "Have I something on me?"

Tabitha nodded. "A wet, clean spot."

"Oh." Hannah stopped scrubbing. She sighed. "I sometimes feel as though I will never be clean again." She got to her feet and turned. "Come, my sister, we must find a different route."

———•◆•———

The forest was ending. Hannah and Tabitha stopped at the edge and made a meal of their red fruit and a large, furry woodland creature

that Little Brother dug out of a burrow and shared with them. Then
the three of them stood and looked out across the expanse of a great
field stretched before them.

The trail of Nephi and his people could be seen straight ahead.
A short distance into the treeless region, a series of hills started. The
tracks disappeared around the first.

"Tomorrow, Mother Hannah?" Tabitha asked.

Hannah sighed and nodded. "Tomorrow, Dearest One."

The two women turned back and found shelter nearby—inside
the bole of an enormous tree. The tree was slumped to one side, as
though it had simply become tired of standing upright. The middle
part had rotted partially away, leaving a space just big enough for two
women and their four-footed companion to curl up in.

The black night was around them, thick and soft and warm. The
jungle alive with the sounds of animals on the cusp of sleep. Or just
awakening.

Tabitha's voice came out of the darkness. "Thank you, Mother
Hannah."

"For what, Dearest One?"

"For bringing me with you."

Hannah sighed. "There was never any question about you coming
with me."

"But there might have been. With the way our people treated
you." The girl was silent for a moment. "I would not have blamed you
if you had just kept on walking."

Hannah smiled into the darkness. "Have you ever listened to
Father Lehi? Or Brother Nephi?"

"Yes."

"What did they teach about revenge or anger or cruelty?"

"That revenge belongs to the Lord. That anger and cruelty have
no place among the Lord's own people."

"You were listening."

Tabitha stirred. "I was."

"I have forgiven our people, Tabitha."

The girl sucked in a breath. "Even—?"

"Even Father Lemuel and my s-son, Samuel."

Silence for a moment.

"How that must have hurt you."

Hannah sighed. "The pain of the stones was nothing to the pain of the betrayal."

"But you can forgive them?"

"They have been led astray."

"So your anger is turned to King Laman?"

"*Laman,*" Hannah emphasized the word, "is not my king. And not yours either."

"I am sorry. It is just that we had to—"

Hannah interrupted. "I understand. But he is not *my* king." She settled more comfortably against the wall. "I have only one king. My Lord. I will bow to no one else."

"I did not want to."

"Of course, Dearest One."

"So is it *Laman* you are angry with?"

Hannah sighed again. "No. Not even him. I think my anger is turned more toward the Father of All Lies. The one who lead Laman down that dark path of greed and treachery."

Again Tabitha was silent. "And then Laman leads—"

"Yes. The Lord of Lies leads Laman, who leads Lemuel, who leads Samuel. It is a forever chain. The chain of the forever damned."

"But you said you forgive them. If you forgive them, how will they be damned?"

"*I* forgive them, Dearest One. But they, indeed all of us, will have to answer to divine justice. Each of us will have to pay for our sins."

"But to be damned."

"Damned is stopped, Dearest One. Like a dam on a river. No progress. No glorious eternal rewards. Stopped. Those who achieve that state will carry on into eternal life, once their debt is paid. But they will only be able to progress so far. Their choices here will dictate their rewards there. Some blessings they never will be able to receive."

The two of them settled after that, each finding slumber in the thick darkness.

Sometime later, Hannah awoke to the sounds of Little Brother moving around. Reaching out, she touched his wiry hair. "What is it?"

The animal circled a few times and lay down once more, huffing quietly.

Then Hannah heard the sound of something hitting the ground outside. Pelting it. Something like—she gasped and shot to her feet, hitting her head on the solid part of the tree above her. "Ouch!"

"Mmm? What is it?" Tabitha's sleepy voice came out of the blackness.

Hannah swallowed her panic. "It is raining, Dearest One," she said as evenly as possible.

"Oh. I like the rain."

Hannah sniffed softly. She, too liked the rain. Coming from the arid lands of Jerusalem, the sound of rain was always welcome. Until now. When one realized that the onslaught of life-giving droplets of water could soon obliterate the precious tracks they had been following.

How would they find Nephi and his people?

———— • ♦ • ————

Dawn brought only grayness.

As soon as it was light enough to see, Hannah was out of their shelter and gazing about her at the soggy landscape.

"Are you all right, Mother Hannah?" Tabitha emerged, sleepy-eyed.

"I am well, Dearest One."

Tabitha stretched and yawned. "I was having the most glorious dream. We were at Grandfather Ishmael's home in Jerusalem. I have never seen it, but Mother and you and others have described it so well. Anyways, I dreamed I was there and you and I were working in the garden. And it started to rain and we were laughing and dancing in it . . ." She broke off. "It *is* raining."

Hannah nodded.

The girl gasped and spun about to look across the treeless expanse. "The tracks!"

"Gone."

CHAPTER SEVEN

For some time, the two of them stared into the great field.

Finally, water dripping down her face, Tabitha turned to Hannah. "But . . . what will we do?"

Hannah shrugged. Then she turned and walked back to their tree. She patted the trunk as she ducked inside. It looked like she felt—suddenly too tired to go on.

Seconds later, Tabitha joined her there.

For a few minutes, they sat in silence.

Then Tabitha reached across and touched Hannah's arm. "Mother Hannah? What can we do?" she asked again.

"I do not know, Dearest One." Hannah patted the slender fingers. "I simply do not know." She turned her face away so Tabitha would not see the weak tears that were coursing down her cheeks.

She had endured so much and kept on going.

Felt and suffered so much. And still kept on going.

And now she was at the end of the path. There was no way forward. That had been blocked. It was as though the Lord was telling her, "This is as far as you go, Daughter. I never meant for you to succeed. Only try."

Why? Why would the Lord lead them only so far? Protect them and care for them and then abandon them here. Beyond the help of anyone else.

Hannah was numb, her mind empty. Though the air was warm, she felt chilled. Shivering, she wrapped her arms around herself.

For the first time, she felt truly alone.

Then she felt the familiar fluttering in her belly.

Hannah gasped, sliding a hand over her stomach. There it was again. She was not alone. Someone else was depending on her.

"Mother Hannah?"

Hannah smiled slightly. Make that *two* someones.

A red tongue licked her hand.

And one more.

A scripture often quoted by Nephi suddenly came to her mind. *"Be of good courage, and he shall strengthen your heart, all ye that hope in the Lord."*

Did she have hope in the Lord? Did she truly believe the things that Father Lehi and Brother Nephi had been saying?

Could she go on?

Another kick from within.

She blotted her tears on the sleeve of her tunic, took a deep breath and straightened. She could go on. Her heart swelled within her.

She *would* go on.

"Mother Hannah?"

She turned to Tabitha. "We go on, Dearest One. Once the rains have stopped, we go on."

———————◆———————

She checked Tabitha's bandage again, but the bleeding had stopped and the wound seemed to be knitting normally.

The rain had continued unabated throughout the morning. Little Brother had gone on a hunt and brought back another large rabbit.

After the three of them had eaten their fill, Hannah laid the hide of the animal out in the rain. In a short time, the warm water had washed it clean, and she brought it back under the trees, rolled neatly, and stowed in her pack with all of the others. Hannah smiled. She was gaining quite a collection of animal skins.

Turning to her companions, she said, "Well, I suppose we should be on our way."

Tabitha leaned out of their shelter and peered up into the dripping trees. "Could we not remain here one more day? It is already past the middle hours. We would not get far before nightfall. Perhaps by tomorrow, the rains will have stopped and we will be able to proceed in relative comfort."

Hannah shrugged. "Are you not worried about the tracks?"

"Mother Hannah, the tracks are lost to us. The rains already fallen have taken care of that."

"I guess you are right." Hannah sighed. She, too peered up into the trees above them. "Perhaps it *will* be better tomorrow."

But the rains continued unabated through the night.

———— ◆ ————

By morning, the entire landscape had turned a dull greenish-gray. And, even here under the trees, the ground had become soft. Hannah and Tabitha stood at the edge of the forest and looked out across the soggy countryside.

"What do you think, Mother Hannah?"

Hannah sighed as she looked up at the fat, gray clouds. "I think we may as well go on, Dearest One. This rain shows no signs of abating. We cannot spend days here waiting for the weather to clear. Each day, the people of Nephi are drawing further and further from us. We must go on."

"Where do we go?"

"The tracks led there." Hannah pointed. "We will go there." She looked up. "And then we will trust in the Lord."

"Perhaps he erased the tracks because he wanted us to trust in him completely."

Hannah blinked and looked at Tabitha. "I never thought of that, Dearest One, and I think you are right. The Lord wants us to trust in him for a time and not the evidence of our eyes."

"Faith is believing something you cannot see with your eyes."

Hannah smiled. "And now it is your turn to teach me."

They started forward. Their tunics, headcloths, and hair were immediately soaked. But the rain was warm and Hannah realized that, if she kept moving forward, she really was not that uncomfortable.

The bigger problem proved to be the soggy ground.

Both she and Tabitha were soon ankle deep in a dark brown morass.

Little Brother seemed unaffected by the sticky mud.

Hannah watched as he leapt lightly from grassy hummock to grassy hummock, avoiding the brown mud completely. She frowned and looked back at her companion. "Stay on the grass, Dearest One. Try to avoid the bare patches where the earth shows through."

Tabitha nodded, already winded by her efforts to pull one foot after the other from the sucking mud.

Hannah watched as the girl set a newly-released foot on a thick knot of grass, then pulled the other foot up and did the same.

Tabitha smiled at Hannah in momentary triumph, then suddenly lost her balance and, both hands waving wildly, fell over backwards.

Hannah pulled her feet from the mud and hurried to her companion as fast as she could, careful to keep to the grassy patches. Reaching out, she grasped Tabitha's hand and pulled the girl to her feet.

Tabitha looked down at her muddied tunic, then at the thick, dark muck on her hands. She turned to Hannah, bottom lip quivering and for a moment, tears seemed to threaten. Then Tabitha put her head back and began to laugh.

For a moment, Hannah stared at her. Then she, too, joined in.

For several minutes, the two of them stood there in the pouring rain, soaked and filthy, bruised, battered, and half-starved, and they screamed with laughter. When one would start to get herself under control, the other would go off again.

Finally, exhausted, but feeling strangely lighter, they calmed themselves.

"Well? Shall we continue on?" Hannah asked.

Tabitha nodded. She shook her hands, dislodging what mud she could and the two of them started forward once more.

For most of the morning, they picked their way across the countryside, stepping from knot to knot and trying to avoid the muddier places.

Hannah was grateful for the strong ties on her sandals. The final difficulty would have been for one of them to lose a shoe.

The trail they had seen from the edge of the forest had wound around the first of a series of small hills. Nothing of it remained, but the two women with their four-footed companion continued forward as surely as if it were in plain sight. Hannah's lips moved in a constant silent prayer as she poured out her heart to her Lord.

It was difficult, in the gloom, to tell the time of the day, but shortly after what Hannah assumed to be the middle hour, the two of them stopped near a lone tree to rest.

A short distance away rose one of the higher of the chain of hills, oddly bare in the faded green of the surrounding countryside.

Hannah and Tabitha leaned back against the tree, thankful, for the moment, to be out of the rain.

Tabitha sighed. "How far have we come, Mother Hannah?"

Hannah shrugged tiredly. "Not as far as we think."

"I feel as though I had walked across an entire country."

"I am fairly certain we have not come that far."

Tabitha laughed and straightened away from the tree and pointed. "Look, Mother Hannah! A stream."

"More water." Hannah rolled her eyes.

"But I can finally wash my hands."

"I thought the rain had taken care of that."

Tabitha laughed. "Well, most of it. But not all." She moved away from the tree.

Just then, the ground began to shake.

Confused, Hannah looked around, finally fastening her gaze on the hill that rose over them. It seemed to be—moving. A great wall of mud was sliding down the slope toward them.

She sucked in a breath. "Tabitha! Run!" she screamed.

She saw Tabitha's frightened face look at her, then turn toward the hill. The girl gaped at it blankly, obviously unsure what she was seeing.

"Run!" Hannah screamed again.

Tabitha started to move, but her movements were sluggish and she had taken only a few steps when the wall of mud grasped her, immediately sliding the girl's feet out from under her and carrying her along helplessly.

"Tabitha!" Heedless of her own danger, Hannah started to move away from the tree just as the river of mud reached it.

Gasping, she grabbed the tree and hung on, praying it would hold. She tried to keep her eyes on Tabitha, but the girl was soon so covered in mud that she was indistinguishable from the mess surrounding her.

In moments it was over. The ground had stopped moving and settled.

But nothing was the same.

The entire countryside was changed. A sea of mud covered everything. And somewhere in the mess was her young companion.

Frantic, Hannah released her hold on the tree, then, screaming out Tabitha's name, she waded into the morass.

Little Brother appeared out of nowhere, and as her frantic calls continued, seemed to understand that something terrible had happened. He bounded away from her, making his growling and barking noises.

A short distance away, he began to howl and then dig in the mud.

Hannah struggled toward him, frantic at the enforced slow pace.

Finally, she reached her four-footed companion.

The animal was digging around an arm. Tabitha!

Just behind him, Hannah could see half of the girl's face. She could still breathe!

Hannah joined him, working frantically to dig the girl out.

Their efforts were impeded both by the thick mud which slid back to fill the holes and the water from the constant rain.

Panting, Hannah kept working. Kept digging. Kept pushing. The sweat dripped down into her eyes. She rubbed at them with the back of her hand, leaving a thick band of mud across her face.

Tabitha's eyes opened and the girl watched her two would-be rescuers. Her mouth opened. "Mother Hannah—"

Hannah stopped digging and looked at her. "We are here, Dearest One! We will get you out!"

"Mother Hannah—"

"No! Stop talking! We can do this!"

Tabitha shook her head, or tried to. "It is no use. The mud just slides back."

"Can you move your other arm, Dearest One? Your legs? Anything?"

Tabitha again tried to shake her head. "Leave me, Mother Hannah."

"I will never leave you!" Hannah said fiercely.

"Leave me."

"I will die before I leave you!"

"There will be no dying today."

Hannah spun around.

Nephi and Sam and a group of brothers were standing there, strong and straight in the rain and the knee-deep muck.

Hannah blinked, and then she collapsed into the mud.

CHAPTER EIGHT

*H*annah's hands sank into the morass in a vain attempt to prevent her fall.

"Careful, Sister Hannah!" A hand caught hers and pulled her back upright. Nephi peered at her. "It is Sister Hannah, is it not?"

She gulped and nodded as the tears started to flow. "It is."

"Well, let us help you." Nephi turned to Sam and the others. "A couple of you take Sister Hannah here to safety while the rest of us help dig out—" He crouched down and looked into Tabitha's face. "Who do we have here?"

"Tabitha," the girl whispered.

Nephi smiled, showing strong, white teeth. "Let's get Tabitha out of her very uncomfortable predicament."

A surprisingly short time later, both women were seated in a relatively dry spot beneath an overhang, safely beyond the reach of the river of mud.

The rain still poured down and neither of them was recognizable, even to themselves. But Hannah's heart was singing and she could not stop smiling.

She had done it! With the Lord's help, she had found Nephi and his people!

She sighed and leaned out of her shelter, letting the warm rain run over her face and head.

She felt washed clean.

———————————— • ◆ • ————————————

Sam came over to them. "Sisters, are you ready?"

Hannah nodded eagerly and got to her feet.

Tabitha was a bit slower in standing. Sam reached out a hand and helped support her. She was obviously still feeling the effects of being buried under a wall of mud.

"Let's get you home," he said.

It sounded so wonderful. Like being invited into heaven itself.

The two women were helped to mount a horse, Tabitha in front and Hannah behind, with her arms around the girl in case she weakened during the ride home.

Hannah had never been on a horse before. She felt a little nervous at being so far from the ground. They were certainly much taller than the donkeys she was used to, though not as tall as the camels she had sometimes snatched a ride on.

Tabitha must have been just as nervous. Every time Hannah moved, the girl grabbed her arm.

Hannah patted her shoulder and looked around. "Have you seen Little Brother?"

"The little wolf cub without the tail that was hanging around?" Sam appeared beside them, his brown eyes warm and friendly.

"Wolf?" Hannah blinked.

"Yes."

"I—I guess."

"He's over there." Sam pointed.

Hannah looked. Little Brother was seated out a short distance away, watching all the men warily.

Sam grinned at her. "When he refused to leave, we sort of figured he must be with you."

Hannah looked at the creature. "He is not growling or making a fuss."

Sam frowned slightly. "Does he usually?"

"Oh, yes. He makes a terrible noise."

Sam looked once more at the animal as he grabbed their mount's lead rope and mounted the horse in front of them. "I guess the creature's just glad to be here."

Hannah thought about that. Did Little Brother know as she did that they were all safe now?

One of the men walked past and patted the animal on his head. Little Brother allowed it, even got to his feet and followed the man for a few steps before sitting back down and resuming his watch of the camp. Hannah smiled. Even animals could feel the Spirit here.

Hannah sighed and sat back. This was a far easier way to travel.

———— ◆ ————

Only a pair of hours later, Hannah and Tabitha, along with Little Brother and the group of men, were riding along a short street of neat homes.

Hannah looked up in surprise. One minute, they had been navigating around yet another hill. And the next she was in the bosom of a community.

She straightened and brushed the rain from her eyes. It was as though she had never left Nephi's camp.

The street was nearly identical to the one she had left only ten days before.

There were differences. A large shelter: the hastily-erected, thatched-roofed structure of their early days in the Promised Land, had been constructed. The rest of the street was lined with tents. No stone work had yet been attempted.

No crops grew, although bare patches of earth showed beside nearly every dwelling, attesting to the industry—and faith—of the people of Nephi.

As their little caravan moved along the street, Hannah could see that, even in the unrelenting rain, construction was still ongoing.

Several people were busy finishing the thatching of a roof on a small hut and, beside them, another crew was erecting the walls of yet another cottage.

For a fleeting moment, Hannah pictured the sloth and lassitude of her old community. The unkempt yards. The homes unimproved and already falling into disrepair. Then she smiled. Diligence and faith. Together they produced such comforting results.

Somewhere, Hannah could hear the sound of music—p ipes being played. More than one set in a light, pleasing harmony. She tipped her head to one side and listened. There had been no music in Laman's camp. Everyone had been too busy hunting or slaughtering or celebrating. It was the final sign that they had arrived in the Lord's camp.

"Mother Hannah! Can you hear that? What is it?"

"It is music, Precious One. We are among the People of the Lord."

Their little train stopped and the men began to dismount.

Suddenly, someone screamed Hannah's name.

Hannah and Tabitha both spun their heads toward the sound.

"Hannah! Is it really you?" Moriah was running toward them, her arms out. "It is! It is you!" She laughed joyously. "I knew you would come!"

She grabbed Hannah's tunic and pulled. Both riders slid off, knocking her to the wet street.

Laughing, Moriah got to her feet, now nearly as muddy as the two newcomers. Then she wrapped her arms around Hannah and squeezed tightly. Finally, she loosed her grip, moving back slightly so she could put her hands on either side of Hannah's face and look into it. "Now we are together once more."

Tears made streaks in the mud of both faces as the two women embraced again. Then Moriah smiled and turned to Tabitha. "Is this—little Tabitha? I would hardly have known you, Dearest One!" She touched the girl's face, then drew her into a warm hug. "I am so happy to welcome you home!"

Tabitha, too, began to cry.

There was another cry of: "Hannah!" And suddenly, they were surrounded by more of the people of Nephi. Hannah's sisters Anava and Amanna both gave her warm embraces of welcome, ignoring the mud that caked her.

Then Nephi, leading his horse, approached the chattering group. "Perhaps we should find our two sisters some shelter and a warm meal? Maybe a cleansing and a change of raiment?"

"Oh! Of course!" People quickly ushered the two women toward the cottage that was just receiving its roof.

"You can stay here," Moriah said. "This can be your home!"

Hannah stopped. "But does it not belong to someone—?"

Anava interrupted. "Of course. You!" She grabbed Hannah and Tabitha's hands. "Come along!" She drew them through the door and into the small hut.

Hannah sighed happily as the rain stopped instantly. "The roof seems to be working," she said.

"The floor is damp but we can cover it for now. You wait here!" Anava disappeared through the doorway.

"Here!" Moriah took her place, carrying a mat and two cushions. "You can sit on these while we get things together." She handed the cushions to Hannah and Tabitha and spread the mat. Then took the pillows back, set them on the floor and pressed the two women down onto them.

People began appearing, each of them carrying household fixtures. Rugs. Rush lamps. Sleeping pallets. Blankets.

And suddenly, Mother Sariah was there, thrusting two thick rolls of bread stuffed with meat and cheese into their hands. Hannah nearly dropped hers as she jumped to her feet. She hesitated about hugging the frail woman.

But Mother Sariah had no such misgivings and wrapped her daughter-by-marriage in a warm hug. Then turned and gave her granddaughter, Tabitha, the same.

Hannah began to speak, but Mother Sariah shushed her. "Wait, my daughter. There will be time after you have had a chance to tidy up and get settled. I will wait." She turned and disappeared through the door.

Hannah sat down once more. A few moments later, she put the food she held to her mouth and took a bite. Then she took another. And another. Never had she tasted anything so fine.

Someone brought in a large wooden bowl and a couple of buckets of warm water.

"Here, my dears," Moriah said. "Warm water and soap to wash yourselves and combs for your hair." She looked up as someone brought in a bundle of clothing. "And tunics with which to clothe yourselves."

Hannah put her hand to her head. She had not had anything with which to properly clean herself these past ten days of her journey, other than the cursory splashing she and Tabitha had been able to give themselves at passing streams. Both of them had simply left their hair in an increasingly soiled plait under a more and more unrecognizable headcloth.

Clean, combed hair would seem like such a luxury. And clean bodies? And to be able to finally change her torn and filthy tunic? Miraculous.

Someone had been fitting a door on thick leather hinges and now the people withdrew and closed it behind them, leaving the two women to themselves.

"We will be waiting, my dears." Moriah's voice came through the door. "Come and sup with us!"

Hannah and Tabitha looked at each other. Then each wrapped the other in a warm embrace and let their tears of gratitude flow.

———— ◆ ————

A couple of hours later, two much less muddy and trailworn women exited their small hut and, holding their freshly donned headcloths forward to shield their faces from the rain, stepped into the street.

Immediately, Moriah was waving from the large tent across the way. "Come, my dears! Come where it is warm!"

They hurried over and ducked inside. At once, the combined smells of cooking and melted tallow filled their senses.

"Come!" Moriah indicated the mat on the floor with Mother Sariah, Amanna, and Anava seated around it and food already temptingly arranged across it.

In one corner, Moriah's youngest son, Eamon, and his twin brother, Eadric, were each holding a small set of pipes and blowing earnestly into them. Already they proved they had mastered simple tunes.

Tabitha watched them closely, a wide smile on her face.

Truly, they had reached heaven.

———— •◆• ————

A short time later, the two boys left to play, leaving the women alone.

Amanna peered closely at the scratches on Tabitha's arm. "Well, if this creature was as large and strong as you describe, it truly is a miracle you were not more badly injured."

"There were many miracles on our journey," Hannah said softly.

Moriah put a hand on Tabitha's head. "Getting buried by mud and living to speak of it would also be mentioned."

Hannah smiled. "Our little Tabitha is much stronger than she appears."

Tabitha ducked her head. "I travelled with the Lord's strength. And the Lord's protection."

Hannah nodded. "It is true. We both did."

Anava sighed. "But why did you not come with us?" She looked at Hannah. "On that last day, when I asked you. Why did you not come then?"

"I—I was not of a mind yet." Hannah absently rubbed the lump on the top of her head, under her hair.

"Mother, Hannah was stoned," Tabitha said. "On that last night after you left."

Hannah's sisters stared at her, the blood fading from their faces. "Stoned?" Moriah gasped.

Anava grabbed Hannah's hand. "They stoned you?"

Hannah sighed. Then nodded.

"And Father and Cousin Samuel were there."

Her sisters looked from Tabitha to her.

"Hannah! Why did you not say?" Moriah took a seat beside her. "Are you—Did they—How did you find the strength to make such a journey after such an experience?"

Hannah looked at her sisters and smiled. "We've already been over that."

They nodded, eyes still wide. "Truly, through the Lord all things are possible."

Moriah leaned forward and peered into Hannah's face. "But your injuries. Surely there must be some yet?"

Hannah shook her head. "None that give me any pain." She touched the lump again. "Well . . . one."

Moriah brushed her hand aside and placed her own where it had been. "Sister, there is quite a lump here!"

"It causes little physical pain," Hannah said. "If not for the memories . . ."

"That is the sign of the final blow," Tabitha said. "The last, most significant stone."

Anava put her arm around Hannah's shoulders. "The last stone."

"Dropped by Samuel," Tabitha added. "When he stoned his own mother."

Hannah's head came up and she looked at her husband's daughter. The others went still.

Tabitha took a shaky breath. "I saw it all."

Hannah stared at her. "You did?"

Tabitha started to weep. "I never told you. I could not bear the fact that I . . . did nothing to help."

Hannah's own eyes filled with tears as she reached over and grasped the girl's cold hand. "What could you do, Dearest One?"

"I could have done something!"

Hannah shook her head. "There was nothing anyone could have done. Except Laman." She scrubbed at her face with the sleeve of her tunic and sighed. "For years, he tried to keep a foot on both paths, the Lord's and the world's. When the two began to separate he could keep up the pretence, but only for a while. Finally the differences became too distinct and he had to commit to the one path or the other. And when he did, he and those who blindly follow him were caught. Trapped in the choices they had made. Unable to turn to the right or to the left, but committed to simply walk forward." She looked at her sisters as a tear trickled down her cheek. "My family. Trapped."

Anava squeezed Hannah's arm and nodded. "Oh, Favored One. I am so sorry." She looked at the others. "When one is committed to follow the Father of All Lies, one slides further and further into sin and even depravity until the soul is forever lost."

Moriah looked at Tabitha. "The choices made by your family were made long ago, Dearest One, when their hearts were committed to evil. Of course they can always come back, but generally, when a person commits to follow, they follow."

Hannah put her arm around the girl's slender shoulders. "I am sorry that you witnessed that horrifying event. Sorry that it will be forever printed in your memory as it is in mine. But know this. 'Whoever would lean upon the Lord will gain His strength.'"

Tabitha nodded. "And I will be leaning."

———— ◆ ————

Despite the continuing rain, the moment Hannah and Tabitha finished their meal, Anava, Amanna, and Moriah hurried them out of the house and up the street.

"Everyone wants to see you," Anava panted as they sprinted through the fat drops.

"But we told them we got you first," Moriah said from her other side. "We told them we would share, but only after we got you to ourselves for a while."

A lamp had been lit at the large structure up the street. She and the others hurried to it and when Anava held the door open and dashed inside.

The room was filled with people and Hannah felt her heart fill with joy when they all let out a mighty shout at her appearance.

Nephi came through the crowd and wrapped, first Hannah, then Tabitha, in a warm hug. "My sisters," he said quietly. "I am so very happy to welcome you!"

Hannah's eyes overflowed with tears of gratitude and happiness. "Thank you," she managed, squeezing her voice out over the lump in her throat.

Nephi nodded and smiled, then turned discreetly away, allowing her to blot surreptitiously at her face. "My family, through the help and guidance of the Lord, here are our sisters to join us."

Another cheer went up and his words seemed to be the cue for everyone to surge forward to personally welcome both of them. By the time the youngest of Anava's daughter Esther's eight children had given Hannah a squeeze about her knees, Hannah was so weakened with emotion she was almost overcome.

Then she turned and there were Rachel and Litha.

Hannah felt her eyes widen. And the tears start.

"Sister, I am sorry. We should have taken you. Can you forgive us?" Rachel asked.

Hannah struggled to hold back the tears but in vain. They began to stream down her face.

"We did not think you meant to come," Litha said. "Sister, if we had known, we would have somehow come to you and taken you with us on that last night."

"It is not that," Hannah said, scrubbing vainly at her face with her headcloth. "I mean . . . I—I h-have some news for you."

"News?" Rachel frowned. "For me?"

Unable to force her voice past her tight throat, Hannah nodded toward Litha.

"Both of us?"

Another nod.

Rachel put a hand on Hannah's arm. "Well, tell us, Sister."

Hannah took a deep breath. "It is your . . . sons."

Both of the women gasped. "Our sons?" Litha asked. "Which of our sons?"

Hannah closed her eyes for a moment. Then looked at Rachel. "Your Thaddeus." She turned to Litha. "And your Abishai." Her courage failed her as the two women regarded her intently.

Rachel shook her arm slightly. "Well, what, Sister?"

"They were hunting the great jungle cats and they . . . they . . ." She could not go on.

"Sister, you are frightening us!" Litha said. "Were they hurt?"

"Tell them, Sister," someone said.

Hannah looked up.

Nephi was standing beside them, his eyes steady on her.

She nodded and took another deep breath. "They were k-killed in the hunt."

Rachel and Litha stared at her, their eyes wide with shock.

"*Killed?*" Rachel dropped her hand to her lap. "Thaddeus? Killed?"

Hannah nodded, tears streaming down her face. "I did not see Thaddeus, but Abishai . . ."

"What? What did you see?"

"It is better that they know it all, Sister," Nephi said.

Hannah scrubbed at her face again. "I had just set up my camp for the night. Little Brother was sleeping and did not follow me back to the river for water."

"Little Brother?"

Hannah looked around, but her four-footed companion was nowhere to be seen. In fact she could not remember seeing him after she reached the village.

"Perhaps you should finish your tale, Sister," Nephi suggested.

"Oh. Of course." Hannah shook her head, frowning as herself. "I do not know . . ."

"*Hannah!*" Rachel almost shrieked.

Hannah jumped.

"Be patient with her, Sisters," Nephi said. "This is just as difficult for her."

Hannah took another big breath. "I was at the stream and saw something move in the water." She looked at Litha. "It was Abishai, injured and struggling to stay upright and move to shore. I do not know where he fell in, or how long he was in the water, but when I pulled him from its grasp, he had strength only for a few words before he d-died."

Litha put her hands over her face. "Abishai," she whispered.

Hannah went on. "He told me he and Thaddeus had confronted one of the great jungle cats and wounded it. It had killed Thaddeus and injured Abishai before he jumped or fell into the water." She looked at Litha. "He . . . before he died, he was at peace with the Lord. He said he was going home."

Litha blinked streaming eyes. "Home? He believed?" She turned to Rachel. "He believed! Maybe Thaddeus . . ."

Both women began to sob.

"Brothers and Sisters, perhaps we should give them some space," Nephi suggested, looking around at the silent group surrounding them.

The people slowly filed from the building, many of them stopping to touch Hannah and Tabitha on the shoulder or to squeeze their hands.

Nephi indicated a mat and some cushions in one corner of the great room and they gratefully sank into them.

"Now, Sister," Rachel said through her tears. "Tell us all. I must know every detail if I am to believe this."

Hannah did.

———————•◆•———————

The settlement could talk of little else but Hannah and Tabitha's arrival and the deaths of Thaddeus and Abishai for several days.

Then, just when things seemed to be settling, Little Brother became the next topic of wonder. He had been glimpsed wandering near the settlement by several of the men and a few of the children, but had refused to come closer. Finally, Hannah had gone in search of him and coaxed him inside.

He remained wary, but submitted to entering her hut as long as only she or Tabitha were there. He was an instant hit with the children and, before long, had gotten past his shyness and was one of the People of Nephi.

More than a handful of days had gone by before Hannah was able to talk with the still-grieving Rachel and Litha about their own flight from Laman's camp.

The three of them had come to the House of Assembly after supper to visit in a place protected from the rain.

Sam and a group of brethren had gathered in one corner of the building and were creating beautiful music by the use of strange pipes and two stringed intruments Hannah had never seen before.

Leaving Rachel and Litha, she walked over and watched closely as the men played. Finally, when they paused for a few moments, Sam handed her his pipe. "It is made of bamboo," he said.

Hannah looked at it curiously. She had seen the reed pipes of every description among the people back in Jerusalem, but never a musical instrument made out of bamboo. She shook her head. Bamboo was always used for light, durable shelters and other tools. How remarkable that it could also be used to create such pleasing music.

Next she examined the stringed intruments of the brethren seated next to Sam. Though they resembled the lyre, they, too, had taken their own unique form.

"We do not have the fine materials we had in Jerusalem, so we have had to experiment," Sam told her. "We use gut for the strings and have tried different woods for the body. It has taken some trial and error but we are pleased with the sound."

Hannah nodded. The music was pleasing.

Sam smiled. "We are making a joyful noise unto the Lord!"

The men started to play again, so Hannah rejoined her sisters, waiting at the far end of the building.

She took a seat beside Rachel and the three of them simply sat and listened for a few moments.

Then Rachel put a hand on Hannah's arm. "We would speak, Sister."

Hannah nodded and turned to look at her.

"Litha and I, we have always believed. We just did not dare . . ." She sighed and looked down. "We were not as strong as you."

"Zedekiah and Berachah had their feet firmly planted in Laman's camp," Litha broke in. "Zedekiah threatened Rachel's life when she told him she wanted to join you in listening to the teachings of Nephi." She reached out and lifted Rachel's right hand, "He did this on that last evening when he found the two of us together and suspected what we were planning. It was his final warning."

Hannah gasped. Where Rachel's smallest finger should have been, there was only a half-healed stump.

Rachel doubled up her remaining fingers and tucked her hand out of sight self-consciously.

Hannah put a hand on her sister-by-marriage's shoulder. "I am so sorry this happened to you." She rubbed her face and shook her head. "What horror you must have gone through."

"It was nothing to what you endured, Sister," Litha said. She glanced away. "You endured much, much more." She sighed and turned back. "I am ashamed to tell you what I must . . ."

Hannah put her head on one side and peered into her face. "What is it, Sister?"

Litha took a deep breath. "When the rest of the camp was concentrating on you. Watching you. Suspecting you. That was when Rachel and I found our chance to escape."

Hannah blinked. "And when they all went out that night to kill Nephi?"

She nodded. "They were all talking about you and instructing the women to keep you under their eyes. No one was looking at us. We simply left."

"By yourselves?"

"I had Xander and Gavrilla," Rachel said. "And Litha brought Lana and Leah."

"No other children?"

They shook their heads. "They would not come," Litha said, her eyes filling with tears. "And we dared not say too much for fear they would report back to their fathers."

Rachel looked up, her tears making streaks down her smooth cheeks. "Now they are lost to us. Either in God's kingdom," she paused, and she and Litha squeezed each other's hands, "or forever in the clutches of Laman and his godless ways."

"With my Samuel."

Rachel touched Hannah's cheek. "We understand the pain you feel, Sister."

Hannah put her hand over Rachel's and gave her a small smile. "What we have each walked through has made us stronger. Wiser. We did not do it alone. The Lord was with us."

Both Rachel and Litha nodded.

"Whenever we spoke with you, you assured us that your work in Laman's camp was not yet finished," Rachel said. "What made you change your mind?"

Hannah sighed. "The night after you left—well, Tabitha has told you the story."

"And that is what finally convinced you to leave?"

"That and—" Hannah hesitated. "That and this." She put a hand to her belly.

Rachel frowned. "Hannah? Sister, are you with child?"

Hannah nodded. "In my age—my fortieth year, the Lord has chosen to bless me."

Both of the women stared at her.

"With child?" Rachel asked again.

Hannah nodded once more.

Litha jumped up and wrapped her arms around Hannah. "But Sister, that is wonderful news!"

"You are the first people who know," Hannah said. She smiled. "I am quite sure I will hear of this from Moriah, Anava, and Amanna."

Litha smiled. "When did *you* know?"

Hannah smiled ruefully. "Father Lehi said something. And Mother Sariah."

"But . . . that must have been moons ago!" Rachel said.

Hannah shrugged. "I did not know. Not until I woke up on that final morning. After . . ."

Litha sucked in a breath. "After they stoned you?"

Hannah nodded. "I woke up and . . . that's when I felt it."

"Felt what?"

Hannah looked up—right into Amanna's smiling face. She had come in while Hannah, Rachel and Litha had been intent on their conversation.

"Hmm," Hannah said, grinning. "Before I say anything else, could you collect Moriah and Anava?"

———— ◆ ————

Hannah could hear Tabitha's deep breathing. She envied the girl her ability to just fall into unconsciousness and then stay there. Whenever Hannah closed her eyes, images of her family shot into her mind, complete with sadness, pain, and the nagging feeling that she had not done all she could do to help her son, Samuel.

She tried to keep the thought of them shoved into the back of her mind, but as soon as she was still, she was plagued by memories. Memories of gentler, happier times. Of Samuel during his baby and little boy years. Of shared ideas and ideals and intimacies with Lemuel.

She sighed and turned over on her sleeping mat. Would thoughts of them ever leave her?

Even when she finally succumbed to sleep, her dreams drifted through her years as a daughter, wife, and mother, often ending with her once again watching as her son carried that last stone toward her.

That dream brought her sitting bolt upright, drenched in perspiration and crying out for someone—anyone—to stop the insanity.

Hannah had lost her family. The one thing her father had warned her against in a vision. Somehow she had not fought hard enough. Worked hard enough. Prayed hard enough.

She sighed again. Why were these thoughts always so prevalent during the nighttime hours when sleep eluded her? Probably because that was the only time when her hands were not busy with some task. When her mind was free to travel where it would.

And it chose old, familiar routes.

The room was brightening in the dawn. Already she could hear the birds in the trees heralding the morning. Somewhere a pipe began playing quietly.

Hannah looked around.

She and Tabitha had been given this tidy little hut on their arrival the better part of a month previously. Already it felt more like home than the cottage she had shared with Lemuel and Samuel ever had.

Another pang at the admission. What had she done wrong?

She shook her head and forced her mind back to her inspection. Hers and Tabitha's sleeping mats had been laid out next to the fire in the center of the room. Overhead, she could see the deep blue of the dawning sky through the small smoke hole in the exact center of the thatch.

For a moment, she concentrated on that patch of blue. It looked as though the rains that had brought life to the land, and misery to those trying to build a community, had ceased, at least for a short time.

The world seemed both quieter and noisier. Now that the constant drumming and plash of the rain had ceased, one could hear the other sounds of nature. The calling of the birds. The grunt and bellow of cattle. Bleat of sheep. Even the rusty bray of some of the donkeys.

Just outside her hut, she heard Little Brother's familiar whine. Her and Tabitha's small space did not allow for their four-footed companion to sleep indoors, so he was relegated to the sheltered spot immediately beside their front door.

He still was not happy about it. But he stayed and even brought them the occasional large bird or furry rodent so Hannah and Tabitha knew they still belonged to him.

"Father Nephi!" someone outside called.

Hannah smiled. When had she and her generation moved from 'Sisters' and 'Brothers' to 'Fathers' and 'Mothers'? It had happened so gradually. All at once, the younger generation had started it and it had been accepted.

But she did not feel any older than the young girl who had left Jerusalem so trustingly with Nephi and his brothers over twenty-five years ago.

Except when she thought of Lemuel and Samuel. Then she felt old indeed.

"Father Nephi!" the voice said again. "We are all here. Ready to start."

Hannah frowned. Then she remembered. A group of the brethren were going on a scouting trip to find stone suitable to begin construction of another temple. A temple like unto Solomon's of old. Nephi hoped to find other things as well. Perhaps gold and silver and precious things that would beautify the House of the Lord.

He and Sam as well as their younger brothers Jacob and Joseph had been discussing the trip the evening before, after the devotional. They had agreed that Nephi, Sam, and Joseph would go with a group of sons and grandsons and that Jacob would remain in charge of the village.

Hannah had felt a pang at the thought of their great spiritual leader leaving the village for any reason, but consoled herself that he was leaving a man in charge who honored both his priesthood and his God.

She stood up and reached for her outer tunic, left hanging on a convenient hook on the wall near the door. Throwing her thick braid backward over her shoulder, she arranged her head cloth carefully to cover her sleep-mussed hair and opened the door to step barefoot out into the street.

Nephi and his group were just disappearing into the jungle at the far end of the village.

Jacob was standing, looking after them.

She joined him. "They got an early start."

Jacob turned and smiled at her. "Indeed they did, Sister Hannah."

Hannah smiled. Here, at least, was one who still saw the girl she had been, even though he had been born after their trek had begun.

Jacob went on. "But you know my elder brother. Especially when he is on the Lord's errand. He starts in and gets the task done."

Hannah nodded. "He is truly the Lord's right hand here."

Jacob nodded. "When Father left me his last blessing, he told me to cling tight to Nephi. He said, 'Thy soul shall be blessed, and thou shalt dwell safely with thy brother, Nephi; and thy days shall be spent in the service of thy God.'" He looked at Hannah. "How can one refute the words of a prophet?"

"How, indeed," Hannah said softly.

"Oh, Sister! I did not mean to suggest that . . . I mean that I—I would not bring up . . ."

She smiled and placed a gentle hand on Jacob's arm. "Fear not, Brother Jacob. You have not offended me. Truth is truth. My husband and my son chose not to listen to the great blessings promised by our prophet and your father, Lehi, in return for righteousness. They have chosen, instead, to follow their own hearts and minds—"

"And that of our brother, Laman."

"And Laman," Hannah nodded "down a darker path." She looked at Jacob. "Do you suppose they will ever regret their actions?"

Jacob looked off into the distance, into the broad valley that stretched out before them. "I know they will, Sister Hannah. I know they will regret with their whole soul the choices that took them away from their Lord."

"The weight of a hundred generations of sin," Hannah said softly. A load she prayed every single day that she would be kept from bearing.

"A heavy load to carry, indeed. Especially for those who left the Lord because his work was too great a burden."

Hannah shook her head, feeling the tears prick at her eyes. "A strange turning, for certain."

Jacob heaved a sigh and then turned a smile on her. "But let us not dwell on the past, Sister Hannah, but concentrate instead on the future. What are your plans for the day?"

"There are the usual chores, Brother Jacob, and then Tabitha and I need to tend our garden. There are plants still to be placed and the never-ending weeds to pull."

"By the sweat of thy face." Jacob smiled, and then bowed slightly and turned away. "I will leave you to your duties, my sister, and I will attend to mine."

Hannah watched him walk up the street, greeting more of the early-risers as they came out of their homes.

Men and women were soon about, engaged in the rituals that had heralded a new day since the beginning of time. Grinding grains for bread. Milking goats. Tending stock.

A couple of the eldest young men dashed off into the forest, baskets in hand in search of the sweet red deliciousness that Tabitha and Hannah had discovered and which seemed to grow so abundantly in this part of the forest.

In a few moments, several children, freshly groomed and dressed in tidy, clean tunics, were playing a game with a hide ball. A couple was sitting in the shade of one of the huts, playing a pleasing duet on small pipes.

Everyone greeted Hannah with a friendly wave and smile. Some stopped to engage her in brief conversation before they went on with their tasks.

All were cheerful, busy, and happy.

"Mother Hannah?"

Hannah turned.

Tabitha had awakened and was standing in the door of their hut, outer tunic hastily donned and sleep still heavy in her eyes. "I thought you had left or something."

Even after these weeks together, the girl still suffered from the trauma of her earlier years. Hannah took a deep breath and turned. This was something that she, a childless woman, could do for the motherless girl.

Suddenly, her baby kicked strongly.

Well, she amended. Childless for the present.

"Ready to break the fast with me, Dearest One?"

Tabitha nodded and smiled. "I will fetch milk and cheese." Pulling her head cloth over her hair, she dashed out into the street.

Hannah continued into the hut.

Tabitha stood up. "I think our garden is coming along nicely." She looked around. "The others are a full twenty or more days ahead of ours, but you can hardly tell."

Hannah sat back on her heels and she, too, looked around, using her head cloth to wipe her damp face. "I agree. The ample rains make us all equals."

Tabitha laughed. "I was thinking it must be due to our skill as gardeners!"

"Undoubtedly so."

Tabitha bent over the row and began to pull weeds again. "I wish we could eat the weeds. They seem to grow twice as fast as the plants!"

Hannah laughed. "I'm sure that you can eat quite a few of them. Probably the only difference between those plants we eat and those we do not is taste."

"Except for those mushrooms."

Hannah shuddered slightly. A handful of days before, a couple of the small boys in the settlement, hungry and waiting for their dinners, had found a patch of freshly-sprouted mushrooms. Thinking them the same as those served by their mothers, they had picked and eaten them.

Later, violently ill, they revealed what they had done. Fortunately, quick aid and a blessing of the priesthood soon had them healthy and smiling once more.

But the lesson had been taken by all.

"What is happening?"

Hannah looked up.

Tabitha was looking toward the street.

Hannah followed her gaze. People were hurrying along the street. She could see them in the gaps between the tents and huts. She stood up. "I do not know."

Tabitha got up and trotted to the far side of the house for a better look. "It is Jacob," she called to Hannah. "It looks like some sort of meeting."

Meetings were not unusual in their settlement. Something else they had brought with them from their previous home.

Hannah wiped her soiled hands on her apron. "Well, let us go and see what he has to say!"

Many people had gathered when the two arrived. Jacob was sitting on the raised stone wall of the community well. Hannah and Tabitha quickly took a seat on the ground near him.

Jacob smiled at the two of them, then looked around and stood up. "My beloved brothers and sisters. I have been called of God, and ordained after the manner of his holy order, and consecrated by my brother Nephi, unto whom you look as a leader and protector, and on whom you depend for safety. Behold, you know that I have spoken unto you exceedingly many things. Nevertheless, I speak unto you again; for I am desirous for the welfare of your souls."

He went on to quote from the writings of Isaiah and Hannah closed her eyes at the words of counsel, hope, and salvation; even those of warning and destruction wrapped themselves around her like a warm cloak.

Again, she was struck at the simplicity of the teachings of the prophets. And by the people's inability to follow them.

Jacob's final words, "*I will contend with them that contend with thee . . .*" rang in her ears. How much the Lord loved them. How much He was willing to do for them!

As the people began to disperse, Hannah remained where she was, eyes closed, breathing in the messages of truth she had just heard. Praying silently that she would resist the choices and decisions that could lead her from those simple, profound messages.

"Mother Hannah, I will return to the garden," Tabitha whispered in her ear.

Hannah nodded without opening her eyes. She heard the girl's footsteps as she moved off down the street.

Thinking she was alone, she opened her eyes. Anava, Amanna, and Moriah were all seated on the ground directly in front of her, looking into her face.

Hannah jumped and they laughed.

"We are sorry to startle you, Treasured One," Moriah said. "But we have not spoken in such a long time and would hear how you are getting on."

Hannah smiled at her sisters. "A long time?"

Moriah shrugged. "Well, long to us."

Hannah laughed. "I just spoke to you a matter of hours ago."

"Well it was not memorable. Or long enough."

Hannah laughed again. "What would you like to know?"

"Are you happy here?" Amanna asked. "Are you glad you joined us?"

Hannah smiled. "To hear the words of a prophet spoken at almost every minute of the day? To commune with others who believe as I do? To never have to hide my testimony or my feelings?" She shook her head. "Sisters, I have found Heaven." Her hand slid to her belly and the child that was, again, making its presence felt. "Truly."

Someone shouted at the edge of the village and the four women turned.

"It is Nephi," Anava said happily.

"They must have found what they were looking for," Moriah added.

All got to their feet and hurried toward the group of men emerging from the thick forest.

They arrived just a step behind Jacob, who was embracing his elder brother. "All is well, Brother?"

Nephi smiled. "All is well. We found a great deposit of white marble only a few hundred paces into the jungle in that direction." He pointed.

"A few hundred paces?" Jacob frowned. "Then why did it take you most of the day to return?"

Nephi held out his hand. "Because we were not just looking for marble."

Hannah leaned forward and peered into the wide, calloused palm. Several nuggets of dull gold material rested there.

Jacob's dark eyebrows went up. "Is that . . . ?"

"Gold," Hannah said.

Nephi looked at her and nodded. "Indeed it is, Sister Hannah. How is it that you know?"

Hannah felt her face warm with colour. "Well . . . I—" She paused. "Father had dealings with traders from time to time. Gold was one of their preferred means of payment."

"Of course." Nephi smiled. "What an observant, astute little girl you must have been."

Hannah felt her face grow even hotter. "Well, I was interested in everything."

Moriah laughed. "Indeed you were! Why I remember a time—"

Hannah gripped her eldest sister's arm and whispered urgently in her ear. "Could we please discuss something else?"

Moriah looked at her, mouth open on what she had been about to say. She snapped it shut. "Of course, Dear!"

Everyone was silent for a moment.

"So where did you find the gold?" Jacob asked at last.

Nephi thrust his chin toward the east. "Over there. The Spirit led us in two directions today. West to find the marble and east to find the ornamentation!" He removed the pack he carried and lowered it to the ground. "As soon as we have supped, we will plan how best to fetch both materials."

———— ◆ ————

Hannah, Rachel, and Litha were carding cotton. It was Hannah's first try and, at first, she felt unsure and clumsy.

But Litha was patient and instructive and soon she was making nearly as much headway as her much more experienced sister-by-marriage.

Hannah looked at Litha. "May I ask a question, Sister?"

Litha lifted her head. "Always."

Hannah took a deep breath and bit her lip. "Do you miss your husband?"

Litha looked surprised. She turned her head to gaze out toward the forest. "I miss my Abishai more. Perhaps because I know I will not see him in this life." Her eyes filled with tears that she brushed at impatiently. "But sometimes, yes, I miss my husband." She sighed. "Berachah and I were companions even before you and Lemuel, and he was the choice of my heart. We did not have the difficulties at the outset that you and . . ." She lapsed into silence.

Hannah nodded. "I understand." She, too, looked toward the edge of the forest. "I admit that Lemuel was not my choice. He was the choice of our fathers. But I agreed with their logic and I did grow to love him and see great potential in him."

"He did have great potential," Rachel said.

Hannah looked at her.

Rachel went on. "He did. He was the best of all our brothers at hunting."

Litha nodded. "And he could creep through the landscape without dislodging a stone or bending a blade of grass."

Hannah shrugged. "But in things spiritual, he was lacking." .

Rachel made a face. "I am sorry, Treasured One, but in that you are correct. He preferred to spend time in the countryside rather than in the synagogue with Father."

"I caught glimpses of the man behind the boy," Hannah said. "After the birth of Samuel . . ." She paused.

"Rachel and I were discussing that just yesterday," Litha said. "The months following the birth of his son and the change it made in Lemuel."

"It was the first time he had done something before Laman," Rachel put in. "It made him . . . more of a man in his own eyes, I think."

The three were quiet for a moment.

Hannah looked at Rachel. "And you, Sister? Do you miss Zedekiah?"

Rachel shook her head. "In the beginning, he was attentive and even, at times, kind. But as the years went past, he became more and more—"

"Cruel?" Litha said.

"Not real—yes, okay, cruel." Rachel took a deep breath. "I think he was determined to turn his back on whatever was important to his father."

"But why?" Hannah asked. "He adored his father!"

Rachel shook her head. "He respected him, but he did not believe as Father Ishmael did."

"Oh." Hannah was quiet. "So he was ripe to follow Laman's lead."

Rachel nodded. "Indeed he was. All Laman had to do was present a new path to follow and Zedekiah was on it before two shakes of a lamb's tail."

"Laman pulled a lot of our young men into his wake," Hannah said.

"To their destruction and that of many of the next generation," Litha said.

"True." Rachel looked sad. "Litha and I, as you, Hannah, said farewell to much with each footstep that carried us away."

"Sometimes, I think the worry is more than I can bear," Hannah said. "And I want to run back there and wrap my arms around my son and have all be as it was."

Rachel nodded. "My youngest son and daughter came with me, but two of my sons and my eldest girl did not." Her own eyes filled with tears. "And I know that my Thaddeus will never come to me now."

"But perhaps he has been spared the greater sin," Litha said gently.

Rachel nodded and wiped at her tears with the hem of her apron. "Perhaps. I just know that—"

She was interrupted by the sound of shouting from the edge of the village.

All three women turned.

Several figures were emerging from the trees.

"Ah," Rachel said, rising. "Our scouts have returned."

Hannah turned back to her carding.

"Wait, who is that?" Litha asked.

Hannah looked up again, then followed Litha's pointing finger.

The young men, three of Zoram's sons and two of Sam's, looked excited.

Hannah frowned.

No. Not excited. Upset over something. Then she realized what it was Litha was pointing to.

The men were leading something—someone. Someone who was bound by strong cords.

Slowly, Hannah rose to her feet. A stranger? No. It must be someone from Laman's camp.

Dropping her carding to the ground at her feet, Hannah lifted her tunic hem and began to run, hearing Rachel and Litha fall into step behind her. But as she neared, she could see it was not the familiar face she had been seeking. Feared even.

All three women skidded to a halt.

"Tobias!" Rachel said, recognizing her second-born son. She started forward once more and reached to embrace him.

Her son's lip curled and with bound hands, he struck her away. "Touch me not, traitorous woman!" He leaned forward and spat in the dust at her feet. "Did you think that you could walk away from the rightful king of this land as well as your husband and your family and be received back?" He straightened and lifted his head proudly. "Your treachery will be sung for generations by your children and your children's children!"

Rachel stared at him, her mouth open. Tears welled in her eyes and began to trail down her cheeks. Then she put her hands over her face and sank to the ground, her shoulders shaking with sobs.

The young man stared at her, unmoved. "You cannot influence me with your tears and imprecations."

"She has not said anything yet," Hannah pointed out.

He spun about and stared at her as if he had seen a ghost. "How . . . why . . . how did you get here? I thought you were—"

"Though you and my family left me for dead, my Lord spared me to finish my work here, Tobias. And with his help, I made the trek to join the true prophet."

The young man blinked. "But I saw you. You were d—"

"Only nearly so." Hannah touched her fingers to the almost-healed scar on her head, then straightened and looked at him. "And now you have been given a second chance as I have been. You, too, have found your way into the camp of the Lord's true prophet—"

Now it was Tobias's turn to interrupt. "I did not come to join the deluded followers of the traitor Nephi!" he shouted. "I have been sent out as a scout to discover your whereabouts so our army can find and destroy you!" He lifted his chin. "As is their right as the proper rulers of this people."

Hannah caught her breath. Had things really come to this? With brother ready to put brother to the sword?

Litha was helping Rachel to her feet and she now tried to steer her sister away from the crowd.

But Rachel spun about and flung out a hand toward her son. "Tobias, it is not too late! Come with me now. Come and follow the living prophet! Search your heart. You know the words he speaks are truth!"

Again, the young man recoiled away from her. "I know that you follow the old and outdated teachings of a deluded and power-hungry man and that you will be brought to know the truth at the point of a sword!"

Rachel dropped her hands. "You would take a sword to me?" she asked quietly.

"I—" For the first time, the young man showed some hesitation. For the period of several heartbeats, the two looked at each other. "You left!" he shouted finally. "You abandoned your people!"

"I did not abandon my people," Rachel said firmly, though her voice still quavered. "I *followed* my people."

Her son stared at her for a moment. Then he turned and held out his bound hands to his captors. "Take me where you would. Proceed with your torture and your killing. I am ready."

Zoram's son, Cephus, looked at him. "Torture?"

Another son, Yavin, frowned. "Killing?"

Tobias remained where he was, hands outstretched and chin lifted proudly.

The young men all looked at Cephus, the eldest among them.

He shrugged. "I do not know what to do. Nephi, Jacob, and Joseph are with the gold-seeking party and are not due back until two days hence."

"Ah. So the upstart seeks after gold! I knew his prattle of pursuing only spiritual riches was deception."

Again the group of young men turned to Cephus.

"Perhaps you could take Tobias to the House of Assembly," Hannah suggested.

They all looked at her.

"It is the one building here with stout walls to hold in the foolhardy."

Nodding, Cephus grabbed the end of the rope which bound the young man's hands and the group disappeared up the street toward the synagogue.

Rachel collapsed back against Litha. "You try to put it to the back of your mind," she said. "But then the reality of what you've done settles upon your shoulders and weighs down your spirit once more." She wiped at the tears on her cheeks with the back of one hand. "I gave up my family. Regardless of my reasons."

Hannah slid an arm about her shoulders. "You had no other choice, Sister. You were presented with a branch in the road and you had to take the one way or the other. It was not possible to take both.

Your soul was at stake." She bit her lip. How difficult her own decision had been!

Rachel sighed and nodded. "True. One cannot follow God *and* man." She looked after the group moving away from them. "But sometimes your choices become very painful indeed."

———◆———

Though she remained seated outside her home for the rest of the day, her eyes trained on the House of Assembly, Rachel did not attempt to enter or speak with her son.

Hannah looked at her sister-by-marriage, knowing the helpless gnawing the older woman must be feeling in her heart.

Rather than expose anyone to Tobias's vicious rhetoric, Hannah elected to take his meals to him herself.

She rapped on the lintel of the door and waited a moment.

It swung open on leather hinges to reveal Cephus. "Ah. Mother Hannah," the young man said. He looked down at the bowl she was carrying and smiled. "Taking care of others. As always."

Hannah smiled slightly. "I'm sure your *prisoner* is feeling his lack of food, Cephus."

Cephus nodded. "Indeed he must." He looked across the room.

Hannah had to look carefully to discover her sister's son among the shadows.

"Perhaps I should take it to him?"

Hannah shook her head. "I can manage, Cephus." She noted the truss that held Tobias's arms at a permanent angle and the strong cords binding him. "I am quite sure he will be unable to harm me in any way. Why do you not go and get your own meal? I am certain Belva is waiting."

Cephus nodded. "I am undecided what to do, Mother Hannah. I have never been thrust into the role of prison guard before."

"And certainly not over one of your cousins."

He shook his head. "Nephi has foretold of wars between us, but it is difficult to imagine." He looked at Tobias. "He is kin. How can one lift a sword against kin?"

Hannah felt tears prick at the back of her eyes. "How, indeed."

"I will do as you suggest, Mother, and take my meal. I will be within hearing if you have need. Do not release him."

Hannah nodded and turned toward Tobias. "I have brought you sustenance."

"Take it away, traitorous one! I trust nothing from your hands!"

Hannah smiled and moved forward. "Why would you not trust me, Tobias? I should think it would be more logical for me not to trust you."

He was silent for a moment and she closed the distance between them.

He was difficult to distinguish in the deep shadows here, so far from the door and lamplight. But she could see his eyes gleam in the dim light and knew that he watched her.

She stopped and held out the wooden bowl. "Here, Son. I have brought you meat and herbs, bread, and cheese. Sup. There is no sense in torturing yourself."

He snorted. "We can leave that to the others."

She frowned. "No one here is interested in your pain."

"Ah. You say not, but two have threatened it already!"

"Two from our camp?"

He turned his head. "Do you see anyone else?"

"Of course. That was a foolish statement." She sighed. "Surely there are none in Nephi's camp who will harm you."

He curled his lips. "You still trust him? This man who would divide the kingdom and wrest power away from those who are the rightful rulers?"

Hannah tipped her head to one side and looked at him. "Do you know that the people wanted to declare him king when they reached this place?"

He grunted. "It is not a surprise."

"But did you also know that he refused it?"

He looked at her.

"He refused it, Tobias, because he was desirous that they should have no king. Instead he said he would do for them according to that which was in his power."

"See? He wishes only to gain power." His words carried a little less conviction.

"You know that is untrue, Tobias. The only person who has sought power was Laman."

"*KING* Laman!"

She shook her head and held out the bowl again. "Tobias."

He looked at her.

"Take this meal. It will give you strength."

"For all the treachery *they* have planned." He pointed toward the door with his chin.

Again she frowned. "Son, they have nothing planned."

"I heard them! Two of them. They want my blood!"

"Who?"

"I do not know. They remained near the door and the leader—"

"Cephus."

"Yes. Cephus. He said—"

"That would not happen?"

"Well . . . yes."

"And it will not happen. These people follow a prophet of God. They would not willingly shed the blood of another."

"You do not know!"

Hannah sighed. "Eat, Tobias."

"You may have poisoned the food."

"I will take a little and you shall see." Hannah lifted one of the pieces of meat and placed it on her tongue, drawing it in and chewing slowly. Finally, she swallowed. "See?"

Tobias looked at the bowl of food hungrily.

Hannah studied his bonds, the hands bound together in front of him. The long stake thrust through the crook in his elbows, preventing him from maneuvering.

"Hmmm. Perhaps I shall have to feed you."

"Unless you want to unbind my hands."

"I have been asked not to."

"You do not trust me."

Hannah looked at him. "My brother's son, Tobias, I trusted with my life. But I have seen how much that trust—and that life—are worth. I think we are better if I feed you."

Tobias made a face, and then nodded.

Hannah moved close and lifted a morsel of meat.

Strong, white teeth plucked it from her grasp and the young man chewed rapidly and swallowed. Then opened his mouth for more.

In the passage of only a few minutes, the bowl was empty.

"I . . . thank you, Mother Hannah."

Hannah nodded and smiled. "You may want to think about all we have discussed."

Tobias said nothing. He merely watched as she retraced her steps to the door.

Cephus came in as she reached it. "Ah, Mother Hannah. Has Tobias eaten?"

"He has." Hannah tucked her bowl under her arm. "He has many ideas, Cephus. Not all of them sound."

Cephus nodded and leaned toward her. "And there are those in this camp who would silence those words," he said softly.

Hannah stared at him. "Some of the People of Nephi offer a prisoner harm?"

He nodded again. "They would see me removed so they can take him and do with him as they will. To prevent him from betraying our position."

Hannah blinked. "Have we come such a short distance?"

"Indeed."

———————— ◆ ————————

"Mother Hannah! Come quickly!"

Hannah looked up. Tabitha was standing in the doorway, breathing hard.

"What is it?"

"Anava has gone into the forest to try and find Father Nephi and some of the othersare making threats." She broke off and looked up the street.

"Threats?" Hannah hurried to the doorway and looked out.

Several of the young men and one or two of their wives were standing in the street outside the synagogue. Cephus could just be seen guarding the doorway, his arms folded across his chest. Hannah realized she had been hearing their raised voices for some time. How had she missed this?

She joined Tabitha and the two of them started up the street.

Hannah could see Rachel just ahead of them. She hurried to catch up. The three of them stopped together at the edge of the crowd.

Zoram's son Zalman was speaking. "If we do not take care of this now, we swing the gate wide for more troubles!"

The crowd responded. "Zalman is right!" "Let's listen to him!" "We must handle this now!"

"What are they 'handling'?" Hannah asked Yavin, who was standing beside her.

"If the *Lamanite*—" Yavin twisted the word as he spoke.

Hannah put up a hand and frowned. "Lamanite?"

Yavin smiled slightly. "The followers of Laman. We have decided to call them Laman-ites."

Hannah's frown deepened. "But they are all children of Lehi."

"We are the people of Nephi. So we are Nephites. They are the people of Laman, so they are Lamanites."

Hannah sighed. One more line of separation between their peoples.

"So, as I was saying, if this Lamanite is allowed to live, he may escape. And he will surely tell his people where we are and lead them right to us."

Rachel gripped Hannah's sleeve. "What are they saying?"

Hannah patted the clutching fingers. "Calm now, Sister. Nothing has happened yet." She frowned at Yavin. "The Lord has prevented the people of Laman from finding us thus far. Why do you think he would stop?"

Yavin pointed a hand toward the House of Assembly. "Does this look like the Lord is preventing it? One of them just *strolled* into our town. Father Nephi has said that there will come a time when we will stand, brother against brother."

"If the Lord has decreed it, then perhaps—"

Yavin interrupted her. "We shall work to prevent it!"

"Maybe what we need to be doing is not wasting our time with foolish and threatening gestures, but preparing ourselves."

"Mother Hannah. What we need to be doing is preventing when the opportunity is given us."

"Let us kill the Lamanite!" Zalman shouted. "Before his people come to kill us!"

There was a great roar of response. "Kill the Lamanite!" "Get them before they get us!"

Rachel gasped and clutched Hannah's arm convulsively.

Hannah shook her head, then pushed her way through the crowd, dragging Rachel with her. When she reached the center of the group, she waved her arms and screamed loudly.

Everyone was abruptly silenced. They turned toward her.

She looked around. "Are you really proposing this? That we kill this young man?" She glanced at Rachel. "His mother is standing here beside me. Would you kill her son while she watched?" She touched Zalman's arm. "Would you be the one to wield the sword, Son?" She pointed to different young men in the crowd. "Or you? Or you?"

"We will do what must be done!" Zalman shouted. "As Father Nephi did before us!"

Hannah closed her eyes and uttered a quick prayer for guidance. Then she looked back at the intent young man. "Has the Lord spoken to you, Zalman?"

Everyone was silent now.

Hannah went on. "Taking someone's life is not a simple act. Do you want responsibility of ending someone's existence? You have heard Father Nephi's story. You know that his action, though he was directed explicitly by the Lord, haunts him still."

"Well . . . he did not . . ."

"Did not what, Zalman?"

"Did not have the welfare of the people . . . " The young man stopped.

"Ahh. Now you see. He *did* have the welfare of the people on his shoulders. We would not have the scriptures—and you would not have a father—if Nephi had not acted as directed by the Lord."

The young man was silent.

Hannah touched the healed scar on her head. "We left the people of Laman because of their fondness for violence and settling everything through the use of force. And because they refused to follow the commandments of the Lord." She looked around. "Are we then to become exactly like them?"

"Why are we listening to this woman?" someone shouted. "She has come from them. Perhaps she is one of them! Perhaps it is she who led them here!"

Several people started to speak and Zalman waved them to silence. "They present an interesting premise, Mother Hannah. Have you somehow directed this young man here?"

Hannah stared at him.

"How ridiculous!" Rachel said. "Hannah is one of us. She has suffered more than any of us to be here!"

"And you, Mother Rachel. Defending her. You, too, came from the camp of Laman."

Rachel stared at him, round-eyed.

Hannah distinctly heard the sound of a knife being pulled from its scabbard.

"Perhaps this needs to be settled now."

Rachel gripped Hannah's arm.

"I cannot believe what I am hearing," Hannah said loudly. "Have we left the camp of Laman to follow a prophet of God and instead found exactly what we tried to leave behind?"

"A very good question, Sister Hannah. One I, too, would like to hear the answer to."

Hannah spun around.

Nephi, Anava, and Sam, with Jacob and Joseph close behind, were standing at the edge of the circle.

Hannah felt the stiffening go out of her knees and she sank to the ground, pulling a now-sobbing Rachel down with her.

The crowd moved aside and Nephi, followed closely by Sam, walked to the center.

Nephi touched Hannah's shoulder and reached for hers and Rachel's hands. "Rise, my sisters." The two of them struggled to their feet and stood for a moment next to this great man.

This prophet of God.

Nephi pressed their hands and released them, then turned to survey the now-silent crowd. "When my Anava met us, I could not believe what she was saying. That my people, the people of God, would consider taking the life of a man—and not just any man, their *brother*—out of fear. Or ignorance."

He handed a leather bag to Sam and started to pace the narrow confines of the circle. "I told her she was mistaken." He smiled briefly at his wife over the gathered crowd's heads, then sobered and continued to walk. "I told her my people, the Lord's people, would never consider such a thing." He swung around. "And now I find that, not only are you threatening the life of your young cousin, but also the lives of two of the women of our settlement. *Women!*" He shook his head. "The final and most precious of God's creations! And you propose simply ending their lives. As a *precaution?*"

Hannah saw Zalman look at one or two of the other men. He turned to Nephi. "Father Nephi. We were trying to protect this settlement. We know if this Lamanite should escape that he would immediately bring the army of Laman down on us all." He looked around. "And then many more women—and children as well—will be put to the sword."

Nephi nodded and put his hand on Zalman's shoulder. "I am certain that your only motivation is the preservation of this people, Zalman. But do you not believe that the Lord will protect us? Have you so little faith in God? In his ability to speak through his chosen prophet?" He sighed. "I would not seek to lead this people," he said quietly. "Indeed, I have tried to encourage my elder brothers to take up the burden. But they want to rule. Not lead. So it is left to me. You must trust me when I say that the Lord is directing us. Did he not warn us to leave and separate ourselves from our brethren?" He looked at Zalman. "Did he not preserve us in reaching this fertile valley?" He let his glance pass over the others in the group. "Have we not seen our crops and herds multiplied in the few short months we have been here?"

Some in the circle began to nod.

Nephi turned back to Zalman. "Could we have done any of it without the direction and help of our God?"

Zalman was silent.

"Yes, we should prepare, for we know there will be contentions with the people of Laman. Our brethren. We have been told it is so. But let us not carry the conflict into our own settlement. Let us, instead, stand together as a people. Let us be faithful and obedient and follow our God." He looked around. "My people. I pray continually for you by day, and my eyes water my pillow by night because of you; and I cry unto my God in faith, and I *know* that He will hear my cry. And I know that the Lord God will consecrate my prayers for the gain of my people. Let us trust in the Lord."

He looked at Cephus, still standing in the doorway of the House of Assembly. "Cephus, please bring forth this prisoner who has caused such turmoil in our camp."

Cephus nodded and disappeared. A moment later, he returned with the still-bound Tobias, whom he led to the center of the circle.

Tobias glared at Nephi. "So the time has come, Great Nephi! When you at last show your power—"

"Release him," Nephi said.

Tobias blinked, then stared at him.

"But, Father Nephi," Zalman said. "If we release him, he will go—

Again, Nephi put a hand on his shoulder. "Son. We *must* release him. It is the only way. If we keep him prisoner, we will be doing exactly the same as those who physically bound our sister Hannah—" he glanced at her, "— and continue to spiritually bind everyone else." He nodded. "We must release him and trust in the Lord."

Nephi looked at Cephus and raised his eyebrows.

Cephus pulled out the stake that had been thrust through the bend in Tobias' elbows. Then he drew his knife and sliced through the leather cords that bound the young man's hands together.

Tobias slowly straightened his arms, flexing the stiff muscles.

"Fetch our brother food and water to take on his trip," Nephi said.

"There are provisions to last two days in this." Sam held out the bag Nephi had given him earlier.

Nephi smiled and took it, then turning, gave the bag to Tobias. "Here, Son, take this."

Tobias reached for the bag, looking a little bewildered. "Where are his weapons?"

Cephus stepped forward. "We took them from him when we captured him, Father Nephi."

"And where did they go?"

"I—I am not sure . . ."

"Here, Son, take mine." Nephi pulled his knife from its sheath and handed it to Tobias. The sunlight glinted off the razor-sharp blade. "You must have something to protect yourself during your journey."

Tobias took the weapon, staring at Nephi doubtfully. He weighed the blade in one hand. "Thank you, N-Nephi."

Hannah watched the young man carefully. Here was someone sworn to destroy Nephi if given the chance and Nephi had just handed him the weapon and the opportunity to do it.

Nephi untied his sheath and handed it to the young man as well. "You will need something to carry the blade."

Tobias blinked and took the sheath as well.

"Now, let us ask the Lord to watch over Tobias as he returns to his home."

Nephi bowed his head and closed his eyes.

Hannah gasped. Nephi had untied his sworn enemy, handed him a weapon, and now was standing, eyes closed and helpless next to him.

His faith was far greater than hers. Hannah spent the entire prayer with her eyes on Tobias.

The young man did not participate in the prayer; rather he watched Nephi as the great Prophet of God, spoke to the Lord on his behalf.

Nephi closed his prayer and lifted his head. Finding Tobias's eyes on him, he smiled and put a hand on the young man's shoulder. "Go in safety, Son," he said. "Go with the Lord."

Tobias looked as though he did not quite know what to do or say. Slowly and silently, he edged his way through the crowd to its edge. Then after tying on the sheath and sliding the blade into it, he looped the thick strap of Nephi's travelling bag over his shoulder.

He looked at Nephi one last time, a sharp frown of confusion on his face, then he turned and loped quickly out of the settlement.

Hannah watched him go. A strange thought flitted through her mind that she would see the young man again soon. She shook it off and turned back to look at Nephi. Never had she seen such faith. Truly Nephi was the Lord's chosen prophet.

It was nearly five months since Hannah and Tabitha had joined with the people of Nephi.

The temple was rising. Set back on its own patch of ground, it already stood higher than most of the huts on the street. Men and boys were busily hewing, hauling and hefting stone, their bodies wet with perspiration but their countenances bright and open and cheerful.

Each of the men in the settlement were assigned to one day of labour in six on the Lord's house. The other five days were spent with their own crops, herds, and duties. The seventh day, as always, was dedicated to the Lord.

As the town continued to grow apace with the temple, the crops, and the herds, Hannah could only assume that the allotment of time was working to full effect.

She and the other women tended to the household chores and gardens as well as to the spinning, weaving, and manufacture of the clothing, blankets, rugs, and anything that could be fashioned out of wool; or the cooler and more comfortable cotton that grew plentifully near the great waters.

Hannah was standing in the deep shade cast by the south wall of the temple, chatting with Amanna, Anava, and Moriah and watching the lazy spin of her drop spindle. Her baby had been quite active this morning and did not seem to want her to sit down.

"You must have a cartload of threads by now, Sister," Anava said.

Hannah smiled. "I do have quite a stock." She looked across the settlement. "I am saving up for the next rainy season."

"But that is another six months away!"

Hannah shrugged.

"Or for your confinement," Moriah patted Hannah's swollen belly, "which is much nearer."

Hannah sighed and rubbed her hand across her great abdomen, feeling the almost constant movement of her child. "Sometimes it feels as though the rains will get here first."

Her sisters laughed.

"I know it feels that way, Treasured One," Moriah said. "But even our horses will welcome their newly-born before the rains come. And they have cycles longer than ours!"

Hannah sighed again. "Poor horses."

Moriah smiled. "But each new baby is precious." Again she patted Hannah's swollen belly. "Especially this one who is so anticipated!"

Hannah looked down the busy street.

Lehi and Ishmael's posterity numbered many dozens of persons now, with children, grandchildren and great-grandchildren.

The celebration of marriages was commonplace as the grandchildren continued to find spouses from among their cousins. And the announcement of forthcoming babies nearly as common.

Despite her discouraging talk, as Hannah felt her own burden growing larger within her, her body becoming heavier, and her pace slowing from what it had been, she knew that her time was coming closer.

Later that afternoon, Hannah, with Little Brother lying flat on the ground beside her, was seated just outside the doorway of her home, pulling the leaves from some ripe corn. Her task was nearly completed and she had several deep yellow ears in her basket, ready for drying.

She reached for the last ear, and then stiffened as her hand slid to her belly.

For the past two handfuls of days, she had been enduring short bouts of pain, which had proved to be false. So, for the first few minutes, she dismissed this pain as more of the same. But when it persisted, she threw the last ear into her basket and, ignoring the pile of leaves, collected her basket and got carefully to her feet.

The next wave of pain nearly sent her to her knees. She closed her eyes and bent double, trying to concentrate on staying upright and maintaining her grip on her basket.

Little Brother thrust his nose into her neck.

"Hannah! What is it? The baby?"

Hannah nodded and felt someone take the basket from her arms.

Moriah appeared in front of her and reached for her hand. "Come. Let us get you inside."

Rachel, carrying Hannah's basket, appeared on her other side and took Hannah's other hand.

"My corn," Hannah said weakly.

Rachel smiled. "Do not worry, dear, we will get it to the drying racks."

Hannah nodded and allowed them to lead her into the cool shade of her small hut.

Little Brother whined and paced back and forth.

Hannah heard Tabitha's voice just outside the hut. "Come, Little Brother. Let us go for a walk. This is a place only for women."

The next hours passed slowly for Hannah. Even at the birth of Samuel, she did not recall such pain.

Mother Sariah, who seldom left her tent these days, came to help, though Anava—the community's accepted midwife—was in attendance. Hannah blessed the cool hands and efficient manner of the aged woman.

Mother Sariah might not be as strong as she once was, but her knowledge and expertise had not faded with her physical body. The woman never left her side and Hannah found herself, more often than not, clutching the frail hand for comfort.

When it was time for the baby to make its appearance, it was to Mother Sariah that Hannah turned. "Help me, Mother Sariah!"

The woman smiled and nodded. Then, as Hannah was helped into the birthing chair, she placed a gentle hand on her head. "Trust us now, Treasured One."

And she did.

A short time later, Mother Sariah handed an exhausted Hannah her newborn son. "Mother, here is your son," she said.

Hannah cradled him, looking at the shock of red hair that crowned his head, marvelling at his tightly closed eyes, his fine eyebrows, his perfect mouth and nose. "Did you ever see such a beautiful baby?" she asked again and again.

Mother Sariah shook her head patiently each time, smiling at Hannah's wonder and excitement.

Suddenly, tears were flowing down Hannah's face. Tears she tried to blot against the baby's swaddling.

Though Mother Sariah's eyes were faded in colour, they were not diminished in ability. She spotted the tears immediately. "Treasured One! Why the tears?"

"I'm just . . . so grateful," Hannah whispered, leaning forward and pressing her head against her baby's stomach. "So grate—" Her sobs overtook her and she wept helplessly into the scrap of cloth that Mother Sariah slipped into her hand.

Hannah could feel the woman's cool hand stroking her hair and her cries increased.

"Hush, daughter, hush," Mother Sariah said over and over. "It is a glad moment."

"I know," Hannah gulped. "I feel so blessed!" This last was delivered through a fresh flood of tears.

Anava came and went, tidying and gathering cloths and soiled bedding. She checked with her sister a pair of times, then left her to their mother-by-marriage's expert ministrations.

Finally, though tears continued intermittently, Hannah was able to gain a little control. She glanced ruefully at the soaked piece of fabric that had served her so well. "What is the matter with me?" she whispered.

Mother Sariah smiled. "I think you just had a baby, Treasured One."

"The happiest of times."

Her mother-by-marriage nodded. "And the most emotional. Tears are common."

"I am so grateful for the safe arrival of this new little one."

"You birthed this child without any of the complications of your last labour." Mother Sariah patted Hannah's head once more. "And I remember this hair being dark the last time, not streaked with grey."

"I will enter my forty-first year in a couple of months and have been gifted with a child in my age. As you were."

"And they are gifts indeed."

"A true gift. A blessing. And yet, all I can think of is the people who are not with him and me today."

"Your mother."

"Yes. And Father." Hannah looked away. "And L-Lemuel." Tears pooled in her eyes once more. "He will never know that he has another son. Nor will Samuel know of his new brother." She looked at Mother Sariah, tears spilling down her cheeks once more. "More than ever before, I am feeling the burden of my decision to leave my family."

Mother Sariah squeezed her hand. "To preserve the rest of your family." She sighed. "Every choice we make requires a sacrifice, my dear. Most of them tiny. But some—"

"Some earth-shaking."

"Some earth-shaking." Mother Sariah sat down on the stool placed conveniently near Hannah's pallet. "You were forced to make your decision because they made theirs."

Hannah was silent for a moment. Then she turned to Mother Sariah. "Is there no hope?"

"Daughter, you know there is always hope." Mother Sariah took a deep breath and looked away. "The Savior of us all will come into the world to save us from our sins. From our wrong choices and misdeeds." She turned back to Hannah. "His birth and life and death will give us hope. Hope that we *can* be washed clean. That we *can* be forgiven our mistakes."

Hannah nodded slowly. "If we but put forth our hand and partake of his goodness."

"Follow him and be cleansed."

Hannah looked down at her son. "Then perhaps there will come a time when my son here *will* meet his father. And *will* know his brother."

"Treasured One, because of our Savior, we have hope." Sariah put a hand on the baby's head. "Does your son yet have a name?"

Hannah took a deep breath and nodded. "In the absence of his father, *I* have chosen. He will be known as Benjamin. Named for the youngest son of Jacob and youngest brother of Joseph of Egypt. A strong and faithful young man. A fine example for my son to follow in his life."

Sariah smiled and nodded. "It is well."

———— • ◆ • ————

Little Benjamin was a good baby from his first moments. Happy. Contented. He suckled well and grew swiftly.

It seemed but a day before it was time for his circumcision and naming. Hannah carried him to the House of Assembly, handed him to Moriah, and she and Zoram carried the baby to Nephi.

The rest of the ceremony passed swiftly with Sam standing in for the absent Lemuel.

When Moriah brought her baby back to her, Hannah cuddled him and smiled into her sister's eyes.

It was a good moment.

A short time later, as she was leaving the synagogue with a group of women comprised mainly of her sisters and sisters-by-marriage, Nephi caught up to her.

"Sister Hannah."

The entire group stopped and turned.

"Could we have a word?"

Hannah nodded. "Certainly, Brother Nephi."

"Treasured One, I will take young Benjamin and meet you in your hut."

Hannah nodded at Moriah and handed the baby to her. Moriah and the rest of the women continued up the street. Anava touched her husband's hand and the two of them exchanged a smile. Then she followed the rest.

Hannah turned once more to Nephi. "What is it, Brother Nephi?"

"My wife tells me I have been neglecting you."

Hannah blinked. "Neglecting me, Brother? How? I have food aplenty. I have a comfortable home with every need met." She looked at Moriah, happily bearing Benjamin up the street. "I have a wonderful, healthy son." She turned back to Nephi. "And I have a Prophet of God to follow. Tell me what more I could desire?"

"A husband?"

Hannah caught her breath. She had not expected this. "I—I have a h-husband." She had a difficult time controlling her voice. She cleared her throat and tried again. "I have a husband."

Nephi nodded. "You have a husband who has abandoned the Lord. And you."

"He did not abandon me. I—"

"You made the only decision left to you, considering your options. And condition." Nephi looked pointedly at Moriah, just ducking into the doorway of Hannah's hut bearing Benjamin. "Sister, when one spouse is faithful and the other not, the Lord allows for the

104

dissolution of the marriage in order for the faithful partner to continue to progress."

Hannah stared at him. "Divorce?"

He nodded. "You cannot be expected to remain tied to a man who has abandoned both the Lord and decency. You must continue." He nodded toward the hut where Moriah had disappeared. "Your son must have a father."

"I—um . . ."

He smiled. "I do not expect an answer at this time, Sister. This is an emotional period for you. And the timing could probably be better. Certainly it must be difficult to consider marriage to someone else when you have just delivered the son of your husband." He smiled. "But I wanted to mention it. And let you have as much time as you require to think on it." He touched her shoulder. "There are many men here in the settlement who would gladly take you to wife."

Hannah blinked. There were? She turned silently and made her way up the street, her thoughts a tangle of covenants spoken and broken.

———— • ◆ • ————

"Mother Hannah! It has happened!"

Hannah looked up from her suckling baby. "What is it, Tabitha?"

The girl hurried across the room and settled beside her, aquiver with excitement. "Dan has asked for my hand!"

"Dan?"

"You know. Sam's second son?"

Hannah laughed. "Of course I know Dan." She looked at Tabitha. "I am thrilled for you to gain the notice of such a handsome young man."

"And righteous. Do not forget righteous."

"Of course. That was my first thought."

Tabitha wrapped her arms around herself. "Oh, Mother Hannah! To be asked for by such a family!"

Hannah frowned. "But how did this proposal take place? Do you know Dan?"

"Well . . . we have been talking. You know—in the garden and while he is milking his goats."

"Have you been alone with him?"

"No! Never!" Tabitha sighed. "Always, there is someone nearby." She looked at Hannah. "I fled from those who would carve out new customs and discard those we have clung to for generations. I would not change who I am now!"

Hannah smiled again. "Of course you would not," she said soothingly. "Who did Dan's father approach with his request?"

"Father Nephi. In the absence of my father."

"Ah." Hannah nodded. "It is well."

"Father Nephi proposes that we hold the betrothal ceremony as soon as possible. And the marriage in one year." She looked at Hannah. "So what do you think?"

"I?"

"In the absence of my own mother, who has taken to walking dark paths, I am turning to you, Mother Hannah. I would know your thoughts."

Hannah smiled, feeling suddenly close to tears. "You have my blessing, Dear One. Always. I know with such a man you will be very happy indeed."

"Would you help me plan?"

"I would be honored."

The entire settlement gathered a few days later to celebrate the betrothal. Hannah had never seen Tabitha so happy. The girl glowed with joy.

And her betrothed looked equally giddy.

Nephi and the men of the village had discovered much of gold, silver, and precious things, and Dan's gift to his bride was a beautifully-carved silver headband, which nestled in the girl's dark hair, offering brief glimpses of its finery under her headscarf.

Tabitha bounced over to Hannah following the ceremony. "Mother Hannah! Did you see? Is it not the most beautiful thing ever?"

"Indeed it is," Hannah said, moving the girl's headcloth for a closer look. "Your Dan has rare talent." She placed the tip of a finger under Tabitha's chin and tilted her face to the light. "And he certainly does love you."

Tabitha coloured adorably. "I think he is the handsomest, most talented, most righteous man in the whole village."

"You have to think that," Hannah said, laughing.

"Well, I do!"

———————◆———————

The harvest was upon them. One of several in the year. In this land, the growing seasons were different. Back in Jerusalem, field crops were taken once a year, with lambs being the only double harvest. But here in the Promised Land, crops were harvested and new seeds planted at the same time.

It meant twice the bounty. And twice the rejoicing for blessings received.

Hannah was carrying a basket of dried corn, Benjamin strapped to her body and sleeping happily. As she neared the common fire burning in the centre of the village, she tripped over something and fell to one knee. One of the top cobs of corn jumped out of the basket.

In dismay, Hannah watched it bounce into the fire. She pursed her lips and frowned at the run-away cob as she regained her feet.

Just then, Litha happened by, carrying her own basket filled with dried strips of meat.

The two spoke for a moment, then Litha turned to go.

It was at that moment that something popped in the fire.

Thinking at first it was the usual sound of crackling logs, Hannah paid no attention.

But when other pops followed the first and a flurry of white puffs began to appear, raining about the pit, Hannah moved nearer and peered into the fire.

The kernels on her cob of corn were swelling. And, when they had swelled to a certain point, were exploding into the small white puffs.

Hannah jumped back as two of them, both aflame, bounced in her direction.

Another of the puffs, this one intact, landed at her feet. Curious, she picked it up. Then, remembering it was corn from one of her cobs, she put it into her mouth.

Litha stared at her. "You are not going to eat that!"

But Hannah was already chewing. "It is delicious!" she exclaimed. She moved closer to the fire and, as a couple more of the white puffs rained down in her direction, scooped them up and popped them into her mouth. "Really. Here. Taste one." She grabbed another kernel and handed it to Litha.

Doubtfully, her sister-by-marriage sniffed the small, white puff. Then, shrugging, she too put it into her mouth and began to chew thoughtfully. Her face lit up. "It is good!"

For the next minute, the two stood beside the fire, catching any popped corn kernels that escaped the fire.

Soon they had a crowd around them, watching their antics curiously. "Eat!" Hannah told the people.

After that, the competition for the few puffs that escaped the fire was heavy indeed.

Nephi's fourth daughter, Taavi, grabbed a metal pot and brought it to the fire. Hannah threw another cob into it and jammed on a lid. The two of them then used the nearby tripod and frame to swing the pot over the fire.

In a few moments, all were rewarded with the sound of popping and pinging from the inside of the pot.

When the sounds lessened, they brought the pot out of the heat and gingerly removed the lid.

A great mound of fluffy white greeted them.

A cheer went up and everyone was reaching in for a handful.

In no time, the container was empty.

Hannah threw the spent corncob into the fire, then dropped another into the pot.

This one, too, was soon gone.

"More, Mother Hannah," one of the small children urged.

Hannah smiled at Zoram's young son. "Patience, Eamon. Let us not eat it all at once. Especially since these cobs of dried corn are meant to be used for grinding. For bread."

"But this is so much more exciting!"

Hannah smiled. "It is."

A couple more of the cobs were sacrificed, then the people began to disburse, the women moving toward home and hearth to start the

evening meal and the men gathering to discuss the possible reasons
corn popped.

———————◆———————

The days went past on fleet feet as Hannah devoted her time to her
duties in the village and to Benjamin. Daily, she saw little changes
in her infant son, but, thus far, no resemblance to her husband or
his family. His eyes, nose, and mouth were Hannah's. His bright
hair—changed from its original baby soft and now standing erect on
his little head—that of her elder sister Uzziel. Twinkling, dark eyes
noticed everything and he smiled and laughed readily. Already he was
strong and wanting to roll and get around.

On this morning, he had succeeded in picking up a small, wooden
toy made for him by one of the brethren. Hannah smiled at him as he
crowed happily and waved his prize around, promptly losing it. His
expression changed immediately, his bottom lip quivering as his eyes
filled with tears.

Hannah smiled and handed the toy back to him.

Sunshine was instantly restored.

Hannah picked up her small son and wrapped a length of cloth
around the two of them.

As much as she would rather spend her time watching Benjamin,
she had work to do. She had completely used up her store of yarn
spun from her cotton crop. With a baby outgrowing everything and
in constant need of new clothes, a trip to the cotton field was needed.

With Benjamin strapped snugly against her, she picked up a large,
empty basket and started up the street with Little Brother following
closely.

"Mother Hannah!"

Hannah looked. Tabitha was coming toward her. "What is it,
Dear One?"

"I just wondered if you were going out to pick cotton. And if I
could come along."

Hannah smiled. "Yes. And yes."

"Let me grab . . ." Tabitha disappeared into their hut, returning a
moment later with a basket equal in size to the one Hannah carried.
"I'm ready!"

The two of them, with Little Brother alternating between following them and chasing off into the forest, made their way out of the village and onto a wide trail worn by many feet leading through the forest.

After a short walk, they reached the place near the water where the tangle of cotton bushes grew.

Tabitha set down her basket and started picking at the puffs of white, careful to avoid the sharp boll. As she moved forward among the bushes, she kicked her basket ahead of her.

Hannah did the same and they worked quietly for several moments, each intent on filling her basket.

Hannah straightened, then put her hands against her lower back and stretched it. "Ooh! I am not as young as I used to be."

Tabitha giggled. "None of us are!"

Hannah smiled at her. "Yes. You've reached the great age of sixteen summers. You are definitely—" She broke off. "What is wrong with him?"

Little Brother returned from another foray into the trees and suddenly stiffened and growled. Hannah looked at the pup, puzzled. He was staring at her basket.

He growled again.

Tabitha went still, listening carefully. "Wait! I hear something." She put a hand over her mouth as a strange sound reached them.

The two women looked at each other. "Does it sound like someone saying, 'Sisters?'" Tabitha whispered.

Hannah nodded and put out a hand, shushing her young companion. "Listen!" she hissed.

Silence.

"Perhaps it was just the wind through these branches," Tabitha suggested.

Hannah shook her head and pointed at Little Brother who was moving slowly toward her basket, still growling and with the hair on the back of his neck erect.

The two women remained still and silent for several moments.

Then Hannah shook her head. "Obviously, we were all mistaken." She kicked her basket, but it bumped into something and refused to budge. Hannah lifted it, then gasped and froze.

A hand and arm were just visible in the dark soil beneath the bushes.

CHAPTER NINE

*L*ittle Brother began to howl and Hannah dropped her basket, spilling its fluffy, white contents into the brown soil.

For a moment, she stared at the hand, shocked and transfixed.

Tabitha peered at her, then started forward, stopping when Little Brother stepped in front of her, physically barring her way. "What is it, Mother Hannah?"

"A—" Hannah did not know quite what to say. Finally, "A hand."

"A what?" Tabitha pushed Little Brother aside and came over. "A hand!"

"And an arm."

"Should we see who it is?"

Hannah took a deep breath. Finally gathering herself, she shoved her basket aside and dropped to her knees.

Tobias's dirty, blood-stained face peered at her from out of the bushes.

Little Brother dashed to her and tried to push her away, but she managed to move him aside. The pup wouldn't go far, however, preferring to stay beside her, a constant growl in his throat.

"Tobias!" Hannah gasped.

"Tobias?" Tabitha echoed.

"Quickly, Dear One! Run to the village and fetch help!"

Tabitha disappeared.

Hannah touched the young man's hand. "Tobias are you injured?"

His lips twitched as if he tried to smile. "A bit." His voice was weak and barely discernible.

"Where. Where are you hurt?"

"My . . . back."

Hannah gripped his hand and tried to pull him out from under the bushes, but at his shriek of pain, she stopped.

Somehow, she needed to get him into the open where his wounds could be assessed and help given. Her eyes narrowed. If she could not bring him out, she would have to clear the area around him.

Firmly telling Little Brother to stay where he was, she got to her feet and started pulling at the nearest bush, finally wrenching it from the soil. Then she started on the next and the next. Finally she had cleared a spot immediately surrounding the young man's body and was able to get a clear view. Then she gasped and squatted quickly beside him once more, reaching out with one hand.

Hannah could see the colourful fletching of an arrow protruding from the young man's back. He had been shot. But how? And by whom? And how had he managed to travel with such a wound?

Hannah touched the arrow with gentle fingers, wishing with all her heart that she could simply pluck it out and cast it away. But she knew the folly of such a move. She sat back and tried to decide what to do.

"Tobias?"

Dark eyes drifted open.

"Tobias, can you hear me?"

A slight nod.

"Tobias, who did this to you?"

A slow tear dripped from one eye and across his nose. Another followed it.

Little Brother whined.

"Tobias, who shot you?"

"Told him . . . I b-believed."

"Told who, Tobias? Your father?"

"Told him . . . Nephi was . . . prophet."

Hannah sucked in a breath. "You told someone at Laman's camp that Nephi was the prophet?"

Another slight nod. *"King . . . L—"*

"Yes. Yes. *King* Laman!"

"He said . . . go if I b-believed. King La . . . man. I walked . . . away. He . . . he shot . . ."

His words went through Hannah like a cold blade. *"Laman* shot you?!"

Tobias nodded. *"King* La . . . man. Laughed. F-Father turned away." It seemed to be getting more difficult for Tobias to breath. And speak.

Hannah laid a hand on his forehead. "Tobias, do not try to talk any more. Save your strength, Son. Nephi will be here shortly. He will help you. He will s-save you!"

Tobias shook his head. "Too late for m-me."

"No! It is not too late!" Hannah said fiercely.

Tobias smiled. A real smile this time. "Do not . . . worry. Going . . . home."

Hannah gasped. She had heard almost those exact words from Abishai. "Tobias, no!"

"Go, Son." Hannah jumped as Nephi knelt beside her and took Tobias's hand in his. "Your sins are forgiven you. They really were not yours anyway. Go, Son. Go to God. He is waiting for you."

The lines of pain went out of Tobias's face and he smiled at Nephi. "I . . . believe," he said.

"I know, Son. And God knows. Go. Go to Him."

Tobias nodded slightly, jerkily. "Tell M-Mother . . ." His hand dropped from Nephi's grasp and he seemed to settle into the soil, his eyes suddenly fixed and sightless.

Nephi leaned forward and closed the dark eyes in peace. "I will, Son," he whispered softly. "I will tell her."

Little Brother sat up, threw his head back and howled to the sky.

Hannah shivered and blotted at her tears with the sleeve of her tunic. She rubbed Benjamin's back with one hand and tried to calm her howling pup with the other.

"TOBIAS!" someone shrieked.

Hannah was shoved aside as Rachel threw herself across the body of her son. "Tobias! No!" The quiet air was shattered by the sound of her sobs.

Nephi laid a gentle hand on her back. "He is with God, Sister Rachel."

She blinked up at Nephi with tear-drenched eyes. "He did not . . . he did not . . ."

"He repented, Sister. And his sacrifice has been accepted. He is with God now."

Fresh tears. This time of agony mixed with joy.

Nephi looked at the people who had arrived with Rachel. "Let us give our sister time. I will summon you when there is a need."

The people disbursed, leaving Nephi and Hannah alone with the grieving mother and her son.

For the time it took the sun to pass from morning into afternoon, Rachel cried over Tobias. Nephi and Hannah sat quietly nearby and allowed the mother this last time with her son.

Little Brother trotted nervously back and forth, stopping every few paces to whine or howl.

Finally, Rachel sat back and blotted her tears on her headcloth. "He is at peace."

"And are you, Mother?" Nephi asked.

Rachel nodded and managed a small smile. "I am."

Nephi touched her shoulder, then looked at Hannah. "Sister? Could you summon those who were here before?"

Hannah nodded and hurried off. In a short time, she was back, followed by several of the townspeople.

Nephi looked at them and smiled his thanks. "Take Tobias to the village. We will prepare him there."

Some men moved close and carefully picked up the young man who, such a short time before, had been full of life and promise.

It was a saddened group who began to make their way back to the village.

Nephi had risen to his feet and was staring off into the trees.

Hannah paused beside him. "Is that all there is to this life, Brother Nephi? Pain and suffering?" She sighed and rubbed her forehead. "Sometimes there seems little point in going on."

He looked at her. "There is pain, yes, Sister Hannah. And suffering to be sure. It is sad that we need the opposition to remind us of our duty. To turn our hearts to our God." He sighed. "But much of our suffering is brought on by the choices of men. The evil choices of men."

"Of course, as always, you would call others' choices evil and your own, good."

Hannah looked up, her heart starting to hammer in her chest.

Little Brother appeared suddenly in front of her, his teeth bared, a wild growl in his throat.

Laman was standing not twenty paces away. Hannah could see a couple of men behind him but there was no sign of Lemuel. Or Samuel.

Then she gasped. Standing behind the three kinsmen were two of Laman's daughters, garbed as the men in leather and fur and armed with bows.

Her eyes returned to Laman. Truly he looked every inch the barbarian king with his fur garments, his long, unkempt hair and his wide gold cuffs and golden crown. A bow was slung across his thick body and a sword and smaller knife sheathed at his side.

"My brother. Have you come to make your peace with God?" Nephi asked calmly.

Laman gave a short, sharp bark of laughter. "I could ask you the same question, Usurper!" He turned to watch the group of Nephi's people bear their sorry burden through the trees back to their village. "I am happy to see that you are willing to take care of the boy you murdered."

"*I* murdered?"

"You all but pulled the bowstring. You, who deceived and misled that susceptible young man until the only road open to him was death."

"How can you even think that?" Hannah shouted.

Laman noticed her for the first time. His eyes widened. "Well. Our little shrew is harder to kill than I thought. And is now making life miserable for someone else." He bowed slightly toward her and laughed derisively. "Well, better the Usurper having to endure your presence than me."

Little Brother growled fiercely.

Laman laughed again. "And you have obviously found a protector." The dark eyes scanned the wolf pup, noted the severed tail. "But one a little less than perfect. Rather like you."

Hannah felt as though he had punched her in the stomach, driving all the air from her lungs. Benjamin began to cry and she began to jostle him to quiet him.

Nephi put out a hand and squeezed her arm. "Pay him no mind, Sister," he said softly. "He knows not what he says."

Still bouncing on the balls of her feet to quiet her son, Hannah lifted her chin and turned back to Laman. "Better a man of God than—"

But Laman's eyes were no longer on her. He was staring at Benjamin. "And who do we have here?" he asked softly. "Another arrow in Lemuel's quiver?"

Hannah blinked and put a protective hand over Benjamin's back.

"Shall I tell my brother he has another child?" He looked at Hannah and his mouth twisting into a strange smile. "Or is it even his?" He glanced at Nephi. "Has someone else been tilling my brother's soil?"

Hannah felt her face pucker into an expression of disgust. "Of course not!"

Laman laughed. "As if any would show interest in such as you, Shrew." He turned again to Benjamin. "So it *is* my brother's child." He nodded. "I will inform him."

Hannah felt as though all the blood in her body was about to burst through her head. "No!" she shrieked. "He has taken my only other child away from me! I will not let him have—"

Nephi squeezed her arm again, silencing her. Then he turned to his eldest brother. "Lemuel lost any claim on this child when he conspired to murder his wife," he said quietly. "This boy belongs to Hannah."

"A boy! Lemuel will be very interested to hear it. Iscah managed to present Lemuel with yet another girl, but she ages. Any prospect of producing sons has been abandoned. And we need those sons." He smiled at Nephi. "To inherit the crown of their fathers."

"The only crown we should be interested in, Brother, is that bestowed by the Lord at the end of our earthly journey."

Laman laughed. "You are, if nothing, predictable, Brother. And boring. What care we for some ethereal crown at the end of some pointless journey? It is *now* that should concern us. Ruling *now!*"

"As usual, you see not the riches of righteousness but the riches of the world."

"What else is there?" Laman spread his hands wide.

Nephi closed his eyes. "Have you so little faith, Brother?"

Laman snorted. "What need have I of faith when the whole world is at my feet?"

"The world may be at your feet, but what of heaven? What of eternity?"

"When this life ends, *if* there is more, I will conquer there as I have conquered here."

"You would gain the kingdom of God by the sword?"

Laman's eyes lit up. "Is there any other way?"

"Yes!" Nephi's body shook with intensity. "Yes, Brother. Come to the Lord. Follow His teachings. Walk in His ways. Seek after righteousness and all these things will be added unto you."

Laman laughed. "Why waste my time when all these things have already been added unto me?"

"Only worldly things," Nephi said sadly.

Laman frowned thoughtfully. "You are right in one thing, Brother."

Nephi looked at him.

"I do not yet possess everything." Laman smiled. "I would remind you, Traitor, that it is my right, by birth, to rule *all* this people. The day is not far off when I will realize that right. By the point of a sword if necessary."

Nephi, unarmed and helpless against the tiny army that faced him, straightened and stared fearlessly across the intervening space. "And I will remind *you* that these are the people of God. They follow the Lord's will and the prophet who acts on the Lord's behalf. You do not." He paused for a moment. "But I know that you can. And that you know I speak the truth." He held out his hands. "Search your heart, Brother. You know my words are true. Return to the Lord. Take your place as the elder brother of this people in righteousness."

Laman grunted. "And subject myself to your rule?"

"I do not seek to rule. Only to spread the teachings of the Lord to his people that all may live in righteousness and peace."

"With you at the head."

Hannah heard someone come up behind her. She spun around to see nearly every man—and more than a few of the boys—of the people of Nephi. All carried knives, farm and garden implements, and one or two hefted large rocks. A couple held bows conspicuously.

It should have been a pitiful showing, indeed, against the might of armed warriors, but Hannah felt a surge of gratitude and her fear suddenly melted away. All at once, she remembered something Nephi had said only a few days previously, quoting the Prophet Elisha: *Fear not: for they that be with us are more than they that be with them.*

In her mind's eye, standing with this group of poorly-armed brethren in their ragged line, Hannah suddenly saw the horses and chariots of the Lord.

Laman waved a hand dismissively. "I have come to inform you, *Younger Brother*, that war is coming. A war between the rightful rulers of this people and the Usurper." He and the people around him all reached for their weapons.

Hannah stared in shock as those who, until recently, had called themselves her kin, brandished their weapons above their heads and let loose a mighty shout.

The men and boys around Hannah shoved her behind them and braced themselves for an attack, their pitiful weapons held before them.

Little Brother, sensing a change in the atmosphere, suddenly leapt to his feet and began to chase back and forth, howling wildly.

Though there were only a few men and women with Laman, Nephi's people were hopelessly outmatched in weaponry. But Hannah did not see fear in any of them. Instead, their countenances were firm in their faith in the God of Heaven and Earth.

Laman laughed. "Did you think it would be today?" He looked at his warriors and they, too laughed and lowered their weapons. Laman leaned forward and pointed a wide finger at Nephi. "Hear this, *Brother*! You will know neither the time nor the place when I will attack you. But know this, too, that there will be none who will escape alive. None."

"Then who will you rule, *King* Laman?" Hannah clapped a hand over her mouth as everyone turned to look at her.

Laman stared, narrow-eyed, at her. "Perhaps this spy we sent into your camp will prove helpful after all."

"What?" Hannah gasped.

Laman laughed and made a mock-salute toward Nephi with his sword. "Until later, my *brother*." He looked at Hannah. "And I will be informing my second-in-command of that child's birth." He pointed his sword at Benjamin. "Lemuel will be very interested. I think his son would do far better under his father's care." He nodded at her and his army melted into the forest.

Hannah froze, her heart a lump of cold lead in her chest.

After a few moments, when no further movement came from the forest, the brethren of Nephi slowly lowered their weapons.

Little Brother continued his growling until the sounds of Laman's passing faded into the forest.

Jacob turned to his elder brother. "Command us, Father Nephi. What would the Lord have us do?"

Nephi sighed. "We must prepare for the day spoken of by Laman, my brothers. We must prepare for war."

As the men turned back to the village, Hannah caught up to Nephi. "Brother Nephi, please tell me that Lemuel cannot take my baby. Please tell me he has no claim on Benjamin!"

Nephi looked at her. "Sister, you know he lost all claim on you when he sought to take away your life."

"But can he take my son? Please tell me he cannot take my son!"

Nephi stopped walking and looked suddenly serious. "Only if he can get through me and every other man in this village."

Hannah sighed, relieved. "Thank you."

They started walking again.

"Brother Nephi?"

Again he looked at her. "Is there something else, Sister?"

"Yes." Hannah felt her face flush with heat. "You—you do not believe Laman's words, do you?"

Nephi looked at her and frowned. "I have never believed Laman's words, Sister. But to what are you referring?"

"When he said I was a . . . a sp—" She could not finish.

Nephi's face cleared and he threw his head back and shouted with laughter.

Hannah stopped walking and stared at him.

As did the rest of the men.

Jacob came over to them. "Brother?"

Nephi wiped streaming eyes on the sleeve of his tunic. "I am fine, Brother." He turned twinkling eyes on Hannah. "Sister Hannah has given me just the lift I needed."

Hannah folded her arms in front of Benjamin indignantly. "Well it was not funny to me!"

Nephi laughed again. "Sister, if you knew you the way we know you, you would be laughing too. The idea of the most stalwart, faithful woman I have ever known acting as a spy to the most *unprincipled man* I have ever known, well the idea is—"

Jacob, too began to laugh.

Hannah frowned. Was there a compliment in there somewhere? She decided to take her confusion somewhere else and left the men standing there in the cotton field. Still laughing.

Litha met her as she entered the village. "Hannah! Where are the men? They all ran out of here when someone said they had seen Laman. Is there a battle? Should we be preparing?"

"We should be preparing, Sister, but there was not battle." Hannah turned to look behind her. "And the men are standing there in the forest. Laughing."

Litha blinked and followed Hannah's gaze. "Where? I do not see them."

"Oh, they are there." Hannah pointed. "I will never understand men." She continued to walk up the street, a very puzzled Little Brother walking alongside her.

———— ◆ ————

Tobias was honored and buried early the next morning.

Rachel went where she was led, white-faced but calm through the entire process.

As the family walked there and back, Hannah found that she was staring into the trees much more than usual and jumping at any sound or movement.

121

Laman had said he would attack at any time and in any place. Would a family grieving the loss of their son—a man Laman himself had so callously murdered—and occupied with the process of his burial make a suitable target?

Hannah rubbed her hands across Benjamin's back. What a mixed up world she lived in. She looked toward the head of the winding column of family members. Rachel, her youngest two childrens' hands in hers, was walking between Nephi and Anava, following directly behind the body of her second eldest son, carried on a litter between several of his cousins. Hannah frowned. Lehi had been warned to leave Jerusalem to avoid those who sought to destroy him. The family had been led here, to this land of peace and plenty, where they could follow the teachings of a prophet of God without fear of reprisals.

And, somehow, it seemed they had brought the fight with them.

Already, Rachel had lost two of her sons directly or indirectly to the conflict. And Litha one.

And Hannah's son, Samuel.

Hannah felt an unaccustomed wash of anger pour over her. What had their family accomplished by leaving?

Nephi turned and surveyed his family members, his eyes slowly moving along the column.

When he reached her and saw that she was looking at him, he smiled and nodded before moving on.

Hannah blinked. What was she thinking? They had been brought here to follow a prophet of God.

A prophet of God.

And nothing—certainly not one man bent on power and rule—was going to dissuade them from doing exactly that.

After Tobias's body had been settled in a cave and the entrance blocked with several large stones, the people gathered around Nephi.

"My people," he began. "It is a sad, sad day, when we bury the very light and life of our family."

Rachel's sobs echoed weirdly between the trees and the wall that housed the cave. She was leaning on Litha, who was faring little better than her sister.

Hannah shivered, feeling suddenly . . . strange. As though she were not really here.

Nephi went on. "But even as we give a short farewell to our young brother, we are reassured that we shall see him again. In our bodies we will greet each other and rejoice at our reuniting through the sacrifice of our Saviour, who will come into the world as a ransom. Who will pay the price for our sins and for death and, through that sacrifice, make it possible for each of us to return to our God who awaits us eagerly."

He looked around. "Think of it, my brothers and sisters. Our family reunited once again in peace. In a place where no unclean thing can break through and defile. Where happiness abounds forever." He brushed away a tear. "I look forward to this place. To this time." He smiled. "Soon. But not yet. Not yet."

He reached out a hand to both Rachel and Litha. "My Sisters, both of you have been called upon to send sons forward to that land from which no man returns. Know this: they are safe and happy and will never suffer pain or sickness or hurt or fear or want again. They will simply continue their work from the other side of the veil. Fear not for them. Grieve for the separation, but not for the loss. For truly, there is no loss."

He continued to speak words of comfort and peace.

Finally, as the sun rose above the trees and bathed the land in the first light of a new day, he looked over the gathered people. "Let us return to our lives and our duties. Let us remember this young man—and those who now walk with him—with joy over the time we were together. Not with sorrow over the time we must be apart."

It was a mostly silent group that made their way back to the settlement.

After the evening meal, Hannah and Tabitha gathered with the rest of the people of Nephi in the House of Assembly. A group of young men were playing softly on some pipes while those gathered visited. Hannah looked around. Noticeably absent were Sam and Jacob and several of the older grandsons.

Nephi was standing. Speaking quietly with Joseph.

Hannah tipped her head to one side and studied this youngest of Lehi's sons, born nearly twenty years after Nephi to their mother in her age. Raised during the family's exodus to the Promised Land, he was remarkably sturdy, faithful, and honest.

Hannah shook her head. Why were the eldest sons of Lehi so faithless and the youngest so faithful? Would Laman have been as wicked if he were placed further along in the family? She sighed. It was a fruitless speculation. Things were what they were.

"My family."

Hannah looked up. Joseph had taken a seat and Nephi was standing before them. He looked at the young musicians in the corner and they lowered their instruments.

Nephi nodded. "First of all, I wish to excuse our brethren who are taking up the first of the guard patrols that we will be standing from now and on."

Hannah caught her breath.

He sighed. "It is with a heavy heart that I tell you that we must prepare for war."

Several people in the audience gasped. A general buzz of conversation began as people leaned toward their neighbours and began to speak.

Nephi held up his hands and the noise died away. "My people, I have told you this before. That our coming here to this place would merely postpone what my brother Laman plans. And that his animosity would one day reach out to us. Well that day is coming and we must be prepared." He turned and lifted a long, wooden crate to the nearest chair. Then, he threw back the lid dramatically and withdrew the contents. A single item.

A great sword. The silver blade shone crimson in the last rays of the sun shining through one of the windows. The hilt looked as though it was made of pure gold, inset with many valuable jewels.

Hannah gasped.

Nephi was, once again, holding the Sword of Laban.

Suddenly the thought of war became all too real.

Nephi held it up, turning slowly so everyone could get a good look. "You have all seen this sword. It belonged to Laban and was taken from him by the Lord's direction on that last night in Jerusalem that our family might not perish and die through ignorance."

All eyes in the room were focused on the sword.

"Well, now I have a different purpose for this blade. One that will require everyone's help."

The room was silent.

Nephi took a deep breath and released it. "The Lord has shown me where to find ore to smelt and we are going to use this sword as a master to create dozens of weapons just like it for our brethren."

Zoram's youngest son leaned forward eagerly. "One for each of us, Father Nephi?"

Nephi regarded the boy gravely. "When you are of age, Eadric. Another few years."

Hannah looked at the boy, not yet of an age to lift such a weapon and certainly not strong enough to use one. Two thoughts went through her mind. One, gratitude that her leaders would not be arming their women and children. And second, dismay that they needed to arm anyone. She looked at Nephi. "So we are preparing for a war with our brethren, Brother Nephi?"

"We are, Sister." Nephi sighed and looked over the crowd. "I want you to understand it will not be a war of invasion, but one of defence. Only when we raise our weapons in our own defence will the Lord be with us." He looked down. "But the resultant shedding of blood will be the same." He lowered the sword, sticking the point into the ground. "So we *are* going to arm ourselves to prepare. With this." He pointed to the sword. "But more importantly, with the armour of righteousness."

The people around Hannah nodded.

Nephi raised his head. "I know that each of us hoped our separating from our brethren and leaving them with the land of our first inheritance would suffice to quell their anger and covetousness. But, alas, it has not." He brushed at one cheek. "Their hatred of us, and everything we believe, is strong, and before much more time has elapsed, will escalate from a clash of ideas and ideals to a clash of earthly weapons." He looked away. "It will not be tomorrow. But soon." He looked at Eadric sadly. "And it will last for as long at their ignorance and hatred last, so, Son, you will get your chance to wield your own sword."

Moriah put an arm around her son and pressed him close to her for a moment as her eyes sought Hannah's and the two exchanged a look.

The conflict that had driven them from their home in Jerusalem had followed them here to the Promised Land.

Truly now was the time for every ounce of their spiritual strength.

———————•◆•———————

Now the usual sounds of village industry were nearly drowned out by the constant, almost musical, clang of metal on metal.

The two forges set up by Sam and Nephi rang with the effort of sword after sword being heated and pounded and folded and pounded again. Over and over. Until they finally began to emerge as fine, razor-edged weapons. Identical to the Sword of Laban in everything but jewel-encrusted trim.

Just outside of the settlement, Nephi had set up foundries to smelt and purify the metal, so those not involved with the actual crafting of the swords could provide the fine steel with which they were made.

And not far from there, one could hear the sounds of shouting and grunts of effort of young men being trained with blunted swords or bow and arrows in an arena set up by Joseph on a level patch of ground.

Hannah, with Little Brother behind her, stood at one end of the street and watched in amazement.

What had been a little village growing out of the forest was now a beehive of activity. Where once the brethren could concentrate simply on their building and herding, now they were guarding, patrolling the village perimeter, blacksmithing, and training.

And yet, all seemed cheerful and cooperative. Sure in the knowledge that, even if the weapons and armour being crafted were not strong enough to withstand the blows of the enemy, their armour of righteousness certainly was.

Slowly, the stout little storage shed at the end of the street filled with finely-crafted weapons all neatly and ingeniously stowed so they could be distributed quickly.

Hannah, Little Brother close behind her, paused beside Nephi's little shelter at one side of the street near the House of Assembly. The prophet had set up a stout table under a cloth cover and was busily inscribing on thin gold plates.

"Good morrow, Nephi."

He looked up, then smiled as he got to his feet. "Good morrow, Sister Hannah. You look bright and cheery today!"

Benjamin cooed at his uncle and grinned his wide, toothless grin.

Nephi's smile widened. "As does your son."

"He grows daily," Hannah said, rubbing Benjamin's back with one hand. "He is the sun in my sky."

Nephi nodded, sticking out a finger for the baby to grasp.

"F-Father Nephi," Hannah stumbled over the unfamiliar title. Always, Nephi had been a brother to her. Now, even though she happily acknowledged him as the leader of their people, it was still difficult to remember to address him in the proper manner. "Erm—I have something I would offer."

Nephi, still with Benjamin's baby fingers grasping his larger one, looked at her. "Yes?"

Hannah held out a large bundle.

"What is this?"

"It is my gift to the Lord. For His holy house."

Nephi pulled his finger from Benjamin's grasp and took the bundle, unfolding it to reveal rich furs of every colour and texture. He frowned. "What is this?"

"The furs Tabitha and I gathered on our trek. I had the tanner prepare them and Tabitha and I have stitched them together in what I hope is a pleasing pattern." She watched Nephi's expression closely. "Is it an acceptable offering to our God?"

Nephi spread the large rug and studied it for a moment. Then he looked at her, his smile wide. "It is, Sister."

Hannah took a deep breath and nodded. "It is well." She helped him fold the furs once more and reached for the bundle.

"Do you need me to take them for you?"

Hannah shook her head. "I will deliver them on my way. This is my temple day. Benjamin and I are serving food to the men laboring there today."

"Ah." Nephi looked down. "And your pup?"

Hannah smiled at Little Brother. "He guards the door. Most especially so he can be near to—and entertain—Benjamin."

Nephi smiled. "It is well. All efforts in the building of the Lord's House are gladly accepted." He turned to look toward the great building which now overshadowed the town. "Daily it grows, despite the other duties we have been required to accept."

Hannah lifted her head as the sound of hammers on steel began to ring across the settlement. "Ah. As we now witness."

"Our arsenal grows apace with everything else. Would that we never needed it!"

"Food to break your fast, Husband."

Hannah turned.

A smiling Anava had arrived with a cloth-covered basket under one arm. "Hello, Treasured One," she said to Hannah.

Hannah smiled and gave her a hug. "Hello, Sweet Sister."

Anava handed the basket to Nephi and kissed his cheek, then turned back. "Are you serving at the temple today as well?"

"I am."

"Then let us go together. I have not talked to you for days!"

The two women spent the day preparing and carrying platters of food for the labourers. It was light, pleasing work, given the cooling temperatures, which made a day spent in the close confines of a glowing fire a pleasant experience.

The big meal of the day had been served and the men had drifted back to their duties. Hannah nestled into a private corner to nurse Benjamin. Little Brother had gone to explore.

Anava collected the leavings and stacked everything neatly on her platter. Then she took a seat next to her elder sister. "How it thrills me to see you with your son, Hannah."

Hannah smiled. "It is a constant miracle to me as well, my sister." She tried to smooth her baby's red hair, which resisted her ministrations and remained standing straight up from the tiny head. "Daily, I thank God that he was given to me."

"A blessing that was well-deserved, my sister."

Hannah smiled. "I pray every waking moment, and probably no few of my sleeping ones, that I will remain deserving of His blessings."

"You need not doubt," Anava said. She got to her feet and stretched. "I know of none other more deserving of His blessings."

"If only my faith were stronger."

Anava gave a very unlady-like snort. "There is no one whose faith is as strong as yours, my sister!"

Hannah smiled at her and shook her head. "Sister, if you knew the abundance of doubts I labour under."

Anava closed her eyes. "As do we all." She was quiet for a moment. "Hannah. Have you given any thought to Nephi's suggestion?"

"Which suggestion?"

"That you find a suitable husband in our settlement."

Hannah immediately found her baby's head very interesting.

"Hannah?"

Reluctantly, she looked at her younger sister.

"Have you?"

Hannah sighed. "No. Every time such thoughts appear, I drive them away." She looked at Anava. "I feel bound by the covenants I spoke in the Valley of Lemuel all those years ago."

"Even though the man you spoke those covenants with no longer honors his?"

"Even though."

"It has been nearly a year since you—left—Laman's encampment."

"You mean *King* Laman's . . . "

The two sisters burst into laughter.

"Where is Father Nephi?"

They looked up. Yavin was standing there, breathing heavily.

Anava got to her feet. "What is it, Yavin? What has happened?"

Yavin wiped some perspiration from his face with the back of his hand. "I must speak to him at once!"

"He was there." She pointed. "Scribing. In the village street. But—"

The young man was off before she could finish. Anava turned to Hannah. "What do you suppose that is about?"

———— ◆ ————

"The men did no damage. Merely scattered the sheep and then laughed at Yavin and his two younger brothers when they ran to gather them once more."

Hannah frowned at Tabitha and moved to the doorway of their hut. "But why would they do such a thing? What could possibly be accomplished?"

Tabitha shrugged. "Maybe there is no purpose. Other than to keep us worried. Everyone is talking about it. Lamanites this close to our borders again. It makes us all nervous." The girl slipped past Hannah and looked out into the street.

Hannah turned and did the same.

From her limited view, she could see two separate groups of people standing about, speaking excitedly.

"Oh, here comes Father Nephi," Tabitha said.

Hannah picked up Benjamin and stepped outside.

Nephi was coming down the street. He stopped at first one group, then another and, after he left each one, they all turned and started to walk back up the street.

"I think they are heading for the synagogue," Tabitha said.

"Father Nephi must have called a meeting."

Just then he stopped at the group closest to them. "My people, please join me in the House of Assembly."

Everyone nodded and started up the street.

"I thought as much," Tabitha said.

"Well, let us join with them." Hannah was already in the street and walking with purpose.

It only took a short time for the people to gather. Hannah could see the concern on their faces.

Nephi took his place at the front of the room. "My people, I do not need to ask if you have heard of the incident out in the sheep pastures."

A buzz of conversation was his answer. He raised his hands for quiet. It took a while, but finally, he was rewarded with everyone's attention.

"My brothers and sisters, we need not fear."

Another outburst.

Nephi called out over the noise. "Please, my people, let me finish!"

Gradually, they grew quiet.

"If we are faithful and obey the commandments, we need not fear."

"But those—those *Lamanites* think they can just walk in here and do what they wish!" someone shouted.

Nephi nodded. "We will post guards."

"We already have guards!"

"You are right. We have guards. But we have set them about the village. Now we will set them in the borders of the land."

"Can the Lord simply smite them?"

Nephi looked down at the small boy who had spoken. "The Lord will protect us in his own way, Eamon, but we must do all we can."

"If you would give me a sword, I could go with the patrols."

Nephi smiled at him. "You will have your chance to serve, Son." He looked over the crowd. "We will all have our chance to serve."

Ilka, Nephi's fourteen-year-old daughter, stood up at the back of the hall. "Father?"

He looked at her. "Yes?"

"Could we, my sisters and I, be posted as guards?"

Nephi frowned. "Has it come to this already? That we must arm our women and send them into battle?"

"I am not saying we should be armed. And I certainly am not ready to go into battle. But could we patrol the forest and be a voice of warning to the people?"

Nephi looked thoughtful. "I will speak to the Lord." He smiled at the girl. "And I hope you speak to Him as well."

Nephi spoke a few minutes longer, made some assignments, and then offered a prayer for guidance and protection.

The people returned to their homes.

"I always feel such comfort when Father Nephi prays," Tabitha fiddled with the silver headband she always wore. She sighed. "And when he speaks. He is always so . . . calm."

Hannah nodded. "I know he worries about all of us and shakes his head over the choices we make, but when he talks to us, he is always composed and quiet and encouraging."

"When I hear him, it is always as though the Lord Himself is speaking."

Hannah looked at her young companion. "That is as it should be, Tabitha. When a prophet of the Lord speaks, he does so for the Lord. His words are the Lord's words."

Tabitha walked in silence for a few steps. "So we can always trust him? Always believe him?"

Hannah nodded. "The Lord will not allow His prophet to lead his children astray."

Tabitha frowned. "But what of King Saul and men like him who made mistakes when they were ruling?"

"King Saul was removed from the throne. And though he was ordained by a prophet of the Lord and considered a holy man, he was never *the* prophet."

"Oh." Tabitha turned toward the doorway of their hut. "I am amazed by what you know, Mother Hannah."

Hannah smiled slightly. "I do not know very much, Dear One. But I have read the scriptures whenever Nephi—and time—allows, and I listen to the teachings of Nephi and Jacob whenever I can."

Tabitha nodded and her eyes twinkled as she smiled at Hannah. "Perhaps I should study more."

"That is always a good idea."

———————•◆•———————

Extra guards were posted and, after much petitioning, Nephi had assigned the very first pair of women guards to the sheep pastures— the nearest point to the village.

So far, there had been no contact with the Lamanites.

Half a moon later, Hannah and several of the women were in the gardens in the late afternoon, weeding and harvesting. One of Anava's grandsons, a remarkable boy of three summers was playing softly for them on a little bamboo pipe.

Hannah stood up and fanned her hot face. Something moved in the quiet countryside and her eyes sharpened as she focused on that area.

Yes. Someone running. At first a thrill of shock went through her. Was it someone from Laman's camp? She studied the leaping figure carefully as it approached. Finally, she could see that it was Cephus. The young man seemed very intent on reaching the settlement. What on earth had happened?

Hannah wiped her perspiring face with her headcloth, glanced at Benjamin, happily asleep beneath a tree at the edge of the garden, then made her way to the edge of the garden spot where she assumed the young man would pass.

Her guess was perfect. He came panting up just after she had taken up her post.

"Cephus!" she called when he came into ear shot.

Cephus turned his head, obviously surprised to hear his name spoken and slowed somewhat.

"Cephus, what is it?"

"Lamanite attack. In the sheep pasture. Must get Father Nephi. Not good. Not—"

He sprinted off.

"Another attack?" Rachel asked.

Hannah turned to see that the other women had followed her. Rachel was standing to one side, looking toward the place Cephus had mentioned.

"It certainly sounds like it." Hannah walked over to Benjamin and picked him up. The baby frowned, then sighed and stretched before relaxing back into slumber. "Come, sisters, let us find out." She hurried toward the village.

Cephus was already talking to Nephi when the women arrived. A large group of people had gathered about them.

"We had no warning and no idea they were coming until they were just, suddenly, there, scattering sheep!" Cephus was saying. "We have no idea what happened to the guard. We looked everywhere. Yavin was frantic. Because I run the fastest, we decided I should come here for help. He took Fane and Pallav with him to search." He looked at Nephi. "We could not find them, Father Nephi. I fear—" He gulped and forced out the rest of the words. "I fear they have been—taken."

A gasp went through the crowd and the blood drained from Nephi's face, leaving him looking old and stricken. "That was the women guard." His voice sounded faint. He shook his head. "I tried to tell them the Lord did not . . . but they . . ." He straightened and shouted, "I need all the men!"

In seconds, the street was filled with people.

Normally, a gathering engendered much talk and general noise. But this group was strangely quiet.

Hannah shivered. It was eerie.

Anava hurried to Nephi. "Husband. Is that not the pairing Ilka was with?"

Nephi's face was grey. He closed his eyes and nodded.

Anava clutched convulsively at the bosom of her tunic. "No!" she gasped, sinking to the ground. Several of her daughters gathered around her.

Nephi knelt beside her, sliding his arm about her slender shoulders.

"No!" she shrieked, shrugging him off. "You said . . . you— you . . ." Her tears were running freely now.

"Anava. We do not yet know what has happened."

"But we do know. She kept asking you to pray. And pray. And . . ." She looked at him with tear-drenched eyes. "You knew what the answer was. And yet you kept going back and asking again."

"She wanted so badly to help. I was simply trying to please her."

"You who know we are not here to please man but the Lord!"

Nephi struggled to his feet, looking distinctly unsteady. "But when it is one's daughter . . ."

"All the more reason to follow the Lord."

"Brother, we must do something," Jacob said.

"Let us go and search!" someone shouted.

"We cannot go madly off in all directions!" Jacob said loudly. He looked at Nephi. "Brother, we need the Lord's guidance."

Tears streaked Nephi's face as he nodded. "You are right, Brother. We will pray for direction and to know which way to go."

He sank once more to his knees and bowed his head, offering a heart-felt prayer of supplication and guidance. After he finished, he remained, head bowed, and listened.

Hannah had seen her prophet leader often in prayer in behalf of his people. But never had she heard and felt such power as she now witnessed.

Finally, he raised his head. His dark eyes looked like burning coals in his bloodless face. "I know where Ilka is." He looked around. "I have been shown the way."

Anava's daughters helped her to her feet. "We can get her?" Anava asked. "She will be safe?"

Nephi nodded.

"Oh. Thank you!" Anava threw her arms around her husband. "Thank you!"

Nephi held his wife for a moment. Then he held her gently away. "I must leave immediately."

Anava stared at him. "You?"

He nodded. "Me."

"But—but there are other men. Younger. Stronger." Anava gripped his tunic with both hands. "Laman has sworn to kill you! You cannot simply walk into his lands!"

Nephi interrupted her gently. "It is my mistake, Wife. It is my problem to fix."

Anava swayed slightly and looked as though she was going to faint. Her girls gathered close.

Mother Sariah moved to her side and put her arms around her daughter-by-marriage. "I am here with Anava, Nephi. I will care for her."

Esther, Nephi's eldest daughter, put a hand on her mother's arm. "We all will, Father."

Nephi nodded. "Thank you, my daughter. Thank you, Mother." He turned. "My pack." Someone handed him a leather pack, which he quickly strapped about him. "And my sword."

When the gleaming Sword of Laban caught the afternoon sun, Hannah had to swallow hard and blink rapidly to clear her eyes of tears. The situation had become very real very quickly.

Mother Sariah stepped back as Nephi moved to Anava and wrapped her in his arms. "The Lord directs me, Anava," he said, softly.

"What will you do?" she asked.

Nephi smiled slightly. "I know not. The Lord is in charge." He stepped back.

Anava clung to the sleeve of his tunic. "Can you not take anyone with you?"

"I must do this alone." He gently released her fingers and stepped back. "I will return and I will bring our girls with us. I promise you." He looked at his other daughters. "I promise all of you."

Anava nodded, tears spilling down her cheeks.

Nephi looked at the gathered people. "Check on all our patrols and secure the land." He nodded to Jacob. "See to their spiritual needs."

Jacob nodded. "Always."

Nephi turned and disappeared between two of the dwellings. The rest of the men quickly organized themselves into groups and they, too, left the village.

It was strangely quiet after they left.

"So what do we do now?" one of the women asked.

"We wait," Sariah told her. "And we pray."

"What has happened?"

Hannah turned. Amanna and her two daughters Qiana and Naama were standing there, holding baskets of cotton.

"Where were you?" Anava demanded. "How can you not know?"

Amanna blinked. "We were harvesting cotton, Sister." Her forehead puckered in a frown. "What has happened?"

Hannah moved to her side. "Your daughter—"

"What?" Amanna looked at the two girls with her. She turned back to Hannah and gripped her arm with one hand. "Nadia? Has something happened to Nadia?"

Hannah put her hand over her sister's fingers. "We do not know for certain—"

"Of course we know!" Anava broke in. She looked at Amanna. "Your daughter and mine have disappeared following another Lamanite raid."

Amanna stared at her. "Nadia?"

"Is missing. Both of our girls are missing."

Amanna clutched one of her daughter's hands. "Missing?"

"Nephi has gone to get them back."

Hannah went over to her. "The Lord is directing him, Sister. He will bring both of our girls back. Come. Let us get you to where you can sit."

She urged both of her younger sisters to a patch of cool grass beneath a nearby tree where the street widened into a square. Mother Sariah joined them there. "Let us sit here and wait," Hannah said. When she had gotten them comfortable, she had Amanna's daughters bring the baskets of cotton over and all of them began to clean and card the soft fibers. It kept their hands busy while their thoughts were elsewhere.

The time dragged. Hannah found herself directing many of the women in chores they well knew how to do themselves. No one seemed to want to think. Often, Hannah would find them simply standing over their task, hands idle and eyes fixed on some far point.

Any noise would immediately attract gasps of anticipation and all eyes.

Just after sunset, Tabitha noticed three figures approaching the village. She cried out and pointed and soon every woman had crowded around her, all watching nervously.

A group of men appeared from the trees and moved to intercept the trio. They spoke a moment, then all turned and continued toward the village.

"It is Fane and Pallav!" Amanna shouted. "With . . . someone."

Anava pushed through the crowd. "Is it Ilka?"

"It is Nadia!" Amanna ran to her three children, throwing her arms around them all together and then each in turn.

The group of women smiled happily at their daughter returned. But fresh tears coursed down Anava's and her girls' cheeks.

Mother Sariah put a hand on Anava's arm. "Rejoice for your sister, Dearest One," she whispered. "You too will have your happy ending."

Anava looked at her. "I am grateful for Nadia's return. But this tests my faith, Mother Sariah."

Hannah nodded. "That is what trials do."

Anava turned away.

Soon a chattering group of women had surrounded Nadia.

"But how did you escape?" "What did you do then?" "Were you frightened?"

Mother Sariah held up her hands. "Sisters! Let the girl breathe!"

An instant silence fell over the group.

"Now, Nadia," Mother Sariah moved through the crowd to the girl's side and wrapped her in a warm embrace. "We are very happy to have you safely returned to us." She peered into the girl's face. "Are you strong enough to tell us about it from the beginning?"

Nadia took a deep breath and let it out. "I am, Grandmother. Perhaps it will help for me to speak of it."

"It will occupy us while we await . . . further news," Anava said.

Everyone looked at her and the smiles disappeared. Things were far from over.

"Come and sit, Nadia," Hannah said, directing her to the same patch of grass where everyone had been sitting and carding only moments before. "If it will help you to talk about it, we are your eager listeners."

In a moment, all had found places to sit and were waiting expectantly.

"Ilka and I . . ." Nadia hesitated as Anava made a small sound.

Hannah patted Anava's arm. "Go on, Nadia."

"Well, we were assigned to patrol just around the sheep pasture," Nadia said. "Father Nephi thought it was close enough to the village that we could perform the service and not be in any danger."

Anava gave an unladylike snort.

"Go on," Hannah said.

"We were supposed to remain hidden in the trees and move slowly and carefully, staying in the shadows. But Ilka kept going out into the field to talk to Yavin, so if anyone was about, they were sure to see us."

"Well, they are betrothed," Anava said. "Of course she would want to speak to him. Properly chaperoned, of course."

Hannah nodded as Nadia's eyes sought hers.

"We did not even hear them coming." Nadia's eyes had gotten wide. "It was like Father Lemuel was leading them."

Hannah gasped at the mention of her husband's name. "Was—was he there?"

Nadia shook her head. "No, Mother Hannah. We did not see him." She frowned. "We had just left the field yet again and had taken up a post in the shadow of a large tree. Ilka turned to see if she could see Yavin and someone suddenly grabbed her from behind, putting a hand over her mouth and pulling her into the deeper shadows. I opened my mouth to scream and somebody did the same to me. It was useless to struggle. They were very strong."

Anava was watching the girl closely. "And then what happened?"

"We were lifted and carried off through the trees. They were still so silent. I could not even hear them moving. Both Ilka and I tried to struggle, but it was useless. After a while, I thought I heard sheep bleating frantically and someone calling Ilka's name, but I cannot be certain."

"The Lamanites scattered the sheep after you were taken," Hannah said. "That was when the young men noticed you were missing."

Nadia nodded. "They carried us for quite a while, then stopped in a glade somewhere in the forest. I did not recognize the spot. They put Ilka down and tied her hands. It was then I recognized them. Father Laman's eldest daughter, Gaza, and . . . " she looked at Hannah, "and Father Lemuel's son, Samuel."

Hannah gasped. "You are sure it was Samuel?"

"Yes, Mother Hannah. He has gotten older, but I knew him instantly."

"And Gaza," Mother Sariah said sadly.

"It would seem they are sending their women into battle," Nadia said.

Her grandmother nodded.

"After they had tied Ilka up, they came over to us. It was not until the person holding me released me that I was able to see who it was. Father Zedekiah's son, Jonah."

This time, both Rachel and Tabitha made a noise.

Hannah looked at them and nodded.

"It was obvious they intended to do the same to me, but I kicked Samuel in his . . . manhood and he went down. I wasted no time, but jumped over him and lifted my tunic to my knees. Then I ran."

"You must be fleet indeed, My Hope," Mother Sariah said. "To outrun the very best Laman can send against you."

The girl blushed. "I do love to run."

"So you outran them?" Hannah asked.

"For a while. Then I slid down into the roots of a tree and waited while they passed me." She took a deep breath. "I was a bit worried because they are very good trackers and it was not long before they had followed me right to my hiding place." She frowned. "But then they lost my tracks for some reason."

"Were you praying, My Hope?" Mother Sariah asked.

"I was, Mother Sariah. I was praying that the Lord would make me invisible."

"And He did."

"Well, they did not find me, so I am certain this is so. They stopped right beside my tree. Jonah was very angry that Samuel had let me go. He said something about Jonah holding Ilka for Samuel to take to wife and Samuel holding me for Jonah. And now, because Samuel had been so weak, Jonah was going to marry Ilka himself."

"So they are needing wives from among our girls," Mother Sariah said. "How quickly Laman's evil decisions have twisted back on themselves."

Anava had been listening closely to the conversation and now she dissolved completely into tears.

Hannah moved close and tried to comfort her, but she was inconsolable.

"Why did we come here?" Anava cried out. "Why would the Lord direct us here just to watch our children be taken one by one?"

Rachel got up and moved to her other side. "I do not know the Lord's purposes, Sister. But I do know He has one."

Mother Sariah got slowly to her feet. "Do not make the same mistake I made, my daughter."

Anava looked at her mother-by-marriage in surprise. "You, Mother Sariah?"

"I, too made the mistake of doubting. When Lehi sent our sons to Jerusalem to get the plates. I—Father, forgive me—I called Father Lehi a 'visionary man' and accused him of sending away our sons to die." She smiled slightly. "I think my words were something like: You have led us forth from the land of our inheritance, and my sons are no more, and we perish in the wilderness." She looked around. "Which, of course, was untrue." She looked again at Anava. "Do not, when the skies overhead are dark, allow the power of the Evil One to cloud your life as well. That is when you need all of your faith. And all of your strength."

Anava blotted at her face with her headcloth. "But what do you do with your doubts?"

This time, Mother Sariah did smile. "You bury them deep. So deep that they cannot be found. And you put your trust in the Lord. And in the Lord's chosen servant."

Benjamin was starting to make noises.

Hannah stood up. "Mother Sariah, we need to get food ready. The men may return soon and they will be hungry and the little ones are far past waiting."

Mother Sariah nodded. "Sisters, we must disperse and ready the evening meal."

Anava put out a hand. "Oh, please do not leave me alone! I cannot bear the waiting!"

"We are here, Mother," Esther said.

Hannah took her hand. "You need to provide for your children, Daughter. I will stay with her, if the rest of you want to go."

Mother Sariah nodded. "I, too, will stay."

"I will watch Benjamin and make our meal, Mother Hannah," Tabitha said, reaching for the baby.

Hannah nodded, unwrapped her baby, and handed him to Tabitha with a smile of thanks.

"And we will bring for our mother," Esther said. "Come sisters."

Soon Hannah, Mother Sariah and Anava were the only people left in the square.

Hannah handed Anava the carders and set the half-empty basket of raw cotton beside her, but her younger sister seemed unable to settle and was continually dropping the tools to get up and pace about the little square.

Some of the men began to trickle back into the town by twos and threes. All reported the town secure and the guard set before they left to find their dinners.

Throughout the evening people came and went, some staying to visit and some moving on after only a word or two.

Tabitha brought Benjamin to Hannah for a last nursing before putting him to bed, then took the yawning little boy back to the hut.

As the time grew later, Hannah began to encourage Anava to find her bed. "You need rest, Sister."

"How can I sleep?"

"Perhaps if you relax your body, sleep will follow."

It took an effort to convince her, but finally Hannah and Mother Sariah were able to escort Anava to her home where they saw her tucked up and comfortable. Hannah lit a small lamp and turned to Mother Sariah. "It is time you sought your own bed, Mother."

She nodded. "Yes, Daughter. I am feeling my age."

"Go. Rest."

Soon Hannah and Anava were alone. They talked little. The combination of the dark and the quiet made them meditative.

After a while, Hannah could tell by her even breathing that Anava had finally found sleep. She settled herself on the cushions on the floor and sought the oblivion of rest.

———————◆———————

For two days, nothing was heard from Nephi. His people carried on with their chores and duties, but all were simply marking time. Waiting for that moment when their prophet would return to them. At the start of the third day, Hannah, still serving her younger sister by sleeping in Anava's hut, woke with a start, wondering, at first where she was. Nothing looked familiar in the fine, grey first light of another morning.

Then memory washed over her and she gasped and sat up.

Realizing then what had awakened her.

Ilka was kneeling beside her mother's pallet. She and her mother were sobbing quietly as they held each other.

Hearing another noise, Hannah glanced around.

Nephi was leaning against the doorpost, his face expressionless as he watched his wife and daughter.

Her heart singing praises to God for Ilka's safe return, Hannah rose stiffly to her knees and then to her feet. She smiled down at the two women and nodded at Nephi who seemed not to notice her. She slipped quietly past him and headed to her own hut. The joy she had felt at seeing Ilka safe with her mother melted quickly away, replaced by unsettled feelings that bloomed suddenly inside her.

What was wrong?

She crept through the shadows, trying not to awaken either Tabitha or Benjamin as she sought her own mat.

It seemed moments later that noises of cheering and elation crept through the closed door and roused her once again.

Benjamin started to cry and she pulled him to her for his morning feed.

Tabitha opened the shutters on one of their two windows and looked out into the street. "Something has happened, Mother Hannah!"

"Ilka has returned with her father."

Tabitha spun around and looked at her. "What? When?"

Hannah managed to smile. "It was very early this morning. Before the sunrise."

"The sun is just now rising."

That was why it had seemed like mere moments before. It had been. "So. Not all that long ago."

Tabitha knelt beside Hannah's pallet. "Did you see her? Talk to her?"

"I saw her, yes. But she was with her mother and I felt they needed their time together. I left."

"Ah. So you do not know what happened."

"Father Nephi went and got her back. As he said he would."

"Right." Tabitha leaped to her feet and started to dress. "I am going to find out!" She raked her fingers through her hair and bundled it under her headcloth and in a moment, she was out the door.

Hannah's smile disappeared. She cuddled Benjamin's warm body close.

———— ◆ ————

"So not only did he bring her back, but he managed it without anyone knowing or seeing!"

Hannah nodded as she handed Tabitha a round of bread and heaped some goat's cheese and several slices of cold, roasted lamb on it.

Her thoughts still on her story, the girl rolled the bread and took a bite, then continued. "He crept into the village after everyone had gone to bed. Ilka had been taken to my mother's house. She was still tied up so she could not escape. But Father Nephi crept in, cut her bonds, then had her follow him from the village." She shrugged. "No one even noticed."

Hannah rubbed her forehead and leaned back over the fire, raking the coals evenly. Then she set her small griddle in the center.

"Mother Hannah, did you hear me?"

"I did, Dearest One. I am just . . . thinking about what you said."

"Well it was a miracle, really, because they should have heard him. My mother should have . . ." She paused.

143

"I expect most of them had been pouring strong drink down their throats and were in a stupor rather than a sleep," Hannah said drily. She looked at Tabitha, whose bottom lip was quivering and whose eyes had filled with tears. "Your mother was probably just tired. From all the excitement," she finished kindly.

Tabitha blinked and blotted her tears on her headcloth. "She likes the strong drink as much as Father." She waved a hand dismissively. "I will not think of them. I will think instead about the safe return of our sister."

Hannah put a hand on the girl's arm. "That is best."

"Father Nephi has called his people to the House of Assembly after the morning meal."

Hannah nodded. "Benjamin and I will be there."

———————◆———————

The family was in a mood to celebrate. Smiles and tears of gladness had replaced frowns and cries of sorrow and lively music instead of the melancholy airs that had drifted through the settlement.

Ilka was seated near the front of the room with her mother beside her. A grave-faced Yavin sat close on the other side, hardly taking his eyes from her.

Nephi, closely attended by Jacob and Joseph, was sitting to one side. He looked . . . old. Tired. Hannah studied the face she knew so well. She frowned. He also looked very, very upset or angry.

After a few minutes, he got to his feet and moved to the front of the room. "My people," he said.

Slowly the room quieted.

"My people, we have witnessed a great miracle this day."

There was a buzz of noise and many nodding heads.

Nephi held up his hands and the room went still.

"I followed the Spirit as I was directed and made my way into the wilderness. A day's quick march from here, I came across a hunting settlement nestled in the great rocks at the base of that mountain." He pointed. "Finding a place to hide in the cavity of a rock, I waited while the sun retired and the shadows grew." He took a deep breath. "When it was full dark, I was able to creep from shadow to shadow." He smiled slightly. "I knew not what I should do, but I have always been rewarded for following the Spirit." For a moment, Nephi paused, a slight frown on his face.

Then he looked up. "They had a great fire burning and had just finished what looked like a betrothal ceremony between Ilka," he nodded at her, "and Jonah, Zedekiah's son."

Anava gasped and clapped one hand over her mouth while she gripped Ilka's arm with the other.

Ilka shook her head vigorously and patted her mother's fingers.

Hannah turned to look at Rachel. The woman had her face in her hands. Litha was trying to comfort her. Hannah vowed to speak to Rachel as soon as Nephi was finished here. She turned back to him.

Nephi was looking at his daughter. "Ilka was still bound and had obviously been an *unwilling* participant."

Tears were streaming down Anava's face and Ilka now put a protective arm about her mother's shoulders and rocked her gently, wiping at the moisture on her own cheeks.

Nephi brushed impatiently at his face. "That was the hardest part of all. Waiting." A tear trickled down his face and into his beard. "But the Spirit constrained me and I remained hidden when they led Ilka to one of the tents and then while the men at the fire engaged in the most dreadful orations." He closed his eyes and brushed at another errant tear.

He was silent for a few moments. "When the fire had burned low, and they had finally finished their talking and drinking, they took themselves off to their b-beds for the night." His jaw set. Hannah could see a muscle twitch in his cheek. "I will say this—strong drink makes for deep sleep. No one heard me when I crept through the camp and into the very tent where Ilka had been taken. Though it was very dark, I had no trouble seeing where she was, cutting through her bonds, then carrying her from the village. We came straight here, again without incident."

The room erupted with cheers and praise.

Again, Nephi held up his hands and waited for the people to settle.

"My people, none of this could have happened without the guidance of the Lord. I had no clear idea of what I should do when I left here. The Spirit led and protected me throughout. Your praise should not be for me, but for that God who guided me. Will you join with me in a great prayer of thanksgiving?"

All bowed their heads as Nephi tearfully poured out his heart to the Lord in gratitude for the safe return of his precious daughter.

"There is more to this story, I think," a voice said in Hannah's ear after Nephi closed.

Hannah turned. Moriah was sitting just behind her.

"I agree, Morrie." Hannah turned back to Nephi. "Our gratitude is the same. But there is much more to this story."

Later that morning, Hannah left Benjamin in the care of Tabitha and knocked on the doorpost of Anava's hut. "Good morrow, Sister!"

"Come!" Ilka's voice.

She entered to find Anava seated beside a cold fire, stirring the dead ashes idly. Ilka sat nearby, her eyes on her Mother. She looked up. "We knew you would be coming."

Anava glanced at Hannah, then back down at the stick she was using. "You know."

"Only that there is much more to Nephi's story than he told at the gathering."

Anava sighed. "Much more." Her voice sharpened. "He did not lie!" She looked at her sister. "He just . . . did not tell all."

Ilka broke in. "It looked like a betrothal ceremony, but it was a . . . a . . ."

"It was a marriage ceremony," Anava said dully. She looked at her daughter. "My girl was married to that . . . that *beast*."

Hannah caught her breath. "But surely if she was unwilling, the Lord will not demand the vows be honored."

"Oh, the marriage was performed, but without common consent or authority. It was not 'legal' either in the eyes of man or of God." Anava sighed. "But that did not stop *those people* from acting as though it was!"

Hannah felt her eyes go wide. "You mean he . . . he . . ." Her voice dragged in her throat. "Ilka. Was the marriage consummated?"

Tears spilled down the girl's face. She nodded. "I think so. He was . . . there and I could not move and it hurt. It hurt!" She crumpled, sobbing.

Anava got to her feet and rushed to her daughter, wrapping her arms around her and rocking her back and forth. "There, my darling, it was not your fault. It was not your fault. It is the evil of men. Not of you." She looked at a stunned Hannah. "What can be done? What can we do to . . . undo?"

Feeling slightly faint, Hannah said, "I—I do not know."

"We can find comfort in the Lord." Nephi's voice. "We can find healing and forgiveness and peace."

"Forgiveness?" Anava's head came up. "What does our daughter need to seek forgiveness for?"

Nephi moved to his wife and daughter and put his hand tenderly on his wife's head. "Not for her actions, my Dearest One. But for his."

Anava blinked. "She needs to *forgive* him? For being a *beast*?"

Nephi nodded, his expression grave. "Forgiving him will drop a great weight from her heart."

"Well, forgive *me*, but I do not think she is quite ready for that!"

Nephi nodded. "I know. But she will be." He looked toward the window. "Perhaps someday, we all will."

The four of them sat silently in the room for the time it took the sun to reach the edge of the window. A beam of light shot into the room, touching the rich, dark hair and shaking shoulders of the sobbing girl.

To Hannah, it was almost a caress, sent from Heaven.

Nephi's eyes were on the light also. He sighed. "There is more that we have to discuss."

Anava looked at him. "Husband, can this wait?"

He sadly shook his head. "This must be discussed—and decided—before more of the day passes. Better to get all the suffering done instead of slowly dragging it out."

Anava closed her eyes and tightened her grip on her daughter. "Has she not suffered enough?"

"Perhaps I should find another place to be?" Hannah started to get up.

"No, Sister," Anava said quickly. "I . . ." She looked at Ilka. "*We* need you here."

Silence fell for a few moments, disturbed only by the sobs of the broken-hearted girl.

"We must speak with Yavin," Nephi said at last.

Anava sighed, then nodded. "If it must be done. It must." She looked at Nephi. "I just wish we could take a little time."

"Yavin needs to know," he said steadily. "Then he can choose to act."

"As a righteous man, full of indignation!" Ilka was staring at her father with burning, red-rimmed eyes. "So he can choose to have me stoned, as a righteous man should!"

Hannah gasped. "Oh, please Father, no."

"My daughter, Yavin will not choose to have you stoned. What happened was through no fault of your own."

"Well, he may put me away, then."

Nephi said nothing.

Hannah looked at Anava. Perhaps the worst of Ilka's ordeal had not yet happened.

Nephi turned to Hannah. "Would you stay?"

Hannah blinked. Then nodded.

"I would have you sit over there, please, Sister." Nephi waved a hand toward Anava.

Hannah moved quickly, taking a seat close beside her sister.

Nephi nodded. "And now we will invite in Yavin and his parents."

A moment later, Yavin's eyes went right to Ilka as he, Zoram, and Moriah entered the room, but the girl did not raise her head.

Hannah saw a slight frown of doubt cross the young man's face before he took a seat with his parents on the opposite side of the room.

Moriah looked at Hannah, but Hannah's eyes flooded with sudden tears and all she could do was shake her head helplessly.

"My family," Nephi said. "We have something grave to discuss."

All eyes went to Nephi.

Hannah dabbed impatiently at her eyes with her headcloth and finally she, too, was able to look at him.

"A grave wrong has been committed and it is left to us to right that wrong in the best way we know how."

Again, Moriah looked at Hannah. She shook her head slightly and turned back to Nephi.

"Our little Ilka was . . . mistreated by the people of Laman."

"Mistreated?" Yavin started to get to his feet but his father laid a hand on his arm and stopped him. "What did they do to her?"

Nephi sighed. "There was a—a ceremony performed."

"They married her to Jonah, Zedekiah's son," Anava said softly.

"Married?" This time Yavin did gain his feet. "She's married!"

"Not in the eyes of God, Son," Nephi said. "The ceremony was performed by my brother, Laman, who *was* ordained with the holy priesthood of God, but whose authority has been taken from him because of unrighteousness." He looked at Ilka. "And the bride did not give her consent."

"So she is not married. Then why are we discussing this?"

"Because she—"

"The marriage was consummated, Yavin," Hannah said quietly. "Jonah forced himself on your betrothed while she was bound and helpless."

"I did not want him to," Ilka cried out. "I did not want him! He—It was awful! Awful!"

The blood had drained from Yavin's face, leaving him looking pale and stricken. He sank to his knees. "He—he—"

Ilka nodded.

"I did not arrive in time," Nephi said, tears streaming down his cheeks and into his beard. "I—I *failed my daughter!*" It was a cry of anguish.

For some time, no one spoke. Yavin simply stared at Ilka's bowed head. His parents, pale-faced and shocked, looked from the one to the other.

Finally, Nephi cleared his throat. "I f-found them." His fists clenched. "I wanted to tear his head from his body! Never have I felt such rage, God forgive me! I picked him up and flung him across the tent. He hit something or his head hit something, I do not know. But he did not move after he fell. I cut Ilka's bonds and carried her from the house. We saw no one else as we made our way through the camp and back into the forest."

Ilka was openly sobbing again, as were both Anava and Moriah.

Again, silence fell. A thick silence that seemed to fill the space and make everything move more slowly.

Yavin got to his feet and disappeared outside.

Shocked, Hannah exchanged a glance with Moriah.

Was this, then, Yavin's answer?

Ilka collapsed against her mother. "Does that mean—he does not want me?"

Hannah looked at Moriah again. Her sister shrugged.

Several minutes went past. No one seemed willing—or able—to break the heavy silence.

Finally, Nephi cleared his throat. "In view of this—"

He got no further.

Yavin had returned. His eyes on Ilka, he slipped to his knees on the floor and, as though in a trance, shuffled forward until he was directly before her. He put out a hand and touched her shining hair. "Oh, my love," he breathed. "I am so sorry. So sorry for what was done to you."

Ilka, Anava, and Moriah all lifted their heads and looked at him.

"You have a choice here, Son," Zoram broke in. "Choose the right path."

Yavin nodded, not taking his eyes from the hand that stroked the soft curls. "I can see it was no fault of yours and that no good would come from making you suffer more."

He looked at his parents, then at Nephi and took a deep breath. "Father Nephi, the terrible things done to this lovely girl cannot be heaped at her door." He reached out and took Ilka's trembling hand in his. "It would not be acceptable to ask for her stoning. I feel that is a barbaric practice and should be done away." He exchanged a look with Hannah, who nodded. "Neither would I put her away, though I know that is my prerogative."

Ilka caught her breath as new tears flooded the dark eyes.

"No. Neither of these are what the Lord wants. What I want." He lifted his head, then took her other hand as well. "Instead, I think we should move the marriage forward and speak our vows before a man who holds the proper authority in such ordinances and forgive and forget what has happened in the past. It has naught to do with us. The past happened. It does not define us. Let us move forward. Keep our eyes forward." He lifted Ilka's hands and kissed the one, then the other. "Will you still have me as your husband?"

Ilka caught her breath, then nodded, tears streaming down her face and dripping from her chin.

Yavin turned back to Nephi. "Father Nephi, you have our decision."

By this time, there were no dry eyes in the room.

Hannah looked at Zoram, who was smiling and nodding at his son.

She and Moriah exchanged watery smiles.

———— • ————

The marriage was scheduled for one month hence. Preparations were immediately underway. Animals were chosen and prepared for slaughter. Cloth was woven and garments fashioned.

A new home constructed on Zoram's property to house the newlyweds.

Within three weeks, all was in near readiness.

Hannah was finishing up the work on Ilka's wedding tunic. Benjamin had discovered the whole new world available to a young man on the move and had taken to crawling with a will. Hannah was reminded of her Samuel at the same age. Always exploring. Always . . . She jumped to her feet to fish her son out of yet another near disaster. This time falling into the ashes of the dead fire.

"Now you stay in one spot and play with these." She scattered some blocks and the figure of a horse before the boy.

Crowing happily, Benjamin sat down on his round bottom and grabbed the horse, which immediately went into his mouth.

Tabitha appeared, Little Brother behind her. "Here are the beans, Mother Hannah. I've cleaned them and snapped them."

"Thank you, Dearest One. We will have them with our meal. Benjamin!" She leaped to her feet and grabbed her son.

The little boy had crawled to the waterskin and somehow managed to upend it. Hannah caught him just before the water reached him.

"Mother Hannah, why do I not take him outside to play? It is a beautiful day and some of the young mothers are already out."

"I would be tearfully grateful, Tabitha. I need to finish this for Ilka's wedding next week and time is definitely growing short!"

151

Tabitha laughed. "And you will be just that much more practiced for my wedding three months hence!"

"Indeed I will!"

Tabitha sighed. "Can you believe it is just nine months ago that Dan asked for my hand?"

Hannah looked at her and shook her head.

"So much has happened that it seems much, much longer." She picked up the small boy, and the two of them ducked through the doorway and into the afternoon sunshine, Little Brother again following closely.

Hannah stared into space and thought about those nine months. The girl was right. So much *had* happened! She shook her head and bent over her stitching.

"Mother Hannah, may I speak to you?"

She looked up. Ilka was standing timidly in the doorway. "Of course, My Dear. Please!" She indicated a seat beside her own. "What can I do to please you?"

Ilka sat in the place indicated, then started to fidget, twisting her fingers together and picking at the skin around her fingernails.

Hannah studied her for a moment. "Nervous about the wedding?"

"No. Yes!"

Hannah took another couple of stitches. "Your tunic is nearly ready."

Ilka looked at the mound of cotton in Hannah's lap. "Thank you."

Hannah frowned and looked at the girl again. "Is there something wrong?"

The words came out in a rush. "Oh, Mother Hannah, I—I th-think I am with child!"

Hannah dropped the quill she had been using as a needle and stared at Ilka.

"With child." The girl's eyes filled with tears. "I am afraid to go to my mother and certainly do not wish to go to my father. And I would rather die than go to Yavin. He has already accepted so much!"

"But Ilka, at some point in the future, you will certainly have to— Are you—certain?"

She shrugged. "As certain as I can be. My cycles have been regular for over three years. They are never late and I am half a moon behind."

Hannah caught her breath.

"Mother Hannah, I do not know what to do! If I tell them, Yavin may do . . . anything! But if I try to say it is his when the baby comes early . . ."

Hannah closed her eyes and offered up a quick, urgent prayer. Then she took a deep breath and looked at Ilka again. "Dear One, you are right. Those are the two options open to you. The straight forward path you have already been following. Or the curved and treacherous path that follows deceit in any form."

The girl twisted her fingers together. "What do I do, Mother Hannah? Please tell me what to do!"

Hannah put her hands on Ilka's shoulders and pulled the girl around to face her. "Ilka, you must go on. That is the only way open to us. Pray for strength. Pray for guidance. But go on."

Ilka dropped her head into her hands.

Hannah touched a slender shoulder. "It will not be easy."

Ilka shrugged. "What in this life is?" Her words came out muffled and indistinct. She sat back. "Maybe the best thing would be for me to just jump from the highest cliff."

Hannah gasped. "Daughter, what a thing to say!"

"But think of the peace! Think of all your problems simply being lifted away."

"And a whole new set given when you have to kneel before the Lord and tell Him what you have done with the precious gift of life He gave you!"

Ilka looked away, brushing absently at her tears. "Is there any hope? There is no hope."

Hannah took her hands. "Ilka, you must tell Yavin the truth."

Ilka shook her head fiercely. "Oh, Mother Hannah, I could not do so!"

Hannah put a hand on the girl's arm. "Let him make his decision. He has already proven that he is a man of honor. Allow him to prove it yet again."

The girl was silent for some minutes. Finally, tears making tracks down her face, she sighed and got to her feet. "I will tell him, Mother Hannah. But it will not be easy."

"Nothing in this life is," Hannah said. "Would you prefer to go alone? Or would you like my company?"

Ilka paused halfway to the door. For a moment, she simply stood there, then she turned. "I thank you for your kind offer. But this I will have to do myself."

Hannah nodded. "I will pray for you."

"Thank you." The girl left the hut.

Hannah picked up her needle, but set it down again. Feeling suddenly stifled and restless, she laid the garment aside and went outside.

Up the street, where it widened into a square, Tabitha was sitting with several young mothers, all watching their babies play in the soft grass. Hannah hurried toward them, happy to have Benjamin to take her mind from Ilka and the girl's problems.

For a few blissful minutes, she sat with the younger generation and laughed at the babies' antics.

Then she saw Ilka go into Hannah's hut and come back out. Shading her eyes against the sun, she was obviously looking for her.

Getting to her feet, Hannah hurried toward her. "Ilka! What is it? What happened?"

"Oh, Mother Hannah!" Tears were streaming down the smooth cheeks. "I told him!"

Hannah put an arm around her shoulders and turned her back to the privacy of her hut. "And?"

"And he left."

"Left?"

"Yes. He just stared at me for a moment, his face getting redder and redder. Then he turned and left."

Hannah frowned. "He never said anything?"

"No." Ilka rubbed at her tears with one hand. "What should I do now?"

"Nothing, Dear. You have done all you can." Hannah bit her lip. "I will see what I can discover. You stay here."

Hannah hurried to Nephi's little shelter, but though there were thin, golden plates lying neatly on the workbench, obviously there for when the scribe returned, there was no sign of the prophet.

Hannah turned slowly, surveying the village. Then she spun around and fastened her eye on the temple.

The building, which now dominated the entire village, had been progressing steadily from day to day, despite the changes and occasional shocks that beset the settlement. The roof had been completed and the inner finishing was underway.

Hannah hurried there. Perhaps the workmen had required Nephi's expertise in some of their calculations.

When she entered the front door, Nephi was the first person she saw. He was bent over a work table with Jacob and Joseph, as well as Sam and Zoram.

Hannah hurried over to the men.

"Brother Nephi, may I speak with you?"

Nephi looked at her. "Certainly, Sister Hannah."

He moved away from the table and toward her. "Yes, Sister, what can I help you with?"

Hannah moved to the far side of the room drawing the great man with her. "It is Ilka," she said quietly.

Nephi frowned. "What has happened? Is she all right? Is something amiss?"

Hannah rubbed her face and took a quick breath. "She is with child, Brother."

Nephi stared at her. "With child."

"She just told me this afternoon."

"Is she certain?"

Hannah nodded.

"Have she and Yavin . . . ?"

Hannah slowly shook her head. "It is Jonah's child."

Nephi blinked eyes that were suddenly swimming with tears. "Jonah's child."

"She did not know what to do. She was afraid to go to either you or her mother."

"Afraid?"

"Afraid of disappointing you."

Nephi lifted his eyes to heaven. "And such is the legacy that follows disobedience," he said softly. Tears spilled down his cheeks. "I can blame no one by myself for all this pain and suffering."

"*You*, Brother Nephi?"

He looked at her. "Faithful, stalwart Hannah. You have probably never made a poor choice in your life."

"Brother Nephi. You know of my struggles. My doubts—"

He shook his head slightly. "I made a mistake, Sister. A grave mistake and now my daughter and her future husband must suffer for it."

Hannah frowned at him. "I do not understand."

He sighed. "I went back and back again. Even when I knew the answer was 'no.' It seemed so important to my daughter. I importuned the Lord again and again until, finally, his answer was an exasperated, 'Do as you will. But agree to take the consequences.' Which I took as a 'yes.'" He looked at Hannah. "You would have had the good sense to accept the first answer."

"Oh, Brother Nephi. I am hardly that righteous. Or that smart."

He smiled slightly. "I need to speak to her." He started for the door. "Please find her mother and ask her to join us at her hut."

"Wait, Brother, there is more."

He stopped and turned. "How can there be more?"

Hannah moved closer. "I told her she needed to tell Yavin."

Nephi's eyes widened. "Has he done something? Has he hurt her?" He gripped Hannah's shoulders.

"Brother, you are hurting me."

He released her. "I am sorry. Please finish."

"Ilka is fine. But as soon as she told Yavin, he left."

"Left her?"

"Left the village."

———◆———

Though Hannah and Nephi searched the village, there was no sign of Yavin. Moriah and Zoram both denied seeing him. The gardens, the cotton fields, the fruit orchards, all were checked.

Only when Hannah ran out to the sheep pastures and questioned the young men on duty was she able to find some information.

"Oh, yes, we saw him," Eamon and Eadric said. "His face was all red and he did not talk to us at all. Just walked through the field and into the trees." The boys pointed. "There."

Hannah walked to the edge of the pasture and peered into the trees.

"Greetings, Mother Hannah!" someone said.

She peered into the gloom, finally making out the shapes of Ezekiel and Fane. "Are you the guards here today?"

"We are," Fane said. "Zeke is helping me improve my knife-throwing!"

"Oh. Well, good. Have you seen Yavin?"

"Have we! He almost knocked us down in his haste to make a trail through the trees."

"Did he say where he was going?"

Ezekiel shook his head. "Just something about making things right."

Hannah caught her breath. "O-okay. Thank you." She turned away. She knew where he had gone.

He was hunting for Jonah.

CHAPTER TEN

*H*annah lifted her tunic to her knees and ran as fast as she could for the village.

Nephi met her just outside. "You found him?"

"No. But Zoram's youngest boys say he went past them and into the forest. And Ezekiel and Fane both saw him walking through the trees." She took a deep breath. "I think he has gone to find Jonah."

Nephi shook his head and thought for a moment. Then he looked at her. "Tell no one what you've told me. You say Ezekiel is there in the forest?"

"Yes. He and Fane are guarding there today."

"I need someone—Cephus!"

The young man carrying a load of chopped wood turned and looked at him. "Yes, Father Nephi?"

"I need you to come with me!"

"Could I just finish?"

"I need you now, Son."

Cephus nodded, set his load of wood aside and joined Nephi.

"Cephus will take Ezekiel's job as guard so Zeke can come with me," Nephi told Hannah. "Remember. Tell no one."

Hannah nodded and Nephi and Cephus started running toward the sheep pasture.

"What is going on there? Is that my wood?"

Hannah turned. Moriah was standing beside the pile of wood Cephus had abandoned, watching Nephi and the young man race toward the far field.

"I'm not sure about the wood, Morrie. Cephus was carrying it when Nephi asked his help with something."

"Ah. And is that what he is doing now? Helping Nephi?"

"Yes."

A young boy raced past, holding a cob of dried corn aloft. "I got one! I got one! Come on! Popped corn!"

Instantly, a half-dozen children joined him, racing up the street.

Anava's daughter, Esther, appeared. "James! Come back with that corn!"

A storm of giggles was her only answer. She shook her head, smiled ruefully at Hannah and Moriah and disappeared.

Morrie shrugged and bent down to collect the wood Cephus had dropped. "Well, I guess I will have to just haul the wood myself."

"I will help you," Hannah said.

The day passed with agonizing slowness. Ilka was in Hannah's hut a dozen times, asking if she had heard or seen anything. Each time, Hannah had patiently explained that, as soon as she had a bit of news, however small, she would share it with the worried girl. Finally, in desperation, she came up with some handwork for Ilka to do. That way, she could keep the girl close by and within her sight.

The following morning, there was still no sign of Nephi or Ezekiel. Or Yavin. Cephus had returned when his shift was over, but all he could offer was that Father Nephi had gone into the forest with Ezekiel—and Yavin, he added with a sidelong glance at Hannah—to do some scouting and would return in a day or two.

Ezekiel's wife, Rebecca, had accepted the news in her usual, placid fashion and returned to her duties, caring for their numerous children.

Anava, however, was suspicious. "Why would he leave without speaking to his wife?" she asked Hannah. "It must have something to do with Ilka."

"Why would you think that?"

"Because the girl has been mooning around here for days." Anava said bitterly. Then she sighed and put a hand on her forehead. "Chosen

One, do you remember the happy, contented girl who lived in the same house with you on the outskirts of Jerusalem?"

Hannah smiled at her younger sister. "I do."

"Well I wish with all my heart that I could meet that girl again."

Hannah tapped Anava's head with her finger. "She is in there somewhere, Sister. Just buried by the problems of life."

"And yet we need those problems to strengthen us. I cannot ask to have them removed because I may as well ask to stop progressing."

Hannah juggled Benjamin to one hip and put her other arm around Anava's shoulders. "When our vessel is empty, the Spirit of the Lord is always waiting to fill us once more. Take your problems to the Lord as you did when you were that girl back in Jerusalem. Be filled."

Anava smiled. "I will."

"Sisters!"

Hannah and Anava turned.

Rachel, Litha, and Amanna were hurrying toward them. Each wore an expression of alarm.

"Come at once!" Rachel said. "Mother is calling for us!"

Hannah wrapped her arms around Benjamin. What had happened now?

Anava looked at her. "I think now is not the time to have my vessel filled, Sister."

Hannah felt her heart grow cold. Why did troubles always come in a swarm?

A short time later, Hannah knelt quietly with her sisters and sisters-by-marriage beside Mother Sariah's pallet. Little Brother had followed them and now sat whimpering outside the door.

"My daughters, I have received my call."

"No, Mother," Rachel whispered. "Do not leave us! How can we continue without you?"

The elderly woman smiled. "Do not grieve for me, Precious One. Rejoice for me. My work is finished! I am being allowed to return home!" She looked up toward the roof of her hut. "Remember the words of Isaiah? *He will swallow up death in victory; and the Lord God will wipe away tears from off all faces.* We will only be separated for a time. A very short time. And then, through our Saviour, we will all be together again." She looked at them, her eyes dancing with joy. "I will be with my Lehi!" She gasped and coughed.

"We may be separated for a short time," Hannah said. "But it will still be too long." She took Mother Sariah's hand and kissed it. *Why do troubles come in swarms*, she wondered as she looked at the frail, beloved face. *Why are men tested and tested and tested?* But she knew the answer before she even asked the question. *To be strengthened.* She sighed. Sometimes it took a lot of strength. More, it seemed, than she had.

Mother Sariah laughed. A weak little burst of sound, but it sufficed. "I shall be forever with you, my daughters. For 'daughters' you truly are." She reached out with her other hand and Litha grabbed it.

"Are you ready for the trip, Mother?"

Mother Sariah smiled. "I am."

"Please do not—!" Rachel caught the words back. "Please greet everyone on the other side," she said in a much more subdued voice.

Another smile. "I will."

"Mother! Is it true?"

Hannah turned. Sam, Jacob, and Joseph had come into the room and thrown themselves down on the other side of their mother's pallet.

"My sons." She winced and shifted on her pallet. "Could you help me to sit? I would say what I . . . have to say from an . . . upright position." Her speech was becoming more laboured and breathy.

Sam leaned forward to take her arms and help her sit up. Joseph adjusted a cushion behind her. "Ahh. Thank you." She smiled at them and was quiet for a moment. "My sons . . . and . . . daughters. I would leave . . . my prayer with you for your continued faith. Follow your brother . . . Nephi, who is . . . God's chosen prophet in the land. Stay close . . . to the Lord. Lead . . . your families in . . . righteousness." She leaned back against the cushion, her face pale as new wool.

"Mother, conserve your strength," Jacob said. "Let us fetch the children so you can speak with them."

Again that small smile and a merry twinkle from her eyes. "I have . . . spoken with them, Son. They are more perceptive than their . . . parents and have been coming . . . in to visit with me all week!"

Jacob looked slightly ashamed. "Mother, I am so sorry."

She patted his arm. "With all that has been happening, I cannot . . . assign blame, Son. The children are . . . free from the . . . worries that have . . . beset us and have . . . the time . . . for visiting with . . . useless old . . ."

Hannah gasped. "Useless?"

Mother Sariah suddenly lifted her head. "Lehi? Husband? Is that you? Where . . . are you, Dear? I—I cannot . . . see you."

Everyone else in the room looked at each other blankly.

"Husband? I am here."

Hannah turned, peering into the shadowy corners of the room. "Mother Sariah?"

The elderly woman turned to her. "Yes, Chosen One?"

"To whom do you speak?"

A slow smile spread across Mother Sariah's face. "Lehi has come for me. With all . . . the important things . . . he has to do . . . he has come . . . for . . . me."

Hannah looked around again.

Jacob squeezed his mother's arm. "What can be of more importance than his eternal companion?"

Her smile widened, the creases in the beloved, aged face deepening. She settled back on her cushion and her expression relaxed.

Her breathing stilled.

Mother Sariah had met her companion and, with him, crossed the veil.

———————•◆•———————

It took several seconds for those who remained to realize what had happened. Rachel reached out and shook her mother's shoulder. "Mother? Mother!"

Mother Sariah's head shifted limply to one side.

"She is gone, Sister," Hannah said, gently.

Jacob leaned forward and placed an ear against his mother's chest. For a few moments, he remained there, his head against her still-warm body. Then he sat back and nodded grimly.

"Oh!" Litha clapped a hand over her mouth, her eyes brimming with tears.

Hannah reached out and closed the beloved eyes, knowing even as she did so that Mother Sariah's spiritual eyes had already been opened on the other side of the veil. For just a moment, Hannah felt envious. Mother Sariah's work was finished. She had remained faithful through the uprooting of her home and the rigors of their twelve-year trek to this new land and the bearing of children in her age in the wilderness. She had weathered the death of her beloved spouse and the treachery of her eldest sons. And had clung closely to the iron rod through it all. Her eternal reward would be a great one indeed.

Hannah felt a tear escape and trickle down her cheek. Then another and another as pictures of this lovely woman and her many roles in Hannah's life played through her mind. Pictures of her as a counsellor and friend. Confidante. Healer. Spiritual leader. And when her own mother had crossed the veil, a new Mother. Hannah was happy for Mother Sariah. She was.

But in agony for herself.

———— • ◆ • ————

Nephi still had not returned, so Jacob, following some fervent prayer, took charge of the burial.

Her daughters bathed and dressed Mother Sariah for her final journey.

When her sons carried her frail body out on the bier, Hannah gasped. Mother Sariah looked peaceful and serene, as though she had truly found her way past the veil and into the Lord's presence.

For an instant, pure joy shot through Hannah. She rejoiced for this woman who had worked so hard, been so much to many and now was receiving her eternal reward.

Would she, Hannah, ever achieve such a prize? She bowed her head and offered up a little prayer in Mother Sariah's behalf. And also a bit for herself.

The grieving family followed the bier to the little cave that already housed the remains of Tobias. Mother Sariah received a place of honour next to her grandson.

After a few inspiring words from Jacob, they returned to the village to eat and drink and reminisce about their matriarch.

The following day, her daughters gathered and distributed Mother Sariah's personal belongings and Sariah's hut, empty for the first time, sat vacant and silent throughout the remainder of the day.

But in a village where housing was scarce, this small hut was soon claimed. Within a day, a young family had taken up residence there.

Hannah stopped and stared when she saw someone come out of Mother Sariah's hut. Someone who wasn't Mother Sariah.

It was Zalman, Zoram's son, and his wife, Naama. They had just welcomed their first child, a robust boy by the name of Saul, but had been unable to complete a home for themselves with the extra war preparation duties thrust upon the young men of the settlement and all that had been happening. Mother Sariah's death had proved a blessing to them in the form of shelter.

Hannah's heart did a funny little dance, then settled into its usual rhythm. Better that the house be used. That it be lived in by a family. She knew that Mother Sariah would not mind. In fact, she would rejoice that her small space brought joy to someone.

It was Hannah who had to adjust.

She greeted the young couple and exclaimed over their dark-haired infant, then excused herself and continued up the street. Hannah had left Benjamin with Tabitha, and the still-fretting Ilka with yet another bit of handwork and was taking advantage of her few idle minutes to gather some flowers to place as a tribute to Mother Sariah.

Several people stopped her to ask if she had heard anything of Nephi or the others and Hannah answered with a sad shake of her head. There had been no news.

Once outside the town, she gathered a large bouquet of wild flowers, intending to lay them on the stone in front of her mother-by-marriage's tomb. Humming quietly to herself, Hannah, with Little Brother following closely behind, retraced her steps from only two days before, when the family had buried their mother.

The trail wound through some rock formations before it ended at the cliff face that housed the cave. Hannah rounded the last turn and stopped abruptly.

Nephi was seated against the base of the cliff. His arms were crossed over his knees and his head rested on them.

Hannah felt a brief surge of thanksgiving at his safe return, then stood for a moment, uncertain what to do. Deciding he needed her to withdraw, she began to back slowly from the clearing. But she had taken only two steps when Nephi raised his head.

"Do not leave on my behalf, Sister Hannah."

She sighed and moved forward, laying her flowers down on the flat rock beside him. "I did not mean to disturb," she said softly.

He half smiled. "I *should* be disturbed."

Hannah looked at him.

He sighed. "My people asked me to be their king, but I refused because I do not believe that a king is what the people—any people—need. They need a spiritual leader. Someone focused on their eternal welfare." He shook his head. "Someone who does not make the mistakes I have made in this past month. Someone whose choices do not threaten both the spiritual and mortal welfare of their people."

Hannah opened her mouth to speak, but Nephi went on. "I have listened to the Lord in all things. Always, His will has been my foremost concern." He shook his head. "But these past weeks, my actions have threatened the lives of my daughter and her betrothed and others, because I was more intent on pleasing my daughter than I was with pleasing the Lord." He flung out a hand as tears made streaks down his face and into his greying beard. "And now, as the final punishment, I was not able to wish my beloved mother farewell as she finished her mortal journey and crossed the veil. I, who should know better! Who should have been where the Lord needed me *when* He needed me." He leaned his head back against the sun-warmed wall. "When *she* needed me."

Hannah sat on a rock nearby. "Mother Sariah was happy to go and went quickly. She understood that you had to do what needed to be done."

Nephi turned his head away.

"Were you able to find Yavin?"

Nephi looked back at her, then put his head down on his knees. "Oh, I found him," was the cryptic reply.

"He is well?"

"Yes. He is well."

Hannah rose to her feet. It was quite obvious from Nephi's clipped answers that he needed time alone.

"Sister Hannah, do not go. I apologize for my rudeness."

Hannah looked at him and found his dark eyes on her.

"Please," he said. "I am sorry. Forgive me."

She sat down again. "It is not for me to forgive, Brother Nephi."

He sighed. "So where do I go for forgiveness, Sister?" he asked softly.

Hannah stared at him. "Surely you know."

"I guess I am asking if I *can* be forgiven for my sins."

Was Nephi really questioning his beliefs? Hannah's world spun for a moment. "I—I do not know what to say."

"Can I be forgiven for my errors and for the pain that just seems to go on and on and on?"

Hannah had no idea how to answer. If Nephi was doubting, what hope did she have? She took a deep, slow breath and sent a frantic prayer heavenward. What could be said? What *should* be said? She looked off toward the distant hills and searched her mind for something—*anything*—that would provide comfort. Suddenly a feeling of calm enveloped her. Hannah breathed a sigh of relief and found she was able to look steadily into Nephi's questioning eyes. "Brother Nephi, I have heard you speak numerous times about forgiveness. About how, through the coming sacrifice of the Savior of the world, we can all be forgiven of our faults and misdeeds." She tipped her head to one side. "Why all of us and not you?"

Nephi looked at her for a few moments. Then he shook his head. "Sister Hannah, as always, you have a way of seeing the gospel from the purest perspective. Of cutting through the fog of misdirection and deception to find the nuggets of eternal truth." He rubbed the back of his neck. "You are right, I can be forgiven. But the bigger question is can I ever forgive myself?"

"You once told me that forgiving ourselves is the hardest of all, Brother Nephi. Why should you be any different than the rest of us?"

Nephi smiled. "Why, indeed."

Both sat quietly for a few moments.

"So," Hannah said finally. "You found Yavin."

Nephi sighed and put his head back against the rock behind him. "I did. This time, I was able to prevent a tragedy."

"He is safe?"

Nephi hesitated. Then nodded. "He will be."

Hannah frowned. "Will be?"

"Laman and I were able to reach an . . . agreement."

"Laman?"

Nephi sighed again. "By the time I reached Yavin, he and Jonah were already bloody from their conflict. Laman's 'warriors' were standing about, cheering at every telling blow—Yavin's as well as Jonah's. It was soon obvious to me that, despite Jonah's training as a hunter, he was outmatched by the fury of the betrayed betrothed. And Yavin was not about to grant any quarter. He had passed beyond reason and wanted only to feel Jonah's heart as it quit beating."

Hannah caught her breath. "It had gone so far?"

Nephi nodded. "Yavin saw it as a form of retribution." He looked at Hannah. "But vengeance belongs to the Lord. I moved between the two of them. When it became quite obvious that Yavin had no intention of quitting, even with me trying to reason with him, I picked him up and carried him physically from the arena."

Hannah thought about the muscular physique of the younger man. "You carried him?"

Nephi smiled. "Even in my age." He let his head fall back against the wall once more. "And that was when Laman decided to step into the ring."

"You fought Laman?"

"No." Nephi shook his head, rolling it back and forth against the wall. "Although I am quite certain that is what he wanted. No, what we did was come to an amicable agreement."

"Amicable? Laman?"

He shrugged. "Yavin had stolen Jonah's bride."

Hannah frowned. "But she was Yavin's betrothed first."

"That was never brought into the discussion."

Hannah blinked. "What?"

"According to Laman, Yavin crept into their camp and stole Jonah's bride. And for that he had to pay."

"But he—but you were the one." Hannah shook her head. "I am so confused."

"Apparently, no one saw me enter or leave and things happened so quickly that Jonah never got a clear look at the person who—" Nephi ground his teeth together, making the muscle in his cheek twitch. "Yavin let them think it was he who had crept into Jonah's tent on that fateful night." He closed his eyes for a moment and rubbed them with one hand. "He also did not tell them about the—b-baby." His voice cracked over the word.

"Good," Hannah said stoutly. "'Tis better that they do not know."

"It was then Laman made his proposal, to 'preserve the young manhood in our camps'."

Hannah rolled her eyes. "So he could use them later for the real conflict he is planning."

Nephi looked at her and smiled slightly. "Quite possibly. We know that he will not make a bargain unless it is to his benefit."

Hannah nodded. "So what was his proposal?"

"He proposed that Yavin pay the 'bride price' for Ilka."

"But she was *Yavin's bride!*"

Nephi said nothing.

"Nephi, she was *his bride!* Why should he have to pay for *his bride?*"

Nephi smiled at her and it was only then she realized she had forgotten to address him formally. She blushed to the roots of her greying hair.

He took pity on her discomfort. "That is what Laman demanded. And that is what Yavin and I agreed upon."

"And what was the price?"

"Sixteen sheep."

Hannah blinked. "So our Ilka is worth sixteen sheep?"

"She is worth vastly more than that. But that number made Jonah happy. So it made Laman happy."

"They'll just eat them."

Nephi smiled again. "Probably. But it is not up to us to decide how the money is used. Only to pay it."

"So when does this payment take place?"

"Ah. That, I was most cautious about. No need for them to come into our camp and no reason for us to go to theirs."

"So?"

"So we shall meet halfway. At a box canyon between us and them."

"We?"

"Yavin and I."

"But it could be a trap!"

Nephi frowned. "I do not think so. Laman had every opportunity to take me prisoner when I went to Yavin's aid. He did not. I think he has not yet worked up the courage to actually murder his brother, despite what he says."

"But each time brings us one step closer."

"That is what truly troubles me."

———————◆———————

Yavin and Nephi left the next day.

Hannah was pleased to see that the betrothed couple had an affectionate—though emotional—farewell. It was quite obvious to Hannah that Yavin had accepted his betrothed's condition as his own and the parenthood of the coming child was no longer an issue.

Ilka moved over to her mother after her father and her betrothed disappeared down the road with their little flock. Anava put her arm around her daughter and hugged her close. Tears always near to the surface, both of them were immediately engulfed.

The rest of the village, after sympathetic glances in their direction, hurried off to their usual duties.

Hannah, Benjamin on one hip, clasped Anava's shoulder gently, then she, too, moved away.

The next two days were devoted to finishing Ilka's wedding clothes.

Her actions proved inspired.

When a triumphant Nephi and Yavin returned on the third day, the wedding of Ilka and Yavin was announced for the following morning.

Hannah was able to present the suddenly frantic girl with her new tunic and headscarf, calming her considerably and the wedding proceeded as planned.

Nephi, still smarting from his mistakes, tried to have Jacob officiate, pointing out that it mattered not *which* priesthood holder performed the ordinance. Just that it *was* a priesthood holder.

But Ilka would have none of it and refused to even set foot in the House of Assembly until her father had taken his place before the altar.

As she watched from the doorway, Nephi shook his head and grimaced to himself, made his way to the altar at the front of the room, removed his shoes, then turned and nodded at her.

Hannah smiled. Here was the strong-willed girl who had pressed her father to return again and again to the Lord for something she greatly desired. Hannah shook her head. Sometimes that strength was an asset. And sometimes it worked against her.

The couple stepped out of their shoes and approached the altar reverently; they knelt facing each other and looked up at Nephi expectantly.

He closed his eyes for a moment, then sighed and turned to his daughter and her betrothed. "Yavin, Ilka, you have travelled a heavy, difficult road here to the altar of the Lord. You have passed through fires that would have stopped most people, and yet you have allowed none of it to destroy you or dissuade you from what you know to be right." He nodded his head. "I commend you for your faith and for your courage."

Yavin reached across the altar and gripped Ilka's hands.

Nephi went on. "The marriage contract is the most sacred covenant you will ever make. It is a three-way contract between the two of you and the Lord. Honor it. Honor each other. By so doing, you will honor the Lord."

In a few moments, the ceremony was complete. Ilka and Yavin kissed over the altar as man and wife.

Nephi brushed at his cheek with the back of his hand as the newly wedded couple got to their feet and stepped together to one side. Then he straightened and looked out at the assembled People of Nephi. "My brothers and sisters, may I present Yavin and his new bride, Ilka."

The House of Assembly was large, having been built to hold most of the camp. Even so, the noise was deafening in the space as everyone began clapping and cheering.

Yavin, his face red in his excitement (and some discomfort) and Ilka, looking very calm and determined, stood for a few moments to receive everyone's congratulations.

Then someone shouted over the noise that it was time for the celebration to begin.

Hannah left with a large group of women to bring in the food and drink. When she returned with a heavy platter moments later, she stopped in the doorway, her mouth open in astonishment.

The room had been transformed. Tables had been erected, decorated, and were already laden with food. Hannah smiled. Truly, when people worked together, miracles could be performed.

Several of the young men had brought out their instruments and were already beginning to play.

The music and celebrations went far into the night. The people seemed loathe to leave, and instead insisted on eating more and more food, drinking the rich wine, and outdoing each other in their storytelling and dancing.

Hannah felt that there was almost a desperate happiness to the entire celebration. As though people partied to forget the trials of the past few weeks. She frowned. Few people knew the entire story and none except those most closely involved—plus Hannah—knew about the upcoming birth of the baby and its unfortunate beginnings.

Perhaps they partied merely because they had the opportunity and it was a way of dropping, for a time, the load each of them carried.

Benjamin was not happy with all the noise and Hannah, feeling the effects of the day as well, decided to retire for the night.

She had just settled her sleeping son on his pallet when there was a soft knock at her front door.

Hannah stepped quietly across the room. "Yes?"

"Hannah?"

She opened the door. Three shadows stood there. Anava, Amanna, and Moriah.

"Come out and sit with us!" Anava said.

"Benjamin has only now gone to sleep."

"We will sit just here where you can listen for him," Anava said, seating herself against the outer wall of Hannah's little hut.

Hannah smiled. "I would love to sit with you."

The four sisters sat together in the soft evening air, listening to the slightly-muted sounds of the continuing celebration.

Anava shook her head. "I do not know where they find the energy!"

Hannah laughed. "Many of them are our age."

"That is what I mean!"

"Actually, I think most of our generation has left to find their beds," Amanna said. "It is the next generation who continues to celebrate."

They sat quietly for a moment and stared up at the moon just clearing the trees across the street from where they sat. Little Brother left his usual sleeping spot near the wall of the hut and flopped down next to Hannah, who began patting his head absently.

"What a beautiful, beautiful night," Anava said.

"Indeed," Hannah and Amanna agreed.

Moriah was quiet.

"Sister?" Hannah asked. "Where are your thoughts?"

Moriah sighed. "Do you ever think about other nights like this one?"

"There have been many." Hannah began.

"I mean when we were home in Jerusalem."

"Oh." Anava made a face. "I think about Jerusalem often."

"Do you remember warm evenings when the moon flooded the world with silver light and we five girls would sleep together on the roof because it was too hot to lie on our pallets inside the house?"

Hannah smiled. "I do remember that."

"And we would try to count the stars," Anava said excitedly. "But there were too many of them. A vast number."

Moriah sighed. "Do you ever suppose that Uzziel remembers as we do?"

The others turned to look at her. A darker blot of shadow against the dusky wall. They did not mention their sister's name often. The memories were painful and it was just . . . easier.

"I—I do not know," Anava said quietly. "She was always so . . ."

"Discontent," Hannah said. She leaned her head back against the wall. "Always she wanted something different than what she had. Always she wanted more."

"Or what already belonged to someone else," Amanna put in.

"Are you still upset with her taking your intended from you, Morrie?" Anava asked.

Moriah shook her head. "No. I really never was. I did not trust Laman and let us face it, trust is the first pillar in a marriage."

"And look where you would be now!" Anava said.

Moriah nodded, then was quiet for a few moments. "Do you suppose she has regrets? Do you suppose she sits there beside the fire, watching the hunters dance and spin—"

"Painted in the blood of their victims," Amanna put in.

"And wonders where she went wrong?"

Hannah shivered. What Moriah described was so close to what Hannah's own experience had been on that last, fateful evening.

Moriah went on. "Do you suppose she remembers being one of the daughters of Ishmael, growing up in the household of goodly parents? Remembers watching Father, and sometimes Mother, make the trek into the city to visit the temple? Prayers and scripture study as a family? Gospel discussions?"

"*I* remember," Anava and Amanna said together.

Hannah nodded. "As do I."

"Or has she forgotten those things and instead thinks of the times when she was most wilful and determined?"

Anava exhaled. "As when Laman gave her that statue? Or one of the numerous times he met her secretly thinking no one would ever discover their treachery?"

Hannah shrugged. "I guess we have our answer, sisters."

They were quiet for a moment. Then Moriah sighed. "Do you suppose that people who have chosen the wrong path ever regret that path? Or remember the right one with longing?"

"I lived in a settlement with Uzziel for a number of years before our final parting and she gave no indication that she had any regrets whatsoever." Hannah rubbed an eye. "She seemed quite contented as the wife of the most powerful man in their village."

"Only powerful in what he could take," Moriah pointed out. "Not in what he had been blessed with."

Hannah half-smiled. "Interesting, is it not, that the Lord stands waiting to give us such riches and glory. But, because of ignorance or impatience or greed, we turn away from Him and, instead, spend our lives and our strength in a pursuit of riches and glory?"

"The temporal instead of the eternal," Moriah said.

Hannah nodded. "I have never understood it."

Moriah smiled. "That is because you have never been tempted by it."

Anava leaned back and looked up at the stars. "Well, I never thought I would say this, but I miss Uzziel. I even miss her sharp tongue and her acerbic wit."

"I miss her, too," Hannah said, softly. "But I miss the Uzziel of my youth. Not the woman who is married to Laman and rules with him in his *kingdom*."

"Are they not one and the same?"

Hannah shook her head. "The one is as different from the other as chalk is from cheese."

Moriah pursed her lips and looked thoughtful. "I cannot help but think that our Uzziel—the one from our childhood—is inside there somewhere."

"Perhaps." Hannah shrugged. "But buried so deeply that she will never emerge."

"So we are back to my initial question. Do you think she has regrets?"

Hannah leaned back against the wall. "I do not think she allows herself regrets."

Anava, too, leaned back against the wall. "I still miss her."

———◆———

"There! Did you see that? He took his first step!" Hannah crouched, arms wide as her son toddled toward her. Little Brother, seeming more concerned than the humans in the room, followed the uncertain steps alertly.

Tabitha looked up from her sewing. "Such a clever little man! I knew he could do it!"

Hannah looked at her. "You did not. You said he could *not* do it."

Tabitha examined her neat row of stitches. "Well he is still so small." She looked over at Hannah. "Hardly more than a babe."

Hannah laughed. "He is ten moons tomorrow!"

"Ten?" Tabitha sat back and counted on her fingers. "You are right!"

"Of course I am right, I am his mother!"

It was Tabitha's turn to laugh. "That does not necessarily follow."

Hannah moved across the tiny room and again squatted and held out her arms. "Come on, baby! Come to Mother."

Benjamin, grinning widely, started forward, then stumbled slightly and sat down abruptly. For a moment, his baby chin wobbled. Then he laughed as Little Brother moved forward and swiped at his baby cheek with a smooth tongue. Hannah picked him up and set him back on his feet. Then began to encourage him once more with smiles and beckoning hands.

"Can you believe it is over a year since we came here?" Tabitha knotted her thread and snipped it neatly with sharp, white teeth.

"Fifteen moons," Hannah said. "Come Benjamin. Come to Mother!"

"And I marry in just one week!"

Hannah looked at the glowing girl and smiled. "Is it really only one week?"

Tabitha nodded and smiled. "One week." Her mouth twisted. "You cannot know how many times I have compared the girl I am to the girl I was such a short time ago."

Hannah looked at her. "I can not see the change. You were a faithful, wonderful girl then. And you are a faithful, wonderful girl now."

"Faithful, yes. But I came to it late." Tabitha looked at Hannah. "I was not born to it as you were."

"We are all converted at some time, Dearest One. Whether we were born to it or not. And I have not been perfect. I have made my mistakes."

Tabitha was silent for a moment. "I guess you are right."

"Of course I am right, I am a—"

"Mother. I know." Tabitha grinned. Then she sobered. "I often wonder how Ilka's story would have changed if I had stayed and married Jonah as I was meant to."

Hannah sucked in a breath. "You cannot think that! Oh, Dearest One, you cannot even consider that because you were saved, she suffered!"

"Think about it. If I had married Jonah, he would not have been hunting for a wife—"

"We do not know he was hunting for a wife. We only know he took advantage when he came upon someone."

Tabitha shrugged. "Well, he would not have been married to Ilka against her will—"

Hannah frowned. "And how do we know that? Perhaps she would have been given to him as a second wife."

"I would have welcomed her as a sister wife. But not if she was unhappy."

"None of this is even worth thinking about. None of it happened. Ilka is happily married to Yavin and their baby is due before the next rains."

"Their baby."

"You know that Yavin has given out that everyone is to consider this child his."

"Do you suppose that he, in his thoughts, ever considers the child's true parentage?"

"You are in an introspective mood today."

Tabitha sighed. "I think it is because I am to be married soon and I am overwhelmed by the blessings that I, the youngest daughter of a sinful man, have been given."

Hannah put her hand on Tabitha's arm. "You can not think of yourself as the daughter of a sinful man. Your father's choices have nothing to do with you."

"What about that scripture that speaks of children suffering for their parents' mistakes even unto the third and fourth generation."

"I wondered about that too," Hannah said. "I could not understand a loving God who would punish innocent children for something they had no part in. But Jacob clarified it for me. He said that parents' choices served as an example to their children. Sinful parents gave sinful examples and righteous parents, righteous examples. Children are much more likely to choose the path they see their parents walk. Thus children of sinful parents would choose a sinful path. At which time, they would be accountable for their own actions."

"Oh. That does sound a bit more fair."

Hannah sighed and smiled. "Our God is a Being of fairness."

"Sometimes it does not seem like it."

"You are thinking of Ilka again."

"Yes, and the terrible things she had to endure. She and Yavin both."

"And Father Nephi."

"And especially Father Nephi."

"All I can tell you is that we learn from our mistakes. Actually, I think we learn more from our times of pain and sorrow than our times of joy." Hannah made a face. "I can not think why that would be, but it is true."

Tabitha nodded and was silent for a moment. "Mother Hannah, I want to ask you something."

"Anything, Dearest One, you know that."

"Well this is . . . personal."

"Ah. We are not discussing Ilka and her troubles any more?"

"No."

"Well, say on."

"Are you considering marrying again?"

Hannah looked at the girl, surprised.

Tabitha rushed into speech. "I mean, you are not young, but you are not in your age yet."

Hannah smiled. "Thank you for that."

"And you should have a companion."

"As Father Nephi suggested some months ago."

"Are you considering it, then?"

Hannah shook her head.

"But Mother Hannah, you could be a second wife to any of the men. Father Nephi, Father Sam, Father Zoram. Or Jacob. Or Joseph. All are good men. All honor their priesthood. Are kind and good to their wives."

"All are excellent men," Hannah said. "All would be wonderful companions."

"But?"

"But I am married. I must keep the covenants I made."

Tabitha frowned sharply. "You are not married! Your husband tried to kill you! It is the same thing."

Hannah was confused. "The same thing? The same as what?"

"Those children being condemned for things their parents do."

"What?"

"It is! Your husband does something terrible and you are forced to leave him. But you remain tied to him and suffer because of that tie forever. And it was nothing you did!"

Hannah blinked and shook her head. "I think I understood that."

"You deserve to be happy, Mother Hannah."

Hannah smiled and put her hands on either side of Tabitha's face. "I am happy, Dearest One."

"But you do not have a companion."

"But I have family. And friends." Hannah looked over at Benjamin, across the room, happily burying his face in Little Brother's back, who retaliated with licks to the fluffy hair. "And I have my little Benjamin." She turned back to Tabitha. "I am truly happy." She made a face. "I have been married. I was married to an eternal companion. A man who did not honor his commitments or his covenants." She sighed. "I was never as happy then as I am now."

Tabitha searched her face. "Truly?"

"Truly."

The girl nodded. "Then I shall not speak of it again."

———————— • ◆ • ————————

Tabitha's marriage was performed quietly a week later, with the two, Tabitha and Dan, kneeling across the altar from each other and Jacob performing the ceremony.

Hannah studied Tabitha's glowing face as the young woman looked at her new husband.

Had she, Hannah, ever looked at Lemuel like that? She tried to remember her own wedding day. In her mind, it had become a jumble of this couple and that couple and taking turns making their covenants. In the year since she had left Laman's camp as one dead, the words spoken more than twenty-five years before and the emotions that accompanied them had become dulled. Blurred. Had the pain of rejection and hatred erased them?

Her mind wandered further. To Samuel's birth. She could still recall the joy of that day. And those spent watching her son grow to young manhood. So not everything had been brushed away.

But her marriage. It was as though it had been truly forgotten.

———————— • ♦ • ————————

Tabitha and Dan had taken themselves away to their new home and the people had finished clearing away all traces of the celebration.

Only the musicians remained, playing one last tune.

Walking carefully in the shadows, Hannah carried a sleepy Benjamin back to their hut and got him settled.

The moon was shining brightly through the open window, throwing a bar of light across Tabitha's empty pallet.

For the first time since her flight from Laman's camp, Hannah suddenly felt lonely.

Then Benjamin rolled over on his tummy, thrusting his little backside into the air and mumbling softly in his sleep.

Hannah looked at him and her expression softened. She was not quite alone. She still had her greatest blessing. She turned on her side and slept.

CHAPTER ELEVEN

*T*he years went by and Benjamin grew. Unhampered by any negative influences, he flourished in his faith, often following after his uncles Nephi or Jacob and plying them with questions far beyond the understanding of a child his age.

On the day he was baptized shortly after his eighth birthday, Hannah knew joy in a faithful son for the first time. As Benjamin's uncle, Sam, lifted him up out of the water, the boy's eyes went immediately to Hannah and he smiled.

Hannah could see no more through the blur of tears.

By his eleventh year, Benjamin had grown in strength and stature and had begun learning the gentle life of a shepherd—taking pride in the health and well-being of his small flock.

There had been no further personal contact with Laman or his people, apart from the infrequent raids on their flocks and herds, and Hannah had long since ceased to worry that Lemuel would one day appear and claim this faithful, fiery-headed son.

The community had grown and prospered as well, marrying and giving in marriage, welcoming many precious children to their fold as well as seeing vast increases in their crops and stock.

The temple had long since been finished. Not quite as grand as that of Solomon because they simply did not possess the fine materials, but beautiful nonetheless, with its curious workmanship, its gold and silver and precious things.

The people remained faithful. Through births and deaths. Marriages. Comings and goings.

There had been times through the years when Nephi, and increasingly, Jacob—as Nephi spent his days labouring over his fine gold pages—would call the people to repent of mistakes they were making. It was a mostly peaceful, prosperous period. Hannah couldn't remember a more tranquil time since they left their home in Jerusalem.

————— ◆ —————

Hannah's heart was singing. In the thirteen years since her second son was born, never had she felt such happiness. Today marked the first time Benjamin had read the prayer at services. She had watched his preparations and been seated in the women's section of the synagogue to witness his success. She knew, for the first time, joy as the mother of a young man bent on righteousness.

As she sat under a tree and watched her young son receive the good wishes of several of his older family members, Hannah could not keep the smile from her face.

Tabitha, her three elder children following closely and her youngest toddling along at her side, stopped in the shade beside Hannah.

"Good morrow, Mother Hannah!"

"Good morrow, Tabitha!" Hannah reached her hands out to the toddler. "I see that little Noah is getting steadier on his feet."

Tabitha sighed. "He wants to walk everywhere. It does slow one down." She turned to her children. "Jamila, would you please take your brothers home? I will be along soon."

The little girl nodded and, taking her two brothers by the hand, moved off down the street.

Tabitha fanned herself with her head cloth. "She is not yet ten, but she is such a help to me."

Hannah was watching the little girl lead her two brothers. "Some of them are born with old souls."

Tabitha smiled. "Indeed they are." She turned to Hannah. "Dan was just telling me of Benjamin's reading during the service today. You must be so proud!"

Hannah smiled. "I am well pleased with him," she said contentedly.

"I would be preparing my Gabriel now. If he had lived."

Hannah nodded and patted Tabitha's arm. "The Lord giveth and the Lord taketh away."

"Praise be unto the Lord," Tabitha whispered. "You think the pain will lessen—and it does—but at times it is all too fresh."

"And it returns as strongly as ever."

Hannah and Tabitha looked up. Rachel was standing beside them. "Good morrow, Sisters. I could not help but overhear. May I join you?"

"Please." Hannah indicated the spot beside her.

Rachel lowered herself slowly to the ground, groaning slightly as she finally settled.

Hannah was watching her. "Have you no relief, Sister?"

Rachel, her face grey and lined from weeks and months of pain, shook her head. "I have missed Mother Sariah's medical knowledge much of the time, but especially of late."

"Have you received a blessing?"

She nodded. "I was told this was my test and that if I endure it well, I will receive my reward." She sighed. "Sometimes the reward seems far off."

Hannah rubbed her sister-by-marriage's back gently. "Does the pain leave?"

Rachel shook her head and leaned back against the tree. "Always it is with me." She rubbed her stomach. "Sometimes it turns from sharp-edged to dull, but that is all."

"What does Nephi say?"

"My brother just shakes his head, sheds tears, and returns to prayer." She summoned up a smile. "But I have hope that someone will be given something."

"I will continue to pray as well, Sister," Hannah told her.

She gripped Hannah's hand. "It is much appreciated."

"Sister Rachel!" Moriah stopped beside them. "Good morrow, Sisters." She turned back to Rachel. "I have been looking for you!"

Rachel smiled up at her. "And you have found me."

"Let me help you to your hut. Our husband thinks he may have found something that will help."

"Zoram is a good, kind man, Sister. He thinks constantly of ways to improve our lives."

"He worries about you and prays for you."

Rachel let Moriah help her to her feet. "Thank you, Dear Sister."

Linking arms, the two women moved slowly up the street.

Tabitha watched them for a while, bouncing her youngest son on her knee absently. Then she turned to Hannah. "Some years ago, I asked you why did you not remarry. When Rachel and Litha accepted Zoram's offer, I thought that you would do the same. It is not good for us to remain alone."

Hannah shrugged. "I have a husband yet living, Dear One."

"I am sorry. That is an entirely personal matter and I have no right to question or interfere."

"You are the same as a daughter to me, Tabitha. Of course you should question. And, at times, interfere."

Tabitha's eyes filled with tears. "Am I really as a daughter to you?"

"You know you are, Dearest One. I have often told you."

"Yes. But this time, I believe you."

Hannah looked at her in mock anger. "Oh, so now I am untruthful and a deceiver?"

Tabitha laughed. "You are the most righteous woman I know, Mother Hannah, and you would never deceive anyone. But the other times you have called me daughter was always when I was in the final stages of childbirth. And we women say many things to encourage at times like those."

Hannah laughed. "Indeed we do. And you have given me many opportunities—and births—to do so. But know this. Always I have been truthful with you, Daughter."

Tabitha took her hand and pressed it. "And I am honored to be so called." She made a grab for her son, who had slid off her lap. "Perhaps I should take this young man and find food for him and his sister and brothers."

"Has Dan taken himself somewhere?"

"He is off with the other cattle herders finding new pastures. The herds have grown so remarkably that we need to be constantly on the search for more grazing."

"A sign of yet another blessing," Hannah said.

"It is true, Mother Hannah. If our herds were not increasing, we would not need new forage." Tabitha got to her feet. "Farewell, Mother Hannah!" Taking her son's tiny hand in hers, Tabitha matched her steps to his toddling ones and resumed her walk down the street.

Hannah resumed her interrupted watch over her son as Benjamin continued to converse with the other men—young and old—of the village.

Finally, he shook hands with several and took a seat beside her. "Mother, you look peaceful."

Hannah smiled. "I *feel* peaceful." She turned to him. "I have great joy in you, my son. At the choices you have made and are continuing to make."

Benjamin smiled. "*I* feel peaceful when I make those choices." He leaned back against the tree. " I do not understand those who would stray from the Lord's ways, Mother. Can they not see the straight path that is before them? Can they not feel the truth in the Prophet's words?"

Hannah looked at him. "You sound as I did so many years ago, questioning your grandfather."

"Ah. I see that you were brilliant as well as beautiful!"

Hannah laughed. "I never considered myself either. Merely someone who saw clearly the path before me." She sighed. "It seemed so simple to me."

"Remember that ye are free to act for yourselves—to choose the way of everlasting death or the way of eternal life."

"Exactly. Why would one choose everlasting death?"

"And what are you discussing so seriously this day?"

Hannah looked up. Jacob and Joseph were standing there, smiling down at the two of them.

Benjamin got to his feet and gave his uncles a slight bow. "Father Jacob and Father Joseph, we were discussing the ultimate choice we all have between right and wrong."

"And how some people seem always inclined to choose the latter," Hannah added. "And why."

"If you could discover the 'why' in that, you would have solved a problem that has tortured the prophets of the Lord since the days of Father Adam!" Jacob said. He glanced around the settlement. "Even here in our little peaceful community, there are those who must always be coached and guided."

"Are we not always to be guided?" Hannah asked.

Jacob smiled. "As always, Sister, your words can not be refuted."

Hannah flushed. "And as usual, I can not keep my tongue behind my teeth."

Jacob and Joseph laughed. "Change not, Sister," Joseph said. "Your outlook refreshes."

"And is needed," Jacob added. He suddenly lifted his head and looked up the street. "Joseph, fetch Nephi. Something has happened." He started up the street at a run.

"I will fetch Father Nephi," Benjamin said. "You go, Father Joseph."

Joseph nodded and started after his brother.

As Benjamin moved off in the opposite direction, Hannah got quickly to her feet and turned to see what had so alarmed Jacob and Joseph..

Two young men, their clothes and hair matted and thick with rich, black soil, were standing in the middle of the street. A group was gathering about them.

They were so coated in dirt that Hannah could not recognize them. She hurried over.

"They are out there. We must hurry and help them!"

Hannah recognized the voice of Rachel's youngest son, Xander.

Jacob nodded. He looked around. "Yavin! Could you and your eldest son fetch a frame?"

The young man nodded. "Isaac! Come, son."

The two disappeared.

"And we'll need another frame. There are two injured."

"I can help," Xander said. "Show me where to find the frame and I can help."

"I have one, Son."

Hannah turned.

Nephi and Benjamin, both breathing heavily, had joined the group. Nephi was holding another frame.

He looked past the houses toward the east. "It is the canyon there, to the east?"

Jacob blinked and nodded.

Nephi waited a moment for Xander to join him, then the two started to run. Several of the young men gathered about ran after them.

Hannah looked at Jacob. "What is happening?"

He turned to her. "A stampede. In the canyon. Two of our men hurt."

Hannah frowned. The cattle they raised were known for their gentle dispositions. "How could they have been induced to run wild?"

Jacob sighed. "It would seem they were forced to it." He looked at Hannah. "By our brethren."

"The Lamanites did this?"

Jacob nodded. "And now we have to see just how bad things truly are." He smiled at her. "Please excuse me."

Hannah nodded. "Of course." She stood and watched as another group of young men charged off out of the settlement. Then she began gathering the women to be prepared for their return.

———— • ◆ • ————

Anava was busily splinting bones and cleaning and wrapping broken skin.

Fane's wife, Harmony, clutching their youngest child in her arms and weeping uncontrollably, was huddled in a corner.

Hannah, her hands busy with minor tasks her younger sister set, let a single tear fall on the broken body before her. When she had seen Fane leave with his brother this morning, he had been happy and brimming with health.

Another tear trickled down her face and she caught it with the back of her hand before it, too, splashed down on her patient. "How could this have happened?" she whispered.

Anava shook her head. "This is the end result of the ugliness of sin, Sister." She dropped a cloth back into a bowl of reddened water. "Here. Could you please hold his foot steady? I have to straighten this leg to get the brace on it."

Hannah nodded and grasped the young man's foot with both hands while Anava pulled the broken bones back into place.

Fane groaned in his stupor.

Hannah looked down at the blood-streaked and dirty face. Deliberately keeping her eyes away from what Anava was doing. Not looking didn't drown out the sounds of the adjusting of bones and joints. And the pain-filled moans of their patient.

Hannah closed her eyes and turned to prayer.

After that, there was little conversation between them other than the occasional whispered instruction and brief acknowledgement.

Finally, Anava sat back and wiped her brow with one hand, leaving a streak of red across it. "There. I've done all I can do." She put her hand gently on Fane's cheek. "If he lives or he dies, it is in the Lord's hands."

Harmony gasped and crawled forward on her knees. "Dies?"

Anava reached out and took the young mother's hand. "*Lives* or dies."

Harmony looked down at her husband's battered face, then clutched her child close. "He *must* live! He *must!*"

Anava nodded. She bowed her head. "Will you pray with me, Sisters?"

"May we join you?"

Hannah turned.

Nephi was standing in the doorway of the hut with a tear-streaked Moriah and Zoram.

Hannah leaped to her feet. "Of course! Come. Come." She moved back to leave room for Fane's parents and Nephi next to the bandaged young man.

"We should anoint and bless him, first," Nephi said.

Hannah moved to the doorway, slipping outside as Nephi began his prayer. She took a deep breath of the clear air and brushed the tears from her cheeks. Then she went in search of some water to cleanse her hands.

"You have come from Fane?"

Hannah nearly tipped the pail back into the well. She caught it just in time, then looked at Yavin.

The young man's dark eyes were searching her face. "Will my brother live?"

Hannah tried twice to find a voice. "Yavin, he is very badly injured. Mother Anava has done all she knows how to do. It is in the Lord's hands now."

Yavin looked over toward Anava's hut. "He is there?"

"Yes."

"Mother and Father are with him?"

"Yes."

"And Father Nephi."

Hannah nodded.

Yavin took a deep breath and rubbed his hands over his face, then clenched them into fists and dropped them to his side. "They came out of nowhere. We had pushed the herd into that canyon. You know. The one with the narrow opening?"

Hannah nodded.

"Fane and Pallav were at the back of the herd, just coming through the gorge. Eamon and Eadric and I had moved into the canyon as the herd spread out. Suddenly, there were several men, all wearing the hides of the great jungle cats. For a moment we thought they *were* jungle cats. The cattle certainly thought so. They turned in a blind panic and started running back through the entrance." He sighed. "Fane and Pallav had no chance to get out of the way. The herd ran right over them."

Hannah shivered.

Yavin looked at her. "It was deliberate, Mother Hannah. Those men meant to injure or kill someone. They chose their time well. Much of the herd had cleared the gorge, but the stragglers and the herders following were still inside with no route to escape."

"They made off with several of the animals, but what do we care about that? We would have given them the cows if they'd only asked."

"They do not think it is manly to receive," Hannah said softly. "Only to take."

"These men were my family, Mother Hannah. The sons of yours and Mother's brothers. Perhaps even your son."

Hannah caught her breath. "Please. No," she whispered.

Yavin was silent for a moment. "How could they do such a thing? How could they deliberately—"

Hannah shook her head. "I do not know."

He took a deep breath. "Have we not suffered enough, Mother Hannah?"

"Yavin—" She reached out to him.

He brushed her hand away. "Have we not suffered enough?" He pointed with his chin at his own hut. "When our women are stolen away and ravished. And our children are—are not—!"

Hannah put her hand on his arm. "Yavin."

He shook her hand off, but turned and looked at her, dark eyes awash in tears. "Have we not suffered enough?"

"Yavin!"

He closed his eyes and let the tears stream down his face to his beard.

"Count your blessings."

He opened his eyes and looked at her, frowning.

"Count your blessings. Do it now! I will do the same!"

He blinked and scrubbed at his tears with the back of his hand. "Uh—well—"

"You have your health," Hannah started for him. "Let us begin there."

"O—okay. My health. But my brother's health—"

"And you have your wife. And your family."

He looked at her.

"Say it!"

"My wife and my family."

"Whom you love very much."

A small smile. "Whom I love very much."

"And you have the teachings of the prophet who speaks for God."

He nodded.

"Say it!"

"Speaks for God. Okay, I have it."

"But are you really grateful? Are you thanking the Lord for those blessings with your whole heart?"

"Of course I am!" Yavin's dark brows lowered in a frown. "Every day I thank the Lord for those blessings."

"Do you? Or do you simply mouth the words?"

Yavin looked at her again.

"What would your life be if any of that was taken from you?"

189

He jabbed toward Anava's hut with one finger. "My brother lies there. Injured!"

"Think of your blessings, Yavin."

He was silent for a moment.

"When bad things happen—and they do happen—it is to remind us of what we do have. To remind us to be grateful for those things."

"My wife and children are not 'things,' Mother Hannah."

Hannah smiled. "I want you to think for a moment of the terrible things that happened to Ilka. And to you. Just for a moment."

He frowned at her.

"Now I want you to think of what you have because of those hardships."

A small smile appeared.

"For one thing, you would not have your most beloved Isaac."

Yavin's expression softened further.

"Perhaps you and Ilka would not be so close if someone had not threatened to pull you apart."

Yavin thought about that for a moment. Then he sighed. "You are right, as always, Mother Hannah."

Hannah waved a hand. "I am not always right." She smiled at Yavin. "But I am always ready to count my blessings."

He nodded.

"Now. About your brother. Father Nephi and your father have given him a blessing and remain to pray for him. You could help by doing the same."

"I will. I do!"

Hannah patted his arm. "Good. And Yavin?"

He looked at her.

"Bad things do happen. They are to remind us to remain faithful. To send us to that God who created us and who patiently waits for us to remember Him."

"I remember Him!"

"But never so much as when something bad happens."

Yavin blinked.

"Now go and pray for your brother. Gather with your wife and children and pour your hearts out to God for him." She took a deep breath and smiled. "He is always listening."

———— • ◆ • ————

By late the next day, the settlement was certain that Fane would live. His younger brother, Pallav, who had been with him in the gorge but escaped with only minor injuries, had taken up a vigil with Fane's wife and with their mother, Moriah. From there, he was able to give constant updates on Fane's progress to anyone who happened by.

Late in the day, as the shadows were growing long, Fane opened his eyes and almost immediately asked for water.

Pallav was ecstatic and, getting to his feet, shouted the news to the entire village.

Hannah hurried to the doorway just in time to witness Anava instructing her three helpers in giving Fane water. "Just sips right now," she cautioned. "Sips. He will want more, but we must let him heal slowly and not try too much too soon."

Pallav nodded and tipped the water skin for the briefest of moments.

"More!" Fane moaned. "More!"

"Mother Anava cautioned against it, Husband," Harmony said. "We must do what she says to ensure you will heal properly."

Fane scowled, but said nothing more.

Anava looked at Hannah. "If his wounds do not become infected, he will live to speak of this experience to his great grandchildren."

"All I care . . . is that I can tell it . . . to my children now," Fane said between gasps.

"Nothing wrong with his hearing," Anava said, smiling.

———— • ◆ • ————

For the next few days, Fane continued to heal.

But as his bruises faded and bones knitted, a new problem arose.

"I have been lying here quite long enough!"

Hannah smiled at him. "I know it seems like a great time, Crowned One, but those bones have really only begun to heal."

He turned to Anava. "Mother Anava! How much longer will I be forced to lie here?"

Anava came over, carrying a platter. "You still have some weeks of inactivity, Fane. Those bones must heal properly before you try to use them or you will never be able to run—and maybe not even walk."

Fane sat back and folded his arms across his chest, looking so much like a small, errant child that Hannah laughed. He scowled at her. "Fine. Now you make jests at my expense."

Hannah put a hand over her mouth. "I am sorry, Crowned One, but your face . . ." She let out another peal of laughter.

Fane slumped back onto his mat and turned away.

"Come, Son," Anava said. "Drink this. It will calm you."

He turned and looked at the mug on the platter. "I am tired of drinking your potions and infusions. I want something to chew! I am starving away to skin and bone. Give me something I can chew!"

"You can chew the spoon!" Anava said, handing him a wooden utensil. "But after you have used it to stir in the honey."

Fane sighed and sat up once more, wincing as he tried to maneuver his bound leg.

"Careful, Son. Do not try to move it too much."

He nodded and reached for the mug. Then, grinning at Hannah, he deliberately put the wooden spoon into his mouth and bit down hard. "Mmm. That tastes so good!"

Hannah laughed again. "I am leaving. I am not needed here."

Anava smiled. "It is a great blessing to see him like this. Well enough to be impatient with his treatment."

Hannah put a hand on her sister's shoulder. "Only you would see the blessing in impatience!"

She met Harmony in the doorway. The young woman was still looking wan and worried, but had a bit more color in her cheeks than she had in the past few days.

"How is my husband today?" Harmony asked. "Does he continue to improve?"

Hannah put her arm around the young woman's shoulders. "He does, Harmony." She turned to look at Fane, who was taking a sip of the drink Anava had prepared. "In fact, he is feeling so much better, he grows impatient with his treatment."

"Oh he cannot do that!" Harmony hurried to her husband's side.

Hannah stepped out into the street.

She could see light streaming from the House of Assembly into the street. Obviously there was a gathering. She hurried toward it.

oBenjamin appeared in the doorway. "Mother, there you are!"

Hannah took his hand. "I was helping with Fane's care."

The boy turned. "Father Nephi and Father Jacob have been talking to us. I thought you should hear what they are saying."

"Always," Hannah said. "Lead on."

They found seats to one side, behind Litha, Moriah and Rachel, the latter slumped over in pain but obviously determined to be there.

Hannah looked at Jacob. It seemed ohe was answering a question one of those sisters had posed.

"Many of our children shall perish in the flesh because of unbelief, Sister Rachel. Nevertheless, God will be merciful unto many."

Rachel started to her feet, then groaned and sank back to her cushion. "Then my Thad-deus? And Tobias?" Her faint voice caught on the word and she sounded breathless.

Moriah put a comforting arm around her sister's shoulders.

"Abishai?" Litha asked.

"Samuel?" Hannah whispered.

Jacob smiled. "Our children shall be restored, that they may come to that which will give them the true knowledge of their Redeemer."

Rachel dropped her head into her hands and began weeping. Litha patted her sister's shoulder, tears streaming down her own face.

Hannah leaned forward and put an arm around each of their shoulders and, with her head close to theirs, shared their grief. And their budding hope and joy.

Jacob continued to speak of the Messiah, whom he called 'Christ.' Of his many miracles. His death at the hands of evil men and his offer of salvation through his resurrection and eternal salvation through his Atonement.

Then he said, "And now, my beloved brethren, seeing that our merciful God has given us so great knowledge concerning these things, let us remember Him, and lay aside our sins, and not hang down our heads, for we are not cast off; nevertheless, we have been driven out of the land of our inheritance; but we have been led to a better land."

Hannah looked at him. They had been cast out. They had suffered terrible losses. But they had been brought here to this beautiful place of milk and honey. Where Nephi and Jacob could speak the words of the Lord without fear of retribution. She looked up toward Heaven and recommitted herself to remembering Him. And praising Him all the day long.

Beside her, Benjamin sighed. "Words of life itself, Mother. And hope for my brother Samuel."

She smiled through her tears and nodded. Benjamin had never met his older brother, but he spoke of him often with love. She wondered if, some day, the two of them would ever be together. Maybe not in this life, but surely in the life hereafter.

She absently watched Litha and Moriah help Rachel to her feet and then half-lead, half-carry her from the room, stopping every few moments so she could breathe and brace herself to continue.

Hannah nodded quietly to herself. Yes they had all suffered and been given great challenges, but for the first time since she had left her son with his father in Laman's camp, Hannah felt stirrings of hope for him.

———— ◆ ————

Fane continued to improve and the next two days passed quietly.

Hannah, Little Brother curled up in the sunshine beside her, was sitting in front of her hut, grinding grains for her and Benjamin's bread when she saw Pallav run past carrying a large, wooden bowl filled with leaves and greenery. "Pallav!" she called. "Where do you go with such speed?"

Pallav just shook his head and continued past her.

Curious, Hannah got to her feet and looked after the young man. He continued up the street to Fane's hut, then ducked inside.

Frowning, Hannah, with Little Brother close behind, followed him.

Just as she reached the hut, Anava came out with Zoram, followed closely by Harmony. Zoram was speaking. "Just put them all into a pot of water and let them steam," he said. "Then crush them and strain out the liquid. Give it to him to drink. Not a lot.

Just a spoonful seems to work wonders with my wife." He frowned. "Although it does not seem to be as effective of late."

"What is wrong?" Hannah asked. "Is there something I can do?"

The three of them looked at her. "Fane is in some pain," Anava said. "Brother Zoram has been instructing us in the use of these leaves." She held out the bowl Pallav had been carrying. She turned and handed it to Harmony and nodded. "You know what to do, Dearest One."

Harmony disappeared.

Zoram smiled and nodded to them and left.

Anava rubbed her hand across her brow.

"You look weary, Sister," Hannah said.

Anava gave her a rather wan smile. "For the first time, I understand what Mother Sariah meant when she said she was wearier than weary."

Hannah put a hand on her sister's arm. "It is the miraculous cost of providing relief. But please know that we are forever grateful for your efforts."

"I do know. In some weary part of myself."

"Has Fane been in pain for long?"

Anava looked at the hut. "No. He woke this morning with some pain in his leg. There is no sign of infection. I am assuming that, despite my advice, he has been doing too much and strained something."

"What are those leaves Pallav brought to you?"

"Those are the newest miracle." Anava turned back to her. "Come. Walk with me."

The two turned together and started up the street.

"Zoram was in the forest, speaking with the Lord concerning Rachel's illness and saw one of the small rodents eating some of those leaves. The animal had been wounded in one of its legs, perhaps in an attack. It stuffed several of the leaves into its mouth. As Zoram watched, it seemed to gain new strength and bounded off as though its wounds did not exist."

Hannah frowned."That quickly?"

Anava nodded. "Zoram says so. He decided to try making a potion from the leaves and see if it could help Rachel with her pain.

It was remarkable. A small spoonful of the distillate gave her relief for hours." She made a face. "Of course it seems to take more and more of the drug now to truly be effective, but it is still remarkable."

"Does it heal her?"

Anava shook her head. "It merely relieves her pain for a time."

Hannah sighed. "Is there nothing that can heal her?"

"Nephi suspects that her pain is caused by something growing within her."

"A child?"

"No. Her time of bearing is long past." She looked sideways at Hannah. "As it is for the rest of us. No, he thinks this is something different. There is a lump that grows in size just here." Anava pointed to her side. "And that seems to be the source of her pain and discomfort."

"Could we cut it from her? With a knife?"

Anava looked at Hannah, wide-eyed. "Cut into her body? While she yet lives?"

"I have seen men wounded there. Remember when Zedekiah fell on that pile of timbers and was stabbed deeply?"

Anava nodded. "Father pulled the stake from him and Mother used her salves to draw out the poisons." She stopped and turned to Hannah. "I wonder if that would work? Mother's salves?"

"Have you tried anything else?"

"Everything I can think of."

"Then what would it hurt?"

Anava, deeply in thought, turned and started toward her hut.

Hannah watched her go. Little Brother nosed her hand. Looking down, she patted the familiar head. Then she looked at him more closely, realizing suddenly that her friend was aging. His muzzle, normally grey in color, had turned quite white.

Hannah knelt down in front of him and held out a lock of her own formerly dark hair, now liberally streaked with great swathes of white. "We are not the youngsters we once were, my friend." She turned to look after Anava. "Age is upon us and there is little we can do about it."

Little Brother bumped her cheek with his nose. His stub of a tail waved back and forth slowly.

Hannah smiled and took his head in both of her hands. "But we shall not wallow in our fears. We shall lift our heads high and go forward with faith and hope."

Little Brother whined and butted her cheek again.

"Exactly." Hannah stood up once more. "Forward. With faith and hope."

———— ◆ ————

A moon later, Anava pronounced Fane mostly healed and able to take up limited activity. This was yet another difficult time for the normally active young man. He was finally able to move around freely, but was hampered by the sticks and wrapping Anava insisted he keep strapped to his leg.

He learned to take a step, then swing his healing leg, then take another step. His gait was lurching and awkward, but he did manage to move around.

He became a familiar sight around the settlement with his step, swing, step.

It was another moon before Anava allowed him to remove the bracing entirely and one more before Fane was again running and moving about as freely as he had before his injuries.

By then, apart from the continuing heightened watch of the guards, the manufacture of weapons, and the training of the young would-be warriors, the village had settled once more into its usual days of quiet industry.

But only for a time.

———— ◆ ————

Hannah woke with a start. Little Brother was howling. The sound was eerie in the grey light of the pre-dawn.

She shivered. Then scrambled from her pallet and hurried to the door. She skidded to a halt when she realized it was standing open.

She glanced across to Benjamin, who was just stirring. "Did you go outside, Son?"

He looked at her and shook his head. "I did not, Mother."

Another howl from outside.

"Perhaps Little Brother—?"

197

Hannah blinked and hurried out.

Little Brother was sitting outside Rachel's hut. He looked at Hannah, then put his nose into the air and let out another long mournful cry.

Hannah went over to him and put a hand on his rough back. "What is it, my friend?"

Little Brother looked at her and whined, then threw his head back and howled again.

It was at that moment Hannah heard screams coming from Rachel's hut.

Death screams.

CHAPTER TWELVE

*H*annah stared mindlessly at Rachel's hut.

Mother!" Benjamin appeared beside her. "Come!" He went past her and into the hut.

People were coming out of their homes all up and down the street and staring in her direction.

Hannah shook her head and followed her son.

Moriah, Litha, and Zoram were sitting beside Rachel's pallet. All were covered noticeably in dirt and both women had torn their tunics at the neck.

As Hannah paused in the doorway, Rachel's son Xander slipped past her and joined the others. Just behind him came her daughter, Gavrilla, already sobbing as she moved around Hannah.

Soon all were kneeling by the simple pallet, mourning the woman who lay upon it.

Hannah moved closer and looked down at the peaceful face.

The lines of pain and fatigue had been smoothed. Hannah saw again the face of her sister-by-marriage as she had looked. Before age and illness and disappointment and pain had marked and twisted it. She crouched down beside the still figure and touched the grey hair tenderly, remembering the night she saw Rachel dressed for her betrothal and again for her wedding. How happy she had been. How beautiful. Her joy could not be contained with the birth of her son Thaddeus and each of her other children, even with the hardships of the trek through the wilderness and the year upon the sea.

Her pain had begun with the treachery of her husband as he followed down dark paths, continued with the death of her sons Thaddeus and Tobias, and had been finalized by her painful disease.

Hannah leaned over to embrace the body.

"No! Touch her not!" Moriah grabbed Hannah's shoulder and pushed her back.

Hannah looked at her sister blankly. "What? What is wrong?"

"She has committed murder!"

Hannah blinked."Mur-der?" Her voice broke on the word. "How . . . why?"

"She has killed the body created for her by God. She has taken her own life!" Moriah melted into tears.

Hannah stopped breathing. Was this true? Her beautiful Rachel? She turned back to the body. How could this be?

"She took . . . all of the . . . p-potion I brewed for her yesterday," Zoram said, his own voice breaking over the words. He held up an empty jug. "The pain was so great." He paused, and then wiped at his eyes with the sleeve of his tunic. "S-she was not in her right mind."

Hannah put out a hand. "She was your wife! And our sister! We must give her her due." She looked down at the still face. "And mourn her properly."

"We cannot mourn her properly!" Moriah shouted, tears pouring down her face. "Her death was not proper!"

Hannah sat there, speechless and confused. For the first time in her life, she did not know what to do.

Someone else had come in, but Hannah was too preoccupied to realize it was Nephi until he spoke. "My brothers and Sisters, we must not judge our sister harshly," he said gently. "Do not presume to know her thoughts."

"We do not need to know her thoughts," Moriah said. "She took her own life!"

Nephi nodded. "And that is grave, yes. But it is not for us to judge. Merely to mourn and bury her." He looked around at the tear-stained faces. "Remember her before she was wracked by such pain she no longer knew what she was doing. Remember the mother. The sister. The wife. Remember the strong, faithful woman who made such sacrifices for her testimony." He sank to his knees beside Rachel's still figure and reached for her hand. "I am quite certain she did not mean to take her own life. I think she just took more and more of the potion because it helped her pain." He shrugged. "How could she even know it would end her life?"

Hannah blinked. "Of course. *I* would not have known."

Moriah turned back to Rachel. "Nor I."

"You see?" Nephi lifted the hand he held. "This is not the hand of a murderer. This is the hand of a gentle soul who lived in constant, unrelenting pain. Who knew that the potion brewed for her by her husband relieved that pain. And who was forced to take more and more of it to achieve a little peace." A tear escaped Nephi's dark eye and trickled down his face. "This is a woman whom our God has just welcomed home." He lifted his head and looked around the circle. "Let us send her off with rejoicing that her work is done. Her journey through." He laid the hand gently back on the still breast and got to his feet. "Let us mourn her as is her due."

But despite Nephi's kind words, there were many in the village who refused to take part in the service to honour Rachel.

It was a small group who accompanied the body to the tomb.

Hannah looked around at the somber faces. Moriah. Litha. Zoram. Rachel's children, Xander and Gavrilla—the only two of her eight who had come out from Laman's camp with her—with their families. Litha's twin daughters, Laura and Leah, who like Rachel's two youngest, had accompanied their mother when she fled Laman. Hannah and Benjamin. And Nephi, Jacob, Joseph, and their wives.

It was a small showing, indeed, from the hundreds that now inhabited their village.

Hannah's tears were as much for her family's stiff-neckedness as they were for a beloved sister.

Nephi spoke briefly, sadly. Paying tribute to the woman who had followed the prophet, leaving home and family to do so. Suffered pain only those who had made a similar sacrifice could understand. And had suffered further, unimaginable pain in her final illness.

He looked at the small gathering. "Judge not, that you be not judged. For with what judgment you judge, you shall be judged: and with what measure you mete, it shall be measured to you again." He signed. "And why behold you the mote that is in your brother's eye, but consider not the beam that is in your own eye?" He turned away. "So shall the Christ speak. His words are suitable for us this day." He started back toward the village, his shoulders slumped with sorrow.

Anava hurried forward and slid her arm through her husband's.

The two spoke quietly for a few moments.

Hannah, hesitant to interrupt, took up a position behind the couple.

Nephi smiled and glanced at her over his shoulder. "Peace, Sister. You are not interrupting."

Anava reached out her hand and grasped Hannah's, pulling her up with them. "Speak with us, for you always have wisdom to share."

Hannah flushed slightly. "Wisdom? All too often I have fears. Doubts."

Anava bumped her with her shoulder. "But not now, surely? Speak on."

Hannah sighed. "I keep remembering Rachel in happier days. Back in Jerusalem. With little Thaddeus and Esther. And even on the trail. Bearing her children and caring for them. She remained stalwart and uncomplaining. Supportive of her husband, even in his wickedness."

Nephi smiled."That is as it should be. Remembering our sister in the good times."

"And not judging her for her actions in the bad," Anava put in.

Nephi sighed. "How quick we are to judge. When we do not understand the circumstances behind the actions. When we do not even know if the actions were deliberate."

"I do not think Rachel meant to take her life."

Anava looked at her.

Hannah gave a quick bob of her head. "Truly. Rachel held life sacred. I believe she was merely seeking relief from her pain. She could have no idea such actions would cause her death."

"I agree with you," Nephi said. He looked around at those following. "But it is not we few that need convincing. Rather is it those we do not see here."

"I will tell them."

Nephi smiled. "I know you will."

———— ◆ ————

Tabitha shook her head. "But, Mother Hannah, she took her life! We can not associate with such people!"

Hannah broke in. "Dearest One, we do not know that." She scraped another slice of meat from the bone she held.

"But—"

"We know only that her death was caused by too much of the pain potion. Did she know that taking more than was recommended would cause her to die? *I* did not know." She looked at Tabitha. "Did you?"

The young woman shook her head.

"There. How can we accuse Rachel of something of which we both were ignorant?"

"But, Mother Hannah, she was the one taking the potion. Surely she, of anyone, would realize the danger."

"How?" Hannah tossed the bone to Little Brother, who had been sitting just outside the open door, his head swiveling from her to Tabitha as he watched their conversation. He caught the treat in the air and moved to the shadows to enjoy it.

Tabitha was silent, thinking. "I think I have made a grave error."

Hannah nodded. "I think you have. But do not despair, Dearest One. We all do. That is what repentance is for."

"But how can I be forgiven when the one I have wronged has already passed through the veil?"

"And the one who makes repentance possible is not yet come to earth." Hannah smiled. "You pray, Dearest One. And you ask to be forgiven. And then you do what you can to correct the mistake."

"But Rachel is gone."

"Then you speak to those who were closest to her. And the most hurt by your actions."

Tabitha nodded. "Yes. That I can do."

Nephi stood at the front of the room and looked out over the gathered people. "My brothers and sisters." He paused for a moment, frowning. "In 600 years from the time our Father Lehi left Jerusalem, the Messiah will be born. He will live out his life among the humble peoples of Israel, teaching and leading. Then he will be crucified by those same people and offer up his life to end death and to save us all from our sins. His teaching will be mighty and his example—unmatched by any of God's children who have walked and will walk this earth. His greatness and glory equal that of God, the Father." He looked away. "His teachings will be spoken until the end of time by the greatest of his prophets." He took a deep breath. "And the greatest of his teachings will concern faith and hope and charity. And it is charity about which I would speak to you today."

There was a rustling among the seated people. Somewhere, a baby cried out and was just as quickly hushed.

Nephi smiled slightly, then sobered once more. "Our sister, Rachel, has died. We have judged her for the circumstances of her dying."

The crowd murmured and Nephi held up a hand until they quieted.

He began to pace. "We, none of us, know exactly what happened that night. We do not know if she took some of the potion and then forgot and took some more. Or if, in a pain-filled haze, simply decided to drink the entire contents." He stopped and turned to the people. "It simply does not matter. All that should matter to us is the fact that our sister, whom we loved, has left us and crossed the veil into our Father's arms. He was grateful to have her come. We should be grateful to have her go. We should rejoice for her. Not judge her."

He repeated the words he had spoken during the walk from Rachel's burial, then smiled. "One last thing I would add, my brothers and sisters. All things whatsoever you would that men should do to you, do you even so to them: for this is the law and the prophets." He clasped his hands together. "My people, we have other things to consider this day. Other worries. Let us not exhaust ourselves about things over which we have no dominion."

He looked down. "And also my soul delights in the covenants of the Lord which he has made to our fathers," he said softly. "Yea, my soul delights in his grace, and in his justice, and power, and mercy in the great and eternal plan of *deliverance from death.*"

He nodded to Jacob and sat down.

Everyone was silent for a few moments. Then Jacob stood, offered a short prayer and indicated that they should all be dismissed.

It was a quiet group that slowly got to their feet and began to find their way to the door.

Hannah saw several of them move over to Gavrilla and stop to speak to her. She craned her neck to try to find Xander, then decided he must be taking a turn with flocks or guarding because she could not see him in the congregation.

Sighing, she turned and joined the stream heading to the door.

Once outside, Hannah lifted her head cloth to protect her face from the heavy droplets pelting from the sky. The rains had started two days before and already the ground was soggy with moisture. Hannah sighed. She knew the divine water was much needed for their crops and herds, but the solemn, grey days threw a net over her spirit and dragged it down.

Benjamin and one of Ezekiel's youngest sons came out from between two huts and ran toward her. She waved. "Benjamin!"

He shook his head as he sped past. "I can not talk now, Mother. I must find Father Nephi."

Hannah turned and watched them go.

Little Brother growled low in his throat.

Nephi had just stepped outside and greeted the two young men with a smile. A smile that quickly faded as they spoke. He beckoned them to follow him back into the House of Assembly.

Hannah frowned. What on earth could that mean?

She sighed and turned back toward her house. Benjamin would tell her.

"Slow down, Dearest One. You can not eat everything in the first bite."

Benjamin swallowed. "I must get back out to the field. I should not even be here."

"Not have a meal with your mother?" Hannah crossed her arms and put on her sternest expression.

Benjamin laughed. "I mean, I am on shift right now and should be out in the field. Especially since—" He hesitated.

Hannah moved closer. "Is something wrong, Son?" She looked toward the doorway. "Something you told Nephi that you are not at liberty to tell me?"

"It is no secret. When we were out in the furthest field this morning, we heard drums."

Hannah caught her breath. "Drums?"

"At first we did not know what we were hearing. Then Father Zoram came out to relieve one of his grandsons and he recognized them. Hide drums. Where animal skins are stretched across great bins formed by hollowed-out trees. He said that people used to have them back in Jerusalem. For music and other things. We have not needed them with our own music. We have found rhythm in hooves and rattles and different reeds."

Hannah frowned. "Who would be playing drums?"

Benjamin sighed. "I may as well tell you for you will hear it soon. Father Nephi thinks that the time of conflict is starting."

"Conflict? But we have long had conflict. To what is he referring?"

Benjamin didn't reply, but stood up and stuffed the last of his bread, meat and cheese into his mouth. "I must go, Mother." He came toward her, gently grasped her upper arms and placed his forehead against hers. "Fear not, Mother Hannah, as long as we remember Him, the Lord is with us."

As he pulled her toward him, Hannah was distracted by her son's height. How tall he was getting! Already much bigger than she. It took a moment for his words to sink in. "Should I be worried?" she asked, belatedly.

"I must go." Benjamin was out the door.

Hannah stepped to the doorway and watched him charge off into the rain.

Should she be worried? The Lamanites had been causing conflict for years. They came in and harassed the herders in the borders of the land, stole some of the animals, and disappeared. Their actions had caused the people of Nephi to increase the guard in all parts of the land and to craft weapons and start the daily ritual of training in swordplay and bow and arrow in the compounds just outside the village.

How was this to be different?

She shivered and looked up at the grey sky.

Already she could feel those drums. They seemed to pound deep into her soul.

War was coming.

CHAPTER THIRTEEN

*A*t first, the sound of the heavy, rhythmic pounding could only be heard in the furthest fields. But three days after Benjamin had alerted Nephi to it, Hannah awoke to them.

At first, she thought she was imagining it. That she had conjured it up in her mind from out of the oppressive reports brought back from the herders and guardsmen. Then she realized she could hear the sounds of alarmed men and women out in the street.

This was not a creation of her imagination.

As the day wore on, the oppressive sound seemed to wind itself around her very heart. Squeezing the peace from her soul one dread beat at a time.

She sought out Nephi, hoping he could give her the words that would quell her trepidation. But Nephi had no words of comfort to give.

She found him in one of the training compounds, speaking to an assembly that included every young man over sixteen years in their village. "My sons," he said. "For sons you truly are, this is the time for faith. And for courage." He sighed. "If we had invaded the land of our brethren, we could not hope for help from our God. But they have come to us, therefore, know that our God is with us. That He will help to defend us, our homes, and our wives and our children. And our very religion. And now I say unto you, my beloved sons, that never has there been so great courage amongst all the Nephites. It has not been needed. Not until this day." He looked toward the borders of their land. "Even now, our brethren are gathered in the borders of the land, ready to charge across it, sweeping all before them."

Ezekiel looked over the assembled men, then turned to Nephi. "Father Nephi, we know that our God is with us. We would not slay our brethren if they would let us alone, but they will not. So we shall go out to meet them in the field of battle. And we shall fight for those things that are most dear to us." He took a deep breath. "And we shall fight in the name of God. And we shall be victorious!"

The rest of the assembly gave a great shout and lifted their swords into the air, then banged them against the heavy, wooden shields they carried.

The sound was deafening and Hannah covered her ears, her eyes drawn suddenly to Eadric, that same person who, as a small boy so many years ago, had been excited at the prospect of wielding a sword. Today, a grown man, he was holding his weapon solemnly, carefully. Obviously aware of the seriousness of his purpose in carrying it and in the covenant he was making as he did so.

Nephi raised his arms. "My sons, let us bow before God. Let us place our lives in His hands."

Every person in the assembly knelt upon the ground and lowered his head.

"Our most gracious Father," Nephi began.

Hannah sat suddenly on a nearby stone, the air gone from her lungs. They were really going to do this. The sons of her brothers were going out to meet other sons of her brothers on the battle field. Brother against brother. Father against son.

She put her head in her hands. How could this be? How could they have come to this? How could the children of Lehi have splintered to the point where hatred would drive them to attempt to murder each other?

A hand touched her shoulder. "Sister?"

Hannah looked up.

Nephi was standing beside her, his eyes on the young men leaving the compound in ordered groups. "You do not agree with what is happening today?"

Hannah stared at him. "It never occurred to me to disagree, Brother Nephi. Only to lament that this course is the only one open to us." She looked away as a tear made its way down her cheek. "My son will be out there on the battlefield. My h-husband."

Nephi sighed and looked up toward the spongy sky. "I lament as well, Sister."

"All these young men. About to be spent and wasted on a field of battle. All sons of our brothers! And ourselves."

Nephi nodded. "How quickly evil has taken hold. In the space of only one generation God has been forgotten and a course toward damnation mapped out and embarked upon." He looked once more toward the faithful young men. "But know this, Sister. These young men will be guarded by angels as they fight this day. Those who stand with us are far greater than those who oppose, and we shall be triumphant in winning the day."

"Can I hope that those same angels will guard my Samuel this day as he is carried along in the churning tide of evil?"

Nephi was silent for a moment. "Pray for him, Sister. Pray for him and for all who have been caught up in this great wickedness."

"Always I pray for him, Brother."

He nodded. "And I will continue to pray as well."

The sight of so many of her beloved young brothers, marching hopefully and faithfully off to battle wielding swords instead of plows, bows instead of shepherd's crooks, filled her with deep despair. And knowing that the enemy they faced was not some nameless, faceless hoard, but brothers they knew all too well, was almost more than she could bear.

"Go and prepare, Sister. Go and do that work for which God fashioned you with a caring heart and willing hands. You and your sisters will be just as instrumental in our success on this day as those who wield swords in your behalf." He looked toward the rapidly disappearing young warriors. "I must go and join our younger brethren now."

Hannah looked at him, incredulous. "You will fight with them? In your age?" She bit her lip, wishing she could recall the words.

Nephi laughed. "The Lord calls His warriors where He can find them. Even I, in my age." He again put a hand on Hannah's shoulder. "And I am happy to answer when He calls."

Her face burning, Hannah got to her feet and hurried into the village.

She paused as she gained the street. There seemed to be a general migration of women toward the House of Assembly. Hannah joined them and there, she found Anava directing willing hands in preparing bandages and ointments. Boiling water. Laying out pallets and linen cloths. And in general, preparing to receive those who offered their lives in an attempt to stem the tide of evil that threatened to overcome them all.

"Be ready and always aware, sisters," Anava said. "Remember to use the potion I have made to keep infection down. Be clean. Be careful. If there is anything you do not feel confident in treating, call me!" She looked around at the sober faces. "One other thing." She paused for a moment, then took a deep breath. "We are here to offer aid, but should the battle reach the eastern slope, we are to remove to our next place of refuge."

Hannah moved over to her. "We are to run?"

Anava nodded. "With every ounce of our strength. I promised Husband before he left."

Hannah took a deep breath. The day grew even more unreal.

The sound of the drums seemed to intensify as the minutes fled past. Then, quite suddenly, they stopped.

Hannah and the women around her looked at each other. What did this mean?

But even as they drew another breath, a great shout filled the air. The sound of hundreds of throats, either screaming defiance of God or begging His blessings as they charged toward each other.

Then there was a great clash of sound. The deadly ring of sword on sword. Sword on shield.

The women moved as one out of the building. Peered past the peaceful street of homes toward the sheep pastures.

211

There was not much they could see—a solid mass of men on the furthest gentle slope, the sunlight glinting and flashing from deadly swords and other metalworks in the group.

Within minutes, carts started coming toward them, pushed to greater speed by drivers who only wanted to deliver their cargo to the waiting ministering hands before they charged back to the battle to collect the next victims.

And then the sense of unreality fled as a nightmare truly began.

———————— • ◆ • ————————

Hannah pushed her headcloth up with the back of her hand and twisted the bandage neatly closed. She looked down the bloody stump of an arm she had been attending. Cephus would serve the rest of his life one-handed. But at least he would live to serve. She carefully covered him with a warm blanket, and then lifted her head. All about her, women were caring for wounded, groaning men. Wrapping bandages around oozing sword cuts. Removing arrows. Tending to the grievous but harder to see crush wounds.

Anava was actually using fine linen thread to stitch a long tear in an abdomen.

Hannah moved closer and recognized Eamon on the pallet. She looked around for Moriah, but caught sight of her eldest sister across the room, tending to someone else.

She took the young man's hand. "Eamon? Can you hear me?"

He turned his head and attempted a smile. "I would know you anywhere, Mother Hannah."

Anava looked at her. "Hold his hand tightly, Sister, while I get these last few stitches in."

Hannah squeezed the bloodied, grimy fingers.

Eamon groaned aloud.

Hannah looked down at the long trail of neat stitches. "Will he recover?"

Anava snipped the last of the thread with a sharp knife and nodded. "The sword caught skin only. It could have been so much worse. So far, we have had no deaths." She looked around and nodded toward the young man Hannah had been tending. "And young Cephus is our greatest sufferer."

She turned back. "The waste! The colossal waste!" She looked up. "Why, Lord?"

Hannah sighed. "The greatest gift He has given us is that of choice. *We* choose to follow Him with it. *They*—" she nodded toward the battle field, "—do not."

"More coming!" someone shouted.

Hannah sighed and turning, hurried to the door. "Bring them in! Bring them in!"

She lost count of the hours as she bandaged, swabbed, comforted and prayed.

The house of gathering filled slowly with groaning, bloodied figures. Sisters did what they could for them, then moved among those who had already been treated to offer a spoonful of Zoram's pain medication, a drink or a word of encouragement.

There were gasps and cries as bloodied, well-beloved faces were brought in with grave wounds, and the sound of prayers being offered became almost as constant as the cries and moans of the wounded.

Then once-familiar faces began to come in. Faces darkened by the blood, now dried, with which they had been painted. Faces not glimpsed by the sisters in the tent since before the parting of the two peoples. Brothers separated from brothers by an abyss of choice.

Lamanites.

At first, shock stilled the sisters' hands.

Then, Anava's voice rose above the din. "They are our brothers still, my sisters. Their leaders have not provided care for them as our leaders have. Treat them as you would your own!"

"But—" someone sputtered.

"They are still our brothers, our sons and grandsons!" Moriah's voice broke as she spoke. "Please. For me. For those of us who may have family still following Laman's path. Help them!"

Those attending fell silent, then, one by one, picked up their tools and went back to work, swabbing away the blood with which the bodies had been painted and then wrapping, bathing, attending, comforting.

They received another shock as, a short time later, a couple of Lamanite women, dressed as the men, were brought in for treatment.

Hannah shook her head. Laman, then, was continuing to arm his women.

She looked up as a shadow darkened the door. She straightened, put her hands to the small of her back and stretched. Then frowned, squinting against the outside light as the figure entered and came toward her.

"Sister Hannah." Nephi's voice.

"Yes, Brother Nephi?"

"We have another wounded soldier."

"Well bring him in! Bring him in!"

Nephi turned and nodded and two men carried in a blood-stained frame, set it beside one of the last free mats and carefully moved the young man from their frame onto it.

Hannah washed her hands in a pail of clear water which Tabitha set beside her, then knelt down. The young man's outer tunic was stained and dirty. And sodden with blood near his midsection. Wasting no time, Hannah separated the garment down the center, then did the same with the under tunic.

Clothing could be easily repaired. Young bodies could not.

She caught her breath and clamped her teeth down on her lip as a stab wound was disclosed. This was not a wound just to the skin. This went deep.

She quickly glanced over the rest of the young man's body. Nicks and scratches only. She turned back. This seemed to be the only grave wound. Carefully, she poured some of Anava's potion into yet another bowl of clear water, dipped in a clean cloth, then began to swab gently at the wound.

Hands gripped hers and she looked up into dark eyes in a darker face. "Mother?" the young man gasped. "Mother! It is you!"

She smiled slightly and started to turn away.

A sigh. "Thank you, Mother." The hands released hers and dropped to the mat.

Hannah nodded and smiled and turned back to her work.

"I have missed you, Mother. I—I know it is too late. But I am so . . . sssorry." The last word was drawn out in a hiss of pain.

Hannah frowned. There was something she was missing. Mother. Not 'Mother Hannah'. And sorry? Sorry? Hannah lifted her head once more and stared into the unfamiliar face. As she looked carefully, familiar features began to emerge. A strong chin. Straight nose. Straight-lipped mouth just barely glimpsed in a thick tangle of beard. Hannah gasped and clapped a hand over her mouth as she stared. "Samuel?" she asked in a small voice.

A slight smile. "Even as you see, Mother."

Hannah felt light-headed. She sat back on her heels. "Samuel?" She leaned forward and -placed a trembling hand on his bearded cheek. She could hardly believe it. "Samuel?" Her thoughts clashed together in confusion. "I—I had not thought to see you again in this world!"

"And I had thought my choices would keep me forever from seeing you."

"What do we have here?" Anava's voice. She sucked in a breath. "Sword wound! Here, Brother, let me help you." She rinsed Hannah's cloth and began to swab at the rapidly-crusting blood on the young man's abdomen. "Hannah, you should have been attending to this!"

Hannah nodded numbly, her hand still on Samuel's cheek and her thoughts a whirl of confusion.

"Hannah!" Anava tapped her arm. "Sister! I need more bandages and could you please get me my sewing kit?"

"It is Samuel," Hannah said breathlessly, looking at Anava. She felt as though she had been exerting herself and needed to stop and simply take in air.

Anava frowned and stared at her. "I—what?"

"Samuel," Hannah said with a bit more force. She sat back and indicated with one hand. "Samuel! He has returned to me!"

Anava turned slowly to look.

"I recognized him the moment I saw him standing there," someone said.

Hannah gasped and looked up.

Nephi was standing on the other side of the mat, watching them carefully. "I was unsure how you would handle the news, Sister, so I decided this was a wounded soldier I needed to accompany."

Hannah looked back at Samuel as though she still couldn't believe he was there.

Nephi moved closer. "Samuel, son, do you mean your mother harm?"

Samuel turned his head and gave a little half-smile. "Based on my actions the last time she and I were together, I cannot fault your asking of that question. But no. I do not intend my mother harm." He turned back to Hannah. "I merely want to bask in her presence."

Nephi nodded. "Then, welcome to our camp, Son. May you stay and be healed." He turned away, toward the door.

Anava had returned to her ministering and now she looked up and wiped her forehead with the back of her hand. "What did he mean by that?"

"I am sure he meant that we would heal our brother," Hannah said. But she couldn't help but wonder if Nephi had been thinking of a more spiritual healing.

"Well this wound is deep, but I think it missed anything important, so if we avoid infection, you should heal quite quickly." Anava looked at Samuel. "It is the Spirit that bore you to us today, son of my sister." She got to her feet. "I will leave you in the capable hands of your mother."

Four men carried in another frame with an unconscious, bloody figure on it. As they set it down, the large man on it roused, stared blearily around for a moment, and proceeded to curse everyone about him weakly.

As if Hannah had not received enough shocks for one day.

The carriers had just brought in Laman, the architect of the pain and sorrow of three generations of people. The man responsible for their current situation—the battle still being fought in the borders of the land.

The House of Assembly suddenly felt very small indeed.

"You cannot keep me here! I tell you turn me loose! Let me go!" Laman's frantically searching hands encountered no weapons.

"The weapons you search for were removed when you were found unconscious among the fallen on the battle field." Nephi handed a sword he was carrying to Sam, who, together with their younger brothers Jacob and Joseph, had joined him beside their eldest brother.

Laman looked up at Nephi, dark eyes black with emotion. "You should have left me to die there!" he spat. "Better to die in glorious battle than to live among the weak and water-willed of the earth!" He turned his head away. "Let me go!"

"Go to what, my brother? You have not provided for the care of your wounded. To what would you go? To the ministering of the woodland creatures, perhaps?"

Laman turned back and glared at him.

"We shall tend to your wounds, Brother. Then you shall be free to leave!"

Laman subsided to a mutter, but kept his eyes on Nephi.

One of the sisters moved closer and paused beside Nephi. "Father Nephi, is it safe?"

Nephi shook his head. "He has been disarmed, Sister, but he is never safe."

Laman snorted but said nothing, merely glared at his younger brother.

The Sister moved forward hesitantly.

"Never mind, Sister, I will care for him." Litha had come up behind the girl, who skittered off gratefully. "Well, Brother. We meet again."

Laman turned from Nephi to glare at Litha. "Ah the unfaithful wife!" He glanced around the room. "And where is my other ungrateful sister?"

Litha straightened and stared at him. "She is dead, Brother."

Laman looked at her. "Dead? Did she anger another husband?"

Litha's face colored slightly, but she gave no other reaction; merely prepared a basin of clean water and potion and began to attend to Laman's wound.

Hannah felt her eyes widen. Laman's arm had been slit open from shoulder to wrist. She could see past the tatters of his tunic sleeve to the bones that formed his very frame.

Litha raised her head. "Anava?"

Across the room, Anava straightened and looked at her.

"Could you come and look at this please?"

Anava came over and examined the wound. "I am afraid this will require a goodly amount of stitching to close." She turned to the victim. "We will have to—" She stopped abruptly and stared. Then she blinked and her eyes lifted to Nephi. "It is L-Laman." Her voice hesitated over the word.

Nephi nodded. "He needs help too."

"But if we help him—"

Nephi reached out and gripped his wife's hands. "If we help him, we will be doing those things the Lord would have us do. We will be His hands here on earth. Remember, despite Laman's choices, our God loves him as He does us."

"I do not need you to speak for me, Brother!" Laman said sharply.

Nephi raised his eyebrows. "I think in matters of the Lord, you do."

Laman scowled but said nothing.

Nephi released Anava's hands. "Do for him what you would do for me, Wife."

Anava nodded and fetched her sewing kit.

"More light!" Nephi called.

Hannah continued to care for Samuel as a mostly silent group stood around Laman's mat and watched Anava tend his wound.

Laman himself said little, merely winced as the needle pierced his skin and stitch after stitch was inserted.

Finally, the wound had been closed, swabbed with potion and wrapped firmly.

"You will not be holding a sword for a while, Brother," Anava said. "Perhaps that is to the good."

Laman lifted his greying head proudly. "I am a man. And will hold a sword when it suits me to do so."

Anava sighed. "You must remove the thread after the flesh knits. It will fester if you do not."

Laman pushed himself upright. He would have risen if Nephi had not stepped in front of him and stopped him. "Brother are we to have no discourse?"

Laman looked at him. "And just what are we meant to discuss? The foolish traditions of our forefathers?"

"We could discuss my sons and daughters," Litha spoke up. "Those who remain with you and their father."

Laman sighed. With barely repressed impatience, he answered her. "I know not what happened to your son, Abishai, Sister. He and Zedekiah's son disappeared while on a hunting trip."

Litha's eyes seemed to glow, but she said nothing.

"The others are as you have seen here or hiding back at the camp on a pretense of supplying the needs of those who remain." Laman rubbed his forehead, the pushing Nephi back, got shakily to his feet. "All are useless to me. As weak and foolish as little baby lambs!" His eyes fell on the mat where Samuel had been lying quiet since Laman's arrival.

Nephi put out a hand. "Brother?"

Laman slapped his hand away, then threw back his head and laughed. "I know you think you have defeated me. But you will not. You cannot!"

Nephi stood in front of his elder brother. They were nearly of a size, large and muscular, both with black, greying hair and beard. Indeed, their familial resemblance was quite remarkable. But where Nephi's eyes remained clear and bright, Laman's had dulled, the skin around them puffy.

When his arm had been exposed, Hannah had glimpsed many scars, puckered and barely healed, criss-crossing the broad expanse. Here was the man who had turned from all he had been taught and who, instead, followed dark paths that led only to death and killing. And he reveled in it!

Nephi was again speaking. "Brother, come back to us. Return to that God you have abandoned and receive of His forgiveness and His blessings."

Laman laughed. "And give up my crown? You truly have been possessed of a devil if you think anything you can offer will entice me back to your foolish ways!"

Nephi's shoulders slumped. "So you insist on continuing this war you have created between us?"

"I did not start it." He put a thumb and finger together and prodded Nephi in the chest with them. "It was you, dear brother, with your prattling on about truth and righteousness. Your bold desire to rule these people. I know my duty and I will not stop until it has been realized."

"Your duty?"

"The rule of this people. It was ordained before we were born. By God himself."

"So you would destroy families. Turn your back on all you were taught."

Laman lifted his head. "I turn my back on those outmoded and ancient beliefs that were blindly followed by our forefathers and have no weight in this day and in this place I brought us to!"

He turned and started to move toward Samuel. "Samuel!"

Samuel gave no indication that he had heard but remained with his head turned away and buried under his arm.

Laman stopped a short distance away. "Come with me now, Son. It is time to turn away from these people and their foolish imaginings and return to truth."

Hannah threw herself across Samuel. "No! You will not take him!"

"He belongs to me. I say he comes with me."

"Well you will be supplying his death sentence, because he has been gravely wounded and cannot get off this mat!"

For the first time, Laman appeared uncertain. Hannah wondered if there was finally someone about whom he actually cared.

Then he stuck his bearded chin forward. "He will come. When he is able, he will come. Or I will come and take him. Either way, he shall be with me!" He looked one last time at Samuel, then turned toward the door. Nephi did not stand in the way, but moved quietly to the side.

Laman stopped in the doorway. "I shall now rejoin my army and we will march through this land and sweep every living thing off it."

Joseph moved up beside his elder brother. "You shall have to travel to find your army, Brother. They have fled like the frightened goats they are."

Laman frowned and disappeared through the doorway. Despite his proud words, his movements were slow and stiff. Members of his army who had been helped by the sisters of Nephi's camp and who could walk got up and followed him.

Samuel and a few others stayed where they were.

Several of Nephi's men started after Laman. "Follow them," Nephi said. "To the borders of our land. They have no weapons and cannot possibly do any harm with our army returning from the battle and ready to engage them at any moment, but see that they leave." He reached for the sword he had handed to Sam and tilted it so the light shining in from the open doorway could play along its length. "I found this lying in the field not far from Laman's unconscious body." He pulled his own sword from its sheath and compared them. Except for the gleaming jewels in the hilt of Nephi's sword, the two were remarkably similar. "Can this be one reason for his enmity?" he asked softly. "Can he covet a sword?"

"He can covet anything he sees but does not possess," Jacob said.

Nephi sighed and shook his head. Then he lifted it, looking around the room. "You have all fought bravely today, ready to sacrifice all you possess for your beliefs. You will receive your reward at the day's end." He turned and left the building.

Samuel looked at Hannah. "Was he speaking to all of us, Mother?"

Hannah smiled. "Indeed he is, Son."

"Of what 'reward' is he speaking?"

Hannah sat back. "I am sure he speaks of the satisfaction of knowing you have done the work the Lord has given you."

"Ah. Then he could not be speaking to me." He sighed and turned so he was looking up into the rafters of the building. "He could not ever be speaking to me!"

"You have been down a dark road, my son. But it is a road from which you can return."

Samuel looked at her. "You do not know the things I have done, Mother. The life I have lived."

"Oh, but I think I do, my son." She rubbed her head. "I know of all the things you have done. And yet, I still tell you that the road you have been traveling is a road from which you can return."

Samuel stared at her. "If only I could believe you."

Hannah took his hand. "Samuel, have I ever lied to you?"

He hesitated. "I . . . thought you had."

Hannah shook her head. "I swear to you that never, in your entire life, have I lied to you or been in any way untruthful."

Tears started in Samuel's eyes. "So many lies," he whispered.

"Son, I have never—"

"Not you, Mother." He turned his face toward the wall nearest the battle field. "Them."

Hannah was silent.

Samuel took a deep, uneven breath and scrubbed impatiently at his cheeks with the sleeve of his shredded tunic. "I did not see the truth." He looked at her. "All my life it stood beside me, clear eyed, and I saw it not."

"But you can see the truth now."

"I can. Perhaps for the first time in my life, I can." His eyes filled again. "But at what cost? At what cost! "

"Samuel, you are here! I am here. Your—your brother is here."

"My brother?"

Hannah smiled. "You have a brother."

Samuel lifted himself on one elbow. "You have married? A second time?"

Hannah shook her head. "No. Benjamin was with me when I . . . well, when I left Laman's camp." She looked down. "It was actually his presence that convinced me I could."

"I thought you were dead. I thought, like everyone in our camp, that when I dropped that final stone, I had killed you."

"I am obviously difficult to kill."

"But my father is not."

"Son, he chose his path. He chose to follow—"

"Because he is dead," Samuel broke in.

Hannah's heart stopped. She stared at him, her mouth open. "He—he—was he here—there?" She pointed toward the battle field. "Did he—was he k-killed there?"

Samuel shook his head. He took a deep breath. "What happened—Mother you must promise me that you will not tell Father Nephi."

Hannah blinked. "Samuel, what happened, Son?"

Another sigh. "He did not agree with Laman's plan to attack the settlement of Father Nephi."

"Then he, too, believed." Hannah was surprised at the brief flash of hope she felt at the thought of Lemuel finding his way back to the Lord, even as his life ended.

"Oh, he did not believe, he was very clear on that. But he did not see the wisdom in wasting our young manhood on the field of battle. He would that Laman should strengthen his kingdom through increase, rather than through battle."

"Oh."

"My father's life ended solely because he disagreed with Laman."

"Then Laman . . . ?"

"When Father turned away, Laman drew his sword and . . . thrust through . . ." Samuel could not finish. He turned his head into the mat and let his tears flow.

Tears streaming down her own cheeks, Hannah put her arm over her son and tried to hug him as best she could. "You were . . . were you there?"

Samuel nodded. "I wish to the heavens I was not." He looked away. "There was no mercy. No . . . discussion. Merely the clash of ideas, then the ending of a life at the point of a sword." He rolled over, rather painfully.

"Samuel, you must remain still."

He nodded. "Laman was so proud of that sword," he said softly. He looked at Hannah. "He had it made to look like Father Nephi's sword. You have seen it. The one Father Nephi carries?" He grunted. "That a thing of such beauty could also be a tool of destruction." He sniffed and wiped his nose on his sleeve. "And, just like that, Father's life was ended."

Hannah wiped at her own streaming eyes. Remembering suddenly and in brief flashes, times of camaraderie, tenderness, and intimacies.

Samuel's face hardened. "And now there is only one thing to be done with *King Laman*."

Hannah gasped and swallowed the rest of her tears. "You are not thinking of doing something to Laman?"

Samuel raised dark eyebrows. "And why should I not? An eye for an eye is the Law of Moses."

Hannah was silent for a moment, her thoughts churning frantically. "Repay evil with evil?"

"Yes."

"Son, who is it that is the Father of all lies?"

Samuel frowned. "I recall you teaching me this." His frown deep-ened. Finally he looked at her. "Satan?"

"Correct. And can he be trusted?"

Samuel's face twisted in thought. "Ummm—I believe not?"

"So will he reward his followers at the end of the day?"

He frowned at her again.

"Son, if you work for someone you do not trust, can you count on payment for work you have done?"

He looked thoughtful.

Hannah touched his hand. A strong, heavily-calloused man's hand. She remembered how soft and white it had been. "And, I prom-ise you this, Son. Neither can you count on Satan to pay for your labors. If you follow him, work for him, it is to your doom."

He nodded, but remained silent.

"And it is Satan who requires that you take a life for a life."

"But it is written."

"I know it is written, Son. But Father Nephi teaches of a better way. Of the way of the Christ who shall come."

"Christ?"

"That is what he shall be called." Hannah turned her head, look-ing across the room. "Father Jacob was telling us only a few days ago."

"Christ."

"Yes. And he shall come in 600 years from when Father Lehi left Jerusalem."

"Another prophet?"

"No. The Savior of us all."

"And how do we know what he will teach, when he has not yet taught?"

Hannah smiled. "Son, what is Nephi?"

He blinked. "A son. A brother. A husband. Father. Grandfather."

"And a prophet."

"Oh."

Hannah's smiled widened. "He has seen this Christ who shall come. He and Jacob also."

Samuel frowned again. "How did they see him. When he has not yet come?"

"You keep forgetting the 'prophet' I have been speaking of."

Samuel sighed. "I cannot, yet, consider Father Nephi anything other than the brother of my father." He looked at Hannah. "Allow me time to ponder."

Hannah nodded and rose to her feet. "I will fetch food and drink, providing Mother Anava permits it." She beckoned to her sister. "Anava, could you please look again at our invalid?"

Anava hurried over and knelt beside Samuel. Deftly, she peeled back the bandage Hannah had applied to the young man's torso. "Hmmm." She reached over to the bowl of potion and wrung out the cloth. Then she swabbed gently at the wound and leaned forward to examine it more closely. "This could have been ugly indeed. A fraction to the one side or the other and your life would have ended."

Hannah clutched the bodice of her tunic.

"But as it is, I think it will heal quickly." She sat back and looked at Samuel. "You are a very blessed young man."

Samuel studied her gravely. "I know that now."

Anava put a hand on his arm. "You have been spared for a reason, son of my sister. Now it is up to you to decide how you will use that gift." She turned to Hannah. "He is allowed water and light foods. Nothing too heavy for the next day. Then we shall see where we are at."

Hannah nodded. "I shall fetch something."

A short time later, she was back with a trencher and a water skin. She sank to her knees. "Here, Son, let me help you." She supported Samuel's head as he lifted it to drink. Then she laid it aside, set the trencher on her lap and fed him bites of soft cheese and fruit.

"Is he really my brother?"

Hannah looked up.

Benjamin was standing beside her, his eyes on Samuel.

She stood up. "He is, Benjamin. Your elder brother, Samuel."

Benjamin continued to stare as though he couldn't quite believe what he was seeing.

"I never thought to meet him!"

"Well, now you shall." Hannah looked at Samuel, then back at Benjamin. "Son, I am so grateful to be able to introduce you to your elder brother, Samuel." She looked at Samuel. "And this is Benjamin."

The two regarded each other for some moments.

Then Samuel held out his hand. "Take my hand in friendship, Brother. I am forever glad to know you."

The two grasped each other's wrists.

"Are—are you here to stay? Is—is our father here?" Benjamin looked around.

Samuel sighed. "I know not if I am here to stay, Brother. I have duties—family—in my other life. And no, our father is not here."

"No. That was foolish of me," Benjamin said sadly.

Benjamin seldom mentioned Lemuel. Hannah was surprised at the depth of feeling in his words. "Not foolish, Son, to want to meet your family."

The boy nodded.

"And how many years have you, Benjamin?" Samuel asked.

"I have just achieved my fifteenth year, Brother."

Samuel nodded. "A great age. I remember when I was that—" He stopped suddenly, his eyes seeking Hannah's.

Hannah felt her breath stop. She remembered clearly what had happened when Samuel was in his fifteenth year.

"I have thrice read in the synagogue," Benjamin said happily. "Father Nephi says I have the spirit of Isaiah."

"A great prophet of our people."

"Yes!"

Hannah looked at Benjamin's smiling face, then turned to Samuel. "Benjamin delights in all things of the spirit."

"As I never did." Samuel looked away. "You finally have a son who pleases you."

Hannah knelt beside him and reached for his hand. "I have *two* sons in whom I am well pleased, Samuel. Two sons."

He turned to her. "How can you be pleased with me, Mother? How? After what I did?"

Hannah sighed and gave him a small smile. "Whose idea was it, Samuel? Yes, you have done some terrible things, but you were urged to do them at another's behest."

He released his hand and held it up. "I did those things of my own free will. I—I followed of my own free will. I and I alone picked up that rock. I—" He closed his eyes. "May God forgive me, I dropped the stone what could have—should have—ended your life. The life

226

of my mother!" He opened his eyes and looked at her. "How can I be forgiven of that?"

Hannah reached out and again grasped his hand. "I have forgiven you, Son," she said steadily.

He caught his breath. "You?"

"I have forgiven you."

Tears began to gather at the corners of his eyes. "How can you forgive me?"

"I love you, Son." Hannah took a deep breath and with her other hand, smoothed the dark hair back from her son's brow. "I have loved you since the day you were born. I will always love you."

"I drove you away."

"Yes. But now we are together again." She tightened her grip on his hand. "And we can stay together forever, if you so wish."

Samuel studied her face for a few moments. "Have you always been like this? Kind? Understanding? Forgiving?"

Benjamin knelt beside Hannah and smiled at his brother. "Have you *met* our mother?"

"I have met her, but I do not think I have ever really known her," Samuel said in a small voice. "And I would like to."

Benjamin laughed. "Then allow me to introduce you. Elder Brother, behold your mother." He looked at Hannah. "And Mother, behold your son."

The tears dripped from Samuel's eyes and into his ears.

Hannah dabbed at them with a clean cloth, then at her own. "It is such a blessing to finally find you, Son."

"And I shall rise up and call you Blessed," Samuel whispered. "As you should have been called from the very first."

———————◆———————

Anava sat back on her heels and wiped her face with a damp cloth. Then she stood up and looked at the women gathered around her. "The battle is finished, my sisters." She turned and surveyed the room, the blanket-draped men arranged in neat rows, the wounded but upright men moving among them, offering care and understanding. "We have been blessed. Though not one of our brethren escaped unscathed, we have lost none to the angel of death this day." She sighed. "Would that I could say the same for our brethren, our sons and grandsons, fighting in Laman's army." She glanced toward the doorway at the two still, covered figures sitting on the road, ready for their final journey. She lifted her head. "Our God has welcomed them and we should rejoice that it is so." She smiled. "And now that the army of Laman has been driven back into the forest, let us take the time, individually and together, to thank our Lord for His goodness." She bowed her head and gave voice to two simple words, "Thank you."

———————— ◆ ————————

Two days after Laman and his army took to their heels, on a bright, hot day, Nephi called his people together in a feast of thankgiving. Frantic preparations ensued with every hearth in the village producing sweet baked goods, meats, and herbs in every colour and texture. Low tables were set up and dishes appeared, set carefully with loving, grateful hands.

Hannah looked down the long tables groaning with every good thing and smiled. Much of the battle had remained atop the far hill and pastures only had been destroyed. The prolific gardens just outside the village had been unscathed and yielded their fruit for the celebration.

Soon, the entire village was seated side-by-side the entire length of the street, with trenchers loaded with delicious food.

Warriors, as yet unable to feed themselves due to injury, were helped by family members and many tears of gratitude were shed.

Samuel, and those like him confined to their pallets, were carried out on litters and placed in prominence.

After some time of feasting and visiting, Nephi got to his feet and waited for the people to quiet down.

It took several minutes but finally, all had focused their attention on him.

"My people, the People of the Lord, we gather today in gratitude." He took a deep breath, then turned to look at the long row of young men lying on their pallets. "We were called into a fight that we did not want against an enemy that should not be an enemy, but we did as we were called to do. In the strength of the Lord we met our brothers on the battlefield and, in the strength of the Lord, we were able to defeat them and send them back into their own lands."

He looked around at all of the people. "There was not a man among you who did not receive a wound that day. And some of you paid dearly indeed." He looked at Cephus, lying in the sun, his wife helping him as he lifted a morsel of meat to his lips with his one remaining hand. "But we did not lose a single soul in the battle and our sons have come home to their families and to retake their lives." He sank to his knees. "Will you join with me in thanking our God for the wonderful blessing of freedom, protection, guidance, and peace?"

As all bowed their heads, Nephi poured out his heart in gratitude to the Lord for His goodness and for His strength. When he closed his prayer a few minutes later, there were few dry eyes and no ungrateful hearts.

Nephi smiled through his tears. "Let us remember, my people, that those who fight with us will always be greater than those who oppose. And that, as long as we stand with the Lord, no army on earth can overtake us. It will only be through sin that our enemy will find the chinks in our armour."

His smile widened. "Let us make sure that there are none!"

Everyone cheered loudly. Then, as was becoming common during celebrations, several flutes and other musical instruments appeared. For the next few hours, as the sun set and a light breeze began to blow, the people sang, danced, and simply sat, enjoying the wonderful spirit that had permeated the assembly.

———————— ◆ ————————

During the long days of Samuel's recovery, either Hannah or Benjamin stayed close to his side, tending to his needs and getting to know the man who was their son and brother. Even Little Brother seemed curious, often lurking around him, sniffing, and wagging his stub of a tail.

They discovered that Samuel had become an accomplished hunter, like his father before him, and had provided much of the game that sustained Laman's camp. Hannah was overjoyed to be told that the family he had mentioned briefly consisted of a wife and three children. She was a little less enthusiastic upon hearing his spouse was the youngest of the daughters of Laman, but when she realized she was a grandmother to two young boys and a girl, she begged for stories about them. Their births. Their lives.

Samuel was happy to speak of them and did so with little encouragement. "The eldest, Jonathan, is strong," he told her. "A hunter. Jon's greatest wish is to supply our family with food. He is already quite proficient with the bow." He smiled. "Our daughter, Mary, is sweet. Gentle." He lifted his hand and touched Hannah's cheek. "Like her grandmother."

"And the youngest son? What is his name?"

"I felt to name him Ishmael, after his grandfather."

Hannah sucked in a breath. "Ishmael!"

"My wife was not—enthusiastic. But she did as I wished. Though she never uses the name."

"Your wife. Is she gentle? Faithful?"

Samuel looked away. "Gentle? No. She has been taught too well by her father. She is very capable of hunting and killing her own game. In fact, she is a better shot with her bow than any of the men in the village."

"But . . . the children."

"They are well cared for. Those women who choose to remain in the village prepare food and care for the children."

"But not your wife. She hunts?"

Samuel nodded. "She often goes out with the men and the other women who wish to join."

Hannah was silent for a moment. "And your other son? Ishmael. Does he show a preference for hunting as you did?"

Samuel shook his head. "He does not. If he could have his way, we'd all be eating corn like the ox. My wife does not think him manly."

"Manly? What *is* his age?"

"He has almost reached his fifth year."

"And he is expected to act as a man. When he is yet young?"

Samuel shrugged. "Was it any different for me?"

Hannah thought back to the time when Samuel was little. Her desperation to keep him a boy after he had caught the eye of the great Laman. She sighed. "No."

Samuel shrugged. "It is the way of the world."

"Not Father Nephi's world."

Samuel looked around at the quiet industry apparent on every hand. At children who shrieked and ran and played. He turned back to his mother. "I am beginning to see that."

"This is the way of God's Kingdom, Son. Not wars and contentions. But peace and industry."

Samuel was silent.

———————◆———————

Samuel was sitting in the sunshine outside Hannah's hut. She had been to the market to purchase cheese and fruit to tempt the invalid's appetite. Nephi rose to his feet from beside the young man as she approached. "And here is your mother, Samuel," he said. "Busy as ever and come to provide for your needs."

Samuel smiled at her. "As she ever has, Father Nephi."

"I shall leave you now, so Sister Hannah can do what needs to be done." He looked at Samuel. "But do not hesitate to send for me if you have more questions, Son." He gripped Samuel's hand and put a hand on his shoulder. "I am happy to answer any of them." He nodded to Hannah and left.

Hannah watched him go, then turned to look at Samuel. "You have questions?"

"Three of Laman's warriors are here with me."

"Yes?"

"And they are anxious to know of things . . . eternal."

"They are coming to you?"

He nodded. "They have exhausted my meager knowledge and I had to turn to Father Nephi."

"You could not find a greater teacher, Son."

"I am realizing that."

Hannah squatted down beside him. "But I have a question. Why are they coming to you?"

"I have wondered that myself," Samuel said. "When there are people of far greater knowledge here than me."

Hannah smiled. "It is the Spirit you carry, Son."

He shook his head. "You are mistaken, Mother. The Spirit would not choose to reside with a sinner."

"Is that how you see yourself?"

"It is what I am."

"Son, we are all sinners. We all make mistakes."

"No one here has made the mistakes I have made."

Hannah smiled. "No. They have made different ones. They have agonized over them as you do. And they have repented."

"Repentance is for the lesser—"

Hannah held up a hand. "Let me stop you, Son. Repentance is for those who wish to repent. It is not based on the severity of their crimes, but on the size of their hearts and their willingness to give their sins away to know the Lord."

"I have much to give away."

"Then you had better start."

———— ◆ ————

Hannah rejoiced when she saw Samuel again on his feet.

"You are well now?"

He smiled. "Mother Anava has just pronounced me fit and ready to retake my life."

Hannah felt a twinge. "And will you? Retake your life?"

Samuel looked thoughtful. "I have learned much these past weeks. I have been healed both in body and in spirit. My mind is taken up, not with things of the world, but with things of the Spirit." He looked at her. "But now I have a grave problem. I have changed, but my wife has not. My children are with her. I would have them here, but how can I make this happen?"

Hannah put a hand on his arm. "You have begun to pray, Son. Do that. Have faith. The Lord will provide a way." She smiled. "Prayer works. It brought you back to me."

"It is . . . painful. Knowing they are there and I am here. I can now imagine what you must have felt when your child betrayed you and separated himself from you." He shook his head. "The pain of the betrayal must have been great."

Hannah nodded. "But we are given strength when we ask for it, Son. I begged for strength and was given enough to survive and make the journey to the people of Nephi."

"I do not know how you made such a journey. It could not have been easy."

Hannah smiled. "It was not. But I have found, Son, that the important things of life never are."

"I am learning that."

CHAPTER FOURTEEN

*B*enjamin was out of breath. "It is Laman! He seeks to speak with Samuel!"

Hannah looked up from her grinding. "Samuel?" She turned as her elder son got to his feet. "Son, will you—" her voice broke, "—go with him?"

Samuel looked at her. "I know not, Mother. I have my children to think of."

"But you said you would have them here. With you."

"Mother, think. How could I possibly make that happen?"

Hannah felt a great pain in her chest. She gripped the bodice of her tunic. Would she have to let her son go once more? She did not think she could bear it to lose him again. And the grandchildren she had just discovered. Was she never to set eyes on them?

Getting to her feet, she followed him out into the dark, murky day. As she left her hut, Little Brother fell into step behind her.

People all up and down the street were talking together, looking alarmed.

Nephi, his brothers, and several other men, their expressions drawn and worried, were standing in the square, looking toward the sheep pasture where the great, still-recent battle had taken place.

Samuel joined them.

Hannah saw Nephi put an arm around her son's shoulders. The two men nodded at each other.

Hannah moved closer.

"We will go with Samuel," Nephi was saying. "Jacob, Joseph, and I will speak with our Brother."

"But he wants Samuel!" Hannah said. "He wants to take my son!"

Nephi smiled at her. "Sister Hannah, he can not take what does not belong to him."

"But he says—"

"The Lord will provide the way. Have faith."

"I do have faith," Hannah mumbled. "But I also know the treachery of Laman." She lifted her head and straightened. "I will come, too."

Nephi smiled. "There is little to stop you when you have decided, Sister. Come along."

"Mother."

Hannah looked at Benjamin. "I have to go with your brother, Son."

"I would come with you."

Hannah started to protest, but Nephi interrupted. "Come."

Benjamin fell into step with his mother and the others.

They trailed out across the pasture, making their way toward the brow of the hill so recently trampled by the feet of armies and only now beginning to recover. As they grew closer, Hannah could see there was only a small group of four or five people gathered there. Most noticeable among them was the great figure of Laman. Then her eyes were drawn to a woman standing imperiously beside him. A woman dressed as a warrior in fur and leather with shaved head, a bow about her body and a long sword sheathed at her side.

Hannah looked at the others with Laman and the woman, gasping when she realized they were children. A girl and two boys.

She gripped Samuel's arm. "Son. Who are those with Laman?"

Samuel smiled rather grimly. "My wife and children."

"Why has he brought them? Do you think he means to—bargain—for your release?"

Samuel shrugged. "Only Laman knows what Laman will do."

The two groups stopped a short distance from each other.

The little dark-haired, dark-eyed girl who closely resembled Anava and Amanna at a like age spoke up. "Papa!"

She started to run toward him, but was stopped by the woman.

The little girl frowned and looked at the woman. "It is Papa, Mama. I must go to him."

"Not until King Laman says," the woman told her. "You must stay here with me."

The girl looked confused. "But it is Papa."

"Hush. Stand with your brothers."

"Good morrow," Nephi said cheerfully. "Are you well, Brother?"

Laman grunted. "Well enough, Brother. I have come for my son."

"*Your* son?" Nephi raised his eyebrows. "I had thought he was Lemuel's son." He paused. "Lemuel whom you killed."

Jacob and Joseph gasped and turned accusing eyes on Laman. "You killed your brother?" Jacob said. "*Our* brother?"

Laman shrugged. "You speak of what you do not know. I must keep peace in my kingdom. If a life must be sacrificed to do so, so be it."

Samuel stepped forward, his face red with emotion. "It was a mere difference of opinion!" he shouted. "You had no reason to kill him. He would have acceded to your wishes and you know it! It was a holding of power! As is your only way."

Laman stared at Samuel in surprise. "I can see you have been quite long enough with my brother's people. They have filled your head with the same foolish thoughts that plague their own minds."

"Not foolish thoughts, *Laman*!" Samuel spat the word. "Good thoughts. Righteous thoughts. From righteous people."

As they spoke, Hannah kept her eyes on the children a short distance away. Little Brother had moved up beside her and she could see his yellow eyes were focused on the same.

The tallest boy must be John, her eldest grandson. He was so similar to his father at a like age. He was standing stiffly, clutching a bow and trying to look unafraid. The little girl next to him must be Mary. She was gripping the hand of the small, slender boy beside her. Ishmael. A boy with tousled black hair and a thin, ascetic face. Both of the younger children were now looking confused and frightened and ready to burst into tears at any moment.

Hannah felt an old anger stirring.

Laman moved over to John and put his hands on the boy's shoulders. "I have come for my son. I have brought his family to remind him of where his duty lies." He squeezed John's shoulders until the boy winced. "And maybe entice him if he forgets."

"Still using people's children to manipulate and control them, Brother Laman?" Hannah asked.

Laman searched the group for her. Finally, his dark eyes spotted her. "Ah. The shrew!"

Hannah bowed her head. "The same. The one woman who always stood up to you."

Laman's eyes flashed, but he turned away without responding. "So, Samuel. What is your decision?"

Samuel's eyes were on his children, his eyes becoming suspiciously moist. "What would you have me do, Laman?"

"*King* Laman, Husband!" The woman standing beside Laman sounded shocked. "Have you so soon forgotten?"

"I have forgotten nothing, Wife," Samuel said softly. "Including the death of my father unjustly on the eve of battle."

"Unjustly!" The woman sucked the words in with an indignant breath. "How can you say such a thing? You know that King Laman rules and that his word is law!"

"I know that Laman rules." Samuel looked at his uncle. "But I do not recognize him, either as my king, or the maker of my laws."

The woman stared at him open-mouthed. Then turned to look at Laman.

Laman had stepped forward, pushing young John before him. His lip drew wide in a smile that did not reach his black, cold eyes. "So it has come to this." He nodded at Samuel. "You will come and join me, Son, or you will watch your children die."

Hannah gasped and clapped a hand over her mouth. Little Brother glanced at her, then turned back to the children. He growled.

"No!" Samuel cried out. "Spare my children, King Laman! Please! Let us speak a little!" He started forward.

Nephi caught Samuel's arm. "You must trust in the Lord, Son."

Laman pushed John to one side, then grabbed the little girl by the arm and pulled her toward him.

"Papa!" she screamed.

"Laman!" Something in Nephi's voice made Laman stop and look at him. "You would prove yourself by murdering innocent children? Is there no courage left in you?"

Laman hesitated, then curled his lip. "What care I for those things? I am a king. Quite above considering such folly."

"What is a king but the father of his people? You would destroy your people? Your children? Your future?"

Laman remained impassive, his eyes turning back to Samuel and ignoring Nephi.

Nephi took a deep breath. His next words rolled out of him like thunder. "Laman, stop this instant, or the Lord Himself will call those who will defend these innocent children!"

Laman looked around, unaffected. "I do not see him, Brother. Or those he calls." He turned toward Nephi. "You, perhaps?" He laughed. "When could you defeat me?" Still holding the terrified, now-sobbing little girl with one hand, he reached out with the other and put his hand on the hilt of his sword then looked again at Samuel. "Let this be on your head, my son."

"He will do it, Husband!" Samuel's wife said, moving to Laman and putting a hand on his shoulder. "He has the power!"

Hannah stared at the woman, shocked that she would impassively allow her children to be sacrificed by their grandfather.

Laman pulled the sword from its sheath. It came easily with a long hiss.

Samuel dove forward, but something leaped past him in a blur of greying fur, flying claws and razor teeth. Little Brother had sensed the evil threat to a child and was determined to defend the little girl with everything he had.

Startled, Laman turned slightly as the great animal pounced, and screamed as sharp claws raked the side of his face from temple to chin, leaving deep gouges in skin and muscle and across his left eye. The force of the animal's heavy body knocked Laman away from the little girl and yellowed teeth latched onto his muscular arm just above his sword hand, slicing through skin, severing tendon and bone.

Laman screamed again and his sword dropped uselessly from his hand as he fell backwards, pulling his daughter down with him.

Samuel and the other men dove forward. Samuel scooped up Mary and scrambled a short distance away. Nephi picked up Ishmael and Benjamin grabbed Jon's hand. Together, they brought the boys to their father.

Whimpering madly, Laman thrashed about, his good hand over his torn and bleeding face and his injured hand hanging slack. Finally, with his daughter's help, he managed to lurch to his feet and stood there, swaying slightly and looking confused, his left hand clapped tightly over his shattered eye and his right hand dangling uselessly from a shredded forearm.

Little Brother, head lowered and yellow eyes gleaming, now stood stiffly in the space between the two groups. A deep, fierce growl rumbled through his chest and throat.

Laman's daughter belatedly drew her sword and moved to stand defensively between the animal and her father and further attack.

Neither Laman, absorbed in his injuries, nor his daughter who was eyeing Little Brother, appeared to notice that the children no longer stood with them.

"Papa?" Mary said, touching Samuel's face with her two little hands.

"Mary!" Samuel hugged her tightly, pressing his face to her little chest. His sons pushed against him and Samuel dropped to his knees and wrapped his arms around all three together. "My children," he whispered brokenly.

Hannah looked at Little Brother.

The animal was still on guard, head sunk between his shoulders and yellow eyes fastened on Laman and his daughter.

"Little Brother," she said. "Come. Laman will not be the cause any more trouble this day."

Laman frowned on hearing his name, but seemed unable to focus his remaining eye to find who had spoken.

Little Brother joined her, but kept his eyes on Laman and his daughter. Hannah patted the animal on the head. "Well done," she said, quietly.

Laman's daughter lowered her sword.

"Laman!" Nephi said.

Hannah looked up.

Nephi had moved toward his brother, his hand outstretched. "Give me your hand, Brother, and by the power of God, you may be healed."

Laman stared at him, blood dripping from the good hand pressed to his injured face while his damaged hand was held tightly against him. He whimpered. A long pain-filled sigh of sound.

"Give me your hand, Brother, and all of this is done between us."

"Heed him not, King Laman. He will follow after you and force the crown from you!" Laman's daughter, her lips curled with distaste, swung at Nephi's hand with her sword, but missed as he moved faster than she.

"The Lord wears the only crown in His kingdom, daughter," Nephi said calmly. "Come. Join with us here in peace and freedom."

Laman whimpered again, still holding his face.

His daughter lowered her sword and turned to him. "Father, he only wants what you have. He seeks to rule over you. You know this!"

Laman blinked, then twisted slowly to look at her.

"You know this," she repeated slowly. "You have always known." She straightened and looked at Samuel. "I would take my children."

Samuel shook his head. "You will not have them, Wife. I have witnessed their destiny if left in your hands."

The woman narrowed her eyes. "You would have them suffer the same fate as those deluded souls who follow the preachings of a madman?"

"Father Nephi is not mad, Wife. Come. Listen to him and you shall see. For the first time, you shall truly see."

She reared her head back and her lips curled as she took in a breath with a hiss. "I shall not follow the foolish traditions of our forefathers."

"They are not foolish," Samuel said softly. "Come. Listen and you shall know."

"I shall not!" She glanced one last time at her children and slashed down with one hand. "They are not longer my children." She looked at Samuel. "And I no longer recognize you as my husband!" She turned to her father. "King Laman, let us leave this place."

Hannah gasped. "You would leave your children? Your husband?"

The woman looked at her. "They are no longer my husband and children, Traitor." She straightened. "And why do you speak? You, who are guilty of the same actions."

Hannah blinked. "Only when I was forced to do so, Wife of Samuel."

The woman snorted. "And what choice does a man have when his wife repeatedly disobeys him?"

"As you are disobeying your husband?" Hannah asked quietly.

The woman's eyes flashed, but she turned away without reply. "Come with me, King Laman." She put a hand on his arm.

"I—I—" Laman looked confused. He turned back to Nephi.

"My King, we must go now!" His daughter pulled impatiently on his arm.

As he still hesitated, her eyes flashed again as she took a deep breath. "You are the King!" she shouted. "*I* will ensure that your reign is long!"

Laman nodded shakily and allowed her to lead him. The two disappeared into the forest at the edge of the field.

Samuel watched them go, his arms tight around his children.

"Papa? Where are Mama and King Laman going?" little Ishmael asked.

Samuel sighed and looked at his son. "They have chosen to walk a different path from us, Son."

"The one through the forest?"

Samuel half smiled. "Yes."

"Papa?"

"Yes, Mary?"

"I am hungry."

Hannah knelt before the little girl. "Come, Mary. I have plenty of food."

The girl looked at her. "Who are you?"

Samuel rested a hand on Hannah's shoulder. "This is my Mama, Mary. Your grandmother. Mother Hannah."

The girl looked at Hannah. "I like her." She touched Hannah's cheek gently, tracing one of the creases. "Her face is all soft and wrinkly and her hair is white."

"And her heart is pure, my daughter. Come. Let us see what she can teach us."

Hannah smiled and reached for the little girl's hand. "Mary! That is such a pretty name. A pretty name for a beautiful little girl."

"I am in my seventh year."

"Really? That is a great age! When I was your age, we lived far away across the great waters. In Jerusalem. I milked the goats."

She giggled.

Ishamel joined them, grabbing Hannah's other hand and looking up at her with wide eyes. "You milked goats?"

"Yes." Hannah smiled at him.

"Does your little girl milk your goats now?" Mary asked.

Hannah smiled. "I have no little girl." She squeezed the soft hand.

Mary looked up at her. "Can I be your little girl?"

Hannah blinked at sudden tears. "Yes, Dear One. You can be my little girl."

"Papa! Did you hear that?"

Samuel looked down at Mary and smiled. "I did, my daughter. I think it is a good idea." He took her other hand and they all started walking toward the village.

Benjamin moved over to Nephi. "Why would Laman not come to you and be healed, Father Nephi? His injuries were grievous."

Nephi sighed sadly. "Laman has been following his own path for too long. It is not easy to turn when one is so far along."

"But one *can* turn."

Nephi half smiled. "Yes. If one has the strength—or the humility—one can turn."

"That woman was determined he should remain king." Benjamin paused. "But I do not know if he will recover from those wounds. I think his eye was damaged. And I doubt he will ever hold another sword."

Nephi nodded sadly. "His days of being a hunter are most certainly over. And all could have been healed through faith."

"Why does he not believe, Father Nephi? Why does he turn away?"

Nephi sighed. "I do not know, Benjamin. Pride? Ignorance? Even as a boy, Laman was determined to go in his own way. To never bow the knee to anyone."

Benjamin was silent for a few moments. "What will he do now?" He turned and looked toward the spot where Laman and his daughter had disappeared into the forest. "That woman seemed unconcerned about his injuries. Still called him her king. Seemed firm in her support of him."

"Yes, Benjamin. I think she must enjoy a certain standing because of his position."

"It was almost as though *she* was the king."

"And I think that is exactly what will happen," Hannah spoke up. "The next generation will rule."

"And the next generation will move even further down the path of evil shown them by Laman and Lemuel," Nephi said sadly.

———— ◆ ————

"Hannah, precious one, we would speak to you."

Hannah turned. Anava, Nephi behind her, stood in her doorway.

"Come in, Sister, come in." She got to her feet. "Do not hesitate in the doorway!"

Anava smiled and pushed the door wider, then stepped into Hannah's hut.

Nephi followed her into the room.

Hannah set aside her carding, dusted her hands, then wiped them on a cloth. "May I offer you refreshment? A sip of wine? Water?"

"Nothing, thank you," Anava said. A small fire had been lit against the coolness of the day and Anava seated herself beside it, peered up at Hannah and patted the cushion beside her.

Hannah sat down, then looked up at Nephi, who remained standing. "Will you sit with us, brother Nephi?"

He smiled and nodded. "I will, thank you, sister Hannah." He seated himself beside his wife.

"Is there nothing I can do for you?" Hannah asked as the silence stretched.

Anava smiled. "Actually, we were wondering if there was something we might do for you."

Hannah frowned. "I am not sure what you mean."

Anava raised her eyebrows and looked at Nephi, who turned to Hannah. "Sister, I would speak now of commandments. Your husband is dead. Murdered by the hand of one whom we called kin."

Hannah looked down.

Nephi went on. "According to the law given us by our father and prophet Moses, when a man dies, it is the duty of his brother to marry his widow and provide for her and her children."

Her eyes sought his as she caught her breath.

Nephi was looking at her intently. "But in placing the matter before the Lord, I am constrained in making such an offer."

Hannah was silent for a moment. Marriage to Nephi? In her age? But she knew, even as the thoughts flitted through her mind that he was right to feel hesitant.

He went on, "However, it is of utmost importance to the Lord that you and your children be well cared for." He waved a hand. "I know that they are grown, or nearly so, but your needs remain. And thus my purpose in visiting with you this day." He took a deep breath. "Sister Hannah I wish to make a pledge to you that as long as I live, I will see that your every need is met."

She smiled. "Brother, I am grateful for your kindness."

He returned her smile. "You have long been the balance wheel in our community and it has been the goal of all of us to see you well supplied." He frowned slightly. "But I feel I need to do this."

"I thank you, Brother." Hannah's smiled widened. "Truly. My life is blessed."

———— ◆ ————

Hannah looked at her two sons and her grandchildren seated around her. All were happily engaged in eating and listening to the lively music of flute and strings. Mary had found a friend in one of the daughters of Tabitha and both were engaged with little dolls and much laughter. Beyond them, the people of Nephi, happiness and content shining from every face, were enjoying the food, the music, and the company of family, friends, and neighbours.

Hannah turned to look over at Nephi. The great prophet. Brother. Leader. For a moment, she saw him, not as the white-haired mature

man he was, but as he had been when they first met. A sober, studi-
ous, intelligent, dark-haired boy who loved the scriptures, respected
his elders, and treated all women with gentleness and kindness.

What a great distance they all had travelled from those idyllic
days in her father's house in Jerusalem.

Hannah smiled and took a deep breath. Surrounded by both of
her sons and her grandchildren, and with a prophet of God to lead
them, her heart felt full to bursting.

Her greatest prayer had, at last, been answered.

DISCUSSION QUESTIONS

1. Why could Laman and his followers not see the tracks leading from the village?

2. Did the Lord provide for and guide Hannah?

3. Is Abishai's death-bed repentance acceptable? Tobias'?

4. Would Rachel's death be considered suicide?

5. Do prophets make mistakes?

6. Does the Lord use animals to move His work forward? Can you think of other examples?

7. Without his daughter's endorsement, would Laman have followed Nephi?

8. What challenges do we have that might compare to Hannah's?

9. Why is a prophet seldom a prophet in his own land?

Acknowledgments

First, to my Heavenly Father, who gave me the words. With all my heart, I thank you.

I would also like to acknowledge my Stringam, Berg, and Tolley families. It is with your encouragement and faith that I carry on.

I must recognize, also, my loyal readers. Thank you! Thank you! You keep me writing!

And a huge thank you to my Cedar Fort team: Hali Bird, for loving my book; Priscilla Chaves, who made it so beautifully visible; Jessica Romrell, for crafting it into something readable; and Vikki Downs, who introduced it to the world. You are the very, very finest!

ABOUT
THE AUTHOR

Diane Stringam Tolley was born and raised on the great Alberta prairies. Daughter of a ranching family of writers, she inherited her love of writing at a very early age. Diane was trained in journalism, and she has penned countless articles, short stories, novels, plays, and songs and is the published author of two Christmas novels: *Carving Angels* and *Kris Kringle's Magic* as well as *Daughter of Ishmael*, the prequel to *A House Divided*. She and her husband, Grant, live in Beaumont, Alberta, and are the parents of six and grandparents of eighteen.